BLOOD RELATIVE

LIZA DROZDOV

For Alexandra and Maxim

as always

ONE

MIST DRIPS OFF her plastic rain cap as she pushes her walker past boarded up stores, vacant lots and empty houses where people used to sit out on their front porches, having a smoke and a drink. But whoever's still here spends all their time indoors, living under siege. She can't make any sense of it; how can there be so much crime in the East Village when there's nothing left to steal?

It's pension day and she'd lined up at the bank with the other seniors, then bought enough groceries to fill the small basket under her walker. She also bought a new vegetable peeler and kitchen knife, but she couldn't manage to fit the knife into the basket and has to carry it balanced on the handle of her walker, wrapped in a plastic bag.

She speeds up as she passes the bus shelter. Dealers use it to conduct business and drunks use it as a urinal so she always gives it a wide berth. Then grabs her shoulders from behind, pushes her inside the shelter and shoves her against the dirty glass. It's a young man with long wet hair hanging over his eyes. He's so close she can see the oily pores across his nose and smell the cigarettes on his breath.

"Give me your money." Her heart races and she shakes her head in terror, clinging to her walker.

"There's no money. Only my groceries," she says, pointing inside the walker's basket. He bends over and starts rummaging around, tossing the groceries out onto the dirty ground, smashing the jam and eggs in rage.

"Where's the money?" He shoves her in the shoulder and she almost loses her balance. "I saw you go into the bank. I know what day of the month it is."

She feels the acid rise in her throat. It's been years since she's seen that kind of anger, years since she felt this fear and it feels for a moment as if time is frozen, as if she's back there. Then she pushes the knife into his chest as far as she can, surprised at how easily the blade slides into his flesh. He looks confused. He's staring into her eyes and still shouting then he staggers back and looks down and sees the handle sticking out of his body. For a moment he looks stunned, as if he doesn't understand what happened before his face goes slack and he crumples to the ground. Cars drive past in the rain, spraying water up onto the sidewalk, their wipers going. Nobody sees a thing.

She waits a moment until she's sure he's dead then she pulls the knife back out of his chest, wipes it on his hoodie and wipes it again with the plastic bag. She picks up the groceries she can save then pushes her walker out of the bus shelter and makes her way along the sidewalk, pausing to throw the knife down the sewer grate.

The memory of how simple it is to kill someone, and the sure knowledge of good it is to take things into her own hands carries her home.

TWO

IT'S SIX-THIRTY IN the morning, half an hour before my shift ends when I get a call reporting a body in a field, which means I won't be clocking out on time this morning. As my car climbs the escarpment I rise out of the mist that lingers by the lake. The pre-dawn light becomes brighter; colours and outlines are now distinct and vibrant. I drive past fields of yellow goldenrod and purple asters and above them I can see the trees have already started to turn, their branches a mix of rich gold and scarlet. A flock of Canada geese flies above my car in a V-formation, so low I can hear their wings flapping.

I have the window down as I'm peering into the grass and bulrushes that line the gravel road, looking for the turnoff when I just catch a flash of high-visibility orange in my peripheral and slow down. It's a kid on a BMX bike, sitting well back from the road. What's he doing out here? It's too early for a kid to be out, or too late, depending on how you look at it.

A few hundred feet along I find the driveway and pull up next to another police cruiser, parked in front of a ten-foot tall chain link fence runs across the drive. I'm relieved the other officer is Decker. I know he isn't going to take the lead on this; Decker just isn't interested in the responsibility.

From the grim look on his face I can tell he's already taken a preliminary look around.

"Hi Gauthier. He's just though here." He pulls open the chain link fence so I can slip through and he follows, but from the way Decker hangs back it's clear he doesn't want to come any closer. I brace myself.

A dead man is sitting on a folding web lawn chair. He's wearing a red and black check lumberjack shirt under a black down vest; dressed warmly, as if prepared to spend some time outside on a cool autumn day. His sleeves are rolled up to above his elbows and his arms hang limp at his sides. I can see deep slashes on both forearms and wrists, running vertically almost up to his elbows. Pools of blood, now mostly dried, have formed on the grass under each hand, and there's a trail of blood trickling down across his palms and fingers. An empty vodka bottle lies a few feet away and about a dozen butts are scattered around his feet. I lean over for a closer look, careful not to touch anything, and see there are both cigarette ends and cannabis roaches.

"Suicide," Decker says.

"Looks like he spent some time. Before." Maybe to relax and get into the mood to die, whatever that mood is.

I straighten and look around. The clearing is surrounded by overgrown bushes and a few narrow trails, possibly made by wildlife, break off into the undergrowth. The abandoned driveway continues on the other side of the fence into a few hundred acres of scrub field, and in the distance I can see huge greenhouses and some kind of warehouse facility.

"Why here?" I ask. "What is this place?"

"The property belongs to Taiga," Decker says. Taiga is one of the largest producers of medical cannabis in the country, and one of the regions best corporate citizens. All the loud opposition to the facility from local residents disappeared after they brought hundreds of jobs to the local economy. Every so often we have to deal with a report of vandalism, but this is new.

"So, what's the message? *Fuck you Taiga?*"

Decker shrugs. "Maybe. Or maybe he just wanted some privacy." That makes more sense. "Nobody comes out here," Decker continues. "Except for the local kids who hang around, drinking and making out." Like the kid I saw on the bike.

I hear a noise and look up. Three large turkey vultures are perched on the top of the fence, watching Decker and me. They've gathered anticipating a feast.

"Sorry guys," I tell them. "Not today." One of them takes flight, flapping his enormous wings as he soars into the granite sky. If we hadn't had the anonymous tip we might not have found the body until the leaves fell, if even then. The vultures, foxes and coyotes would have done away with the carcass in just a few months, dragging his bones and body parts across the fields and leaving just a few scraps of torn clothing behind.

"It's definitely private," I say. I'm thinking aloud, not expecting Decker to engage. "Wonder if the Taiga security team even bothers to patrol back here."

I catch the scent of wood smoke in the air. "Did he make a fire?"

"Not that I can see." Not that he even looked. Decker would never do more than the minimum, without being told, but I need to bite my tongue. I don't need any more trouble with the old guard at the station.

"Maybe you could take a look around," I say, pointing to the trails leading off into the brush. "Check down one of those. See if you can find any sign of these kids you mentioned."

Decker nods and disappears down one of the trails as I call in the report. There isn't much to be done to secure the scene, and no likelihood of anyone walking past and contaminating any evidence. Decker and I will need to stay and wait for the Coroner and the crime scene investigators, but it looks like a suicide, so I doubt it will take long. Any evidence and impressions still need to be recorded so I get out my notebook and camera and began documenting the scene while we wait.

I finish my call and wait, breathing in the rich scent of autumn in Niagara: ripe straw cut and drying in the fields, plump late wine grapes hanging in clusters from the vines and rotting apples that have fallen from the wilding trees along the windbreaks that line the field.

"There's the remains of a bonfire down that way," Decker reports when he returns. "Some empty beer cans. Used condoms."

"Nice. Any bike tracks?" I take a guess.

"Yeah. Lots." Decker shrugs. It isn't important to him. He's just the first responder who's going to pass it off on whoever comes along next: Coroner, FSU, or Major Crime Unit. I make a note to get some casts of the bike tracks, in case they are relevant.

"What did he come out here for?" I say. "Why here, in the middle of nowhere? Couldn't he decide to die at home?"

"I'd say he came for the view."

Decker's response brings me up short and I stare at him for a moment before following his gaze.

We're standing high up on the escarpment and there's a clear view of the silvery lake, with just a slight shimmer of waves lapping the shore. In the distance the black line of the horizon is slashed open revealing deep orange and red. It's dawn. As I watch the band of orange spreads and the sun is just rising over the lake. From the position of his chair the dead man could have seen the golden sunrise, the ball of fire as it rose up from the black water.

"He came for the view," I echo. Maybe Decker is more intuitive than I give him credit for. "What was the weather like yesterday?"

"Not a cloud in the sky," Decker says.

"Good for him." I nod in approval at the dead man. "Makes sense. Looks like he's been dead about a day."

"So, you think he's been here since night before last? Drinking, smoking, possibly thinking it over, then he does the deed," Decker says. "He watches the sun come up on his last day on earth."

I nod, looking at the long vertical slashes in the dead man's arms. "Where's the blade?" I ask, looking through the grass. Decker blinks. "Did you see one?" He shakes his head.

"But I found this, on the ground next to him." He holds up a note, already placed into a clear plastic evidence bag.

I glare at him. "Don't suppose you took a picture before you bagged it?" I ask, already knowing the answer. Decker shrugs. He doesn't care about procedure. He just wants to get home to bed after his night shift. I lean in to read it in the poor light.

I didn't want to leave a mess. Sorry for everything.

It's pitiful. I blink back the tears and don't dare meet Decker's eye, in case it betrays my feelings. *Didn't want to leave a mess.* Did he have any experience with suicide? With the mess of blood and brains that the dead leave behind in their final howl as they leave the world? Someone has to clean it up, once they're gone. Looks like our guy did his best to make sure his blood will just be washed away by the rain. Once the lawn chair and his body are removed, it'll be as if he'd never even been here. It's like he'd wanted to wipe himself right off the face of the earth.

"That was thoughtful of him," I say, careful to cover my emotion. "We'll need to confirm the handwriting. And where's the blade? It didn't walk away by itself."

Decker raises his eyebrows and looks up at the vultures but I ignore him. The birds did not fly off with it.

"Forecast calls for rain in the next hour," Decker says, looking at some grey clouds moving in from the west. "Hope the investigation team will be here soon. Need to get it tented off." What he really means is so he can go home.

I pull on my nitrile gloves and start to go through his pockets. No ID. No wallet. No keys. I straighten and take another look at the body.

"So, how did you get out here?" I ask him. "Who are you?" The sun comes up over the horizon, its light reflecting in the dead man's eyes.

THREE

DECKER AND I wait while the investigation team takes photos and finally removes the body. Waiting is something I've become very good at: waiting at the scene of a crime; waiting in my patrol car for a call; waiting in silence while a suspect thinks of a plausible lie to tell. I have an anxious moment as the Coroner pulls up, but when Lewis Yun steps out I breathe a sigh of relief. It isn't Maja; I'm not ready to see her yet. I've been dreading our inevitable meeting and the idea of seeing her, of talking to her again, is just too painful. Luckily there are three Coroners in the region and we don't get that many unexplained deaths, so with any luck I can continue to dodge her indefinitely.

It isn't my first suicide; I've had to deal with dozens since I first joined the Niagara Regional Police force, five years ago. And my first dead body was many years before that, when I'd come downstairs one morning hoping to find something for breakfast before I went to school and found my uncle lying on the couch, dead of an overdose. I'd just gone straight out the door to school with an empty stomach, not for the first time. Then later there was my stepfather, but that's something I try not to think about.

"Damn, I'm beat," Decker says. He's been moaning steadily for the past hour as we wait for first the CSI team to finish up and I've stopped faking sympathy. "I'm only going to get…" he checks his watch, "six hours of sleep, if I'm lucky."

"What's the job tonight?" I pretend to be interested. "Concert? Some big party?" Decker is always first in line for any overtime and paid duty shifts are on offer. I never do any. Not that I can't use the money; it just seems like a lot of the other constables need it more. Some cops, regardless of their skill or talent, go into private security when they retire and some even launch their own businesses. DS Cooper, one of the worst cops on the force, started a company called Limestone Security last year as his retirement plan. Decker works for him too.

Decker nods. "Warehouse Concert Hall. Escorting talent." I do my best to look suitably impressed. "Then I'm back at the station for another night shift tonight."

That's two shifts back to back, on just a few hours' sleep. "How do you do it? *Why* do you do it?"

"Sometimes I wonder myself." He looks miserable. Then he gets an idea. "You know, there's tons of work. Plenty to go around, if you want to take some on."

I give him a big smile. "Thanks," I don't say what I really feel— that I'd rather be dead than go anywhere near Cooper. Decker is a great guy, well, a good guy at least. Why the hell is he hanging around with Cooper? They couldn't be less alike.

I don't want to judge Decker. He clearly needs the money or he wouldn't be doing it. It's not my business. But working for Cooper… no way. There's not enough money in the world for that.

I realize I can't take any more of Decker's whining or helpful suggestions. "Why don't you head back to the station? Clock out," I say. "I can stay here until they finish up."

I leave the scene as soon as the CSI team finishes up and I'm ready to head home for a hot shower and a long sleep. But after I've filed my report at the station, changed out of my uniform and clocked out, I have an idea and suddenly I'm not so tired anymore. Instead of turning left and driving straight home to my cosy townhouse and going to bed, I turn right and drive back toward the canal. I can't shake the image of the kid on the BMX bike, hiding in the bushes near the scene. It's a distinctive bike and I'd recognize it if I see it again so I head toward the park with the skateboard ramp and BMX track. Maybe the kid is there, or someone might know who he is.

I get a coffee from the drive through and stop my car so it's facing the jump park. A few kids are already out, freestyling on the pipes and in the large concrete bowl. None of them have the same bike I'd seen that morning. But it's still early and I have lots of time, so I enjoy my coffee and try not to notice the fatigue settling in.

An hour later, two boys ride up wearing helmets and kneepads. One of them is riding a bike with high-visibility orange trim and detail. I climb out of the car and stroll over to sit on a bench nearby. I'm not in uniform and if they even notice me they'll probably just assume I'm a parent keeping an eye on my kid.

I watch as the two new boys join up with another kid. They ride off to one side of the bowl and get into a huddle, talking intensely about something. The kid I'm interested in is telling a story, a very interesting one from the way his buddies are hanging on his every word. I'm sure he's describing his morning: the body, the cops and whatever else he's been involved in. When I see him pull something out of his pocket and show it to the other boys, I stand up and walk over to them.

"Hi," I say. They break off and look at me warily. I reach into my pocket for my ID. "I'm Detective Constable Gauthier, and I'd like to ask you a few questions." Before I've finished my sentence, they climb onto their bikes and take off, pumping as hard as they can to get away. "Seriously?" I shout after them. "I've got a car!"

I watch them ride off then get into the car and follow in a slow speed chase, staying far enough behind that they don't see me. I watch as first one kid pulls into a driveway, then a few blocks over another one does. I keep well back from the kid on the orange bike and he manages to lose me in the warren of one-way streets in the East Village. Figures he'd live here.

I drive back to the house where the first kid pulled in and knock on the door. After a brief chat with the shocked mother who answers the door, I have the address and name of the kid I'm after: Dennis Sharp, Colbourne Street, the house next to the Speedy Laundromat.

The house is typical of the East Village: a ramshackle two-story dump with a sunken concrete porch, metal awnings over the windows and vinyl siding sloppily hung over the original wood. I've been in lots of houses exactly like it, including the one I almost grew up in, just two streets over.

I knock firmly on the Sharp's front door. A tall heavy woman in a stained t-shirt and yoga pants answers, waving away the smoke from her cigarette. I show her my ID and she looks frightened.

"I'm here looking for Dennis Sharp," I say. "May I come in?" The woman's expression changes from fear to anger and she spins on her heel, leaving the front door open. I take that as an invitation and step inside as I hear her screaming into the backyard.

"Dennis! Get in here right now!" I would not have been surprised to learn that Dennis has wet his pants; I'm a little frightened myself. The woman, who I assume to be Dennis' mother, indicates I should sit down at the kitchen table. She first clears off the remains of the breakfast dishes—coffee cups, cereal bowls, and her ashtray, dumping them straight into the sink as she makes a place for me.

Dennis runs in, out of breath. He takes one look at me and almost runs back out, but his mother grabs his arm and shakes him hard.

"What the hell are you up to now?" she demands. "What did you do?" I watch in silence as he pleads his innocence. His mother is having none of it. "Why are the police here then?" She flings him down into a chair across the table from me and he stays put.

"Remember me?" I smile. He keeps his eyes on the kitchen

floor and won't look at me. "I need to ask you a few questions about where you were early this morning."

"I was asleep, in bed," he lies.

I nod. "So you don't know anything about a body, out by the Taiga facility?" He shakes his head. I glance at the mother who looks as if she might rip her son's head off. "Or about any 911 call that was made at around six o'clock this morning?" He shakes his head again.

I try another tack. "You know Dennis," I begin. "We're able to trace 911 calls, right back to the phone that made them." He looks nervous. "Even if the caller only stays on the phone for just a few seconds." That's half true, assuming we've been able to triangulate the position of the call relative to the nearest tower. Out here in the country with our spotty cell service, it seldom works. But Dennis doesn't know that I'm bluffing. He starts to panic.

"I didn't do anything," he says, daring a glance up at his mother. "I just found him and called."

"So, you were out there last night?" He nods miserably.

"He was staying at his friend's house," his mother interrupts. "That no-good Kyle…" I hold up my hand to silence her.

"So, you and Kyle went out late last night?" I begin again. "You snuck out when everyone was asleep?" Dennis nods. I can easily imagine it: Kids sneaking through the fence at Taiga, maybe on a dare, breaking into the cannabis facility. It's dark, they're nervous. They aren't real criminals, yet. They find the dead guy. They run away. Maybe Dennis can't sleep, either from excitement or he feels remorse for leaving him, so he calls 911 and watches to see what happens next.

"What did you see?"

"Nothing. The guy was dead. Just sitting in a chair. It was freaky."

"Did you take anything?"

"No." I know he's lying. What did the kid take? Money? Drugs? The dead guy definitely had some cannabis; there'd been roaches by the body.

I begin again. "So, you and Kyle were out last night." Dennis nods. "You saw the dead body in the chair." Dennis nods, not paying attention. "And you thought you'd check his pockets?" Dennis nods then realizes what he's admitted to.

He decides to bluff. "Kyle did," he says. "The guy was dead. It's not like he needed any of it."

"Any of what, Dennis? What did you find?"

Dennis reaches into his pocket and withdraws a plastic baggie full of pills and cannabis buds. He slides the baggie across to me. Dennis' mother moans and starts to cry. This is typical East Village crap. Things never change.

"Kyle thought we could sell them," he says. "But he needed me to hold them because his dad..." He stops talking and stares at the floor.

What would Kyle's dad do, I wonder. *Beat him up? Smoke the weed? Sell the pills on the street? Turn the drugs in to the police* was the least likely.

I take another shot. "And you went through his car?"

"There wasn't one," Dennis says.

I don't believe him, but it doesn't matter much. Whatever vehicle the dead guy had been driving was long gone by now; sold, chopped or shipped overseas within a few hours. But it would be nice if there were some way to trace the identity of its owner, the dead guy in the lawn chair.

"What about his wallet?" I ask. "Did you find that?" He shakes his head. I know kids like Dennis. I'd been one myself.

"Dennis," I ask. "Have you got an older brother or sister?" His eyelids flicker.

"Where is he now?"

"*She*," the mother says. "She's upstairs. Asleep."

"Can you please bring her down to speak with me?" I ask. Dennis looks terrified and I know I'm on the right track.

She goes upstairs and I can hear voices, rising louder and louder in volume, escalating into a shouting match. That's followed by a thump that shakes the ceiling above our heads, as if someone has fallen on the floor, then another loud scream. I sit back in my chair, watching Dennis as he listens to the drama unfold above his head. I guess the mother has tried to waken the sister, shaken her, shouted at her, got sworn at for her trouble before she shoved the girl out of bed onto the floor. I smile. *Just another day in paradise.*

Dennis looks nervous, nibbling at his hangnails and staring at the front door. He's probably thinking about making a run for it. His body tenses and I put my foot up on the chair blocking the way out. I shake my head then he settles back down, defeated.

I glance around the kitchen as I wait. The paint on the cupboards is chipped and the laminate countertop has started to peel up at the edges. There are scorch marks all over it. I'd seen a lot of those scorches, usually caused by my stepfather laying his lit cigarette down while he went into the fridge for another beer.

It's all too familiar and I realize the house is exactly the same layout as the one I lived in as a child. Suddenly the back of my neck starts to prickle with anxiety and my heart is racing. I'm staring blindly at the linoleum tiles on the floor that are the identical pattern to those I remember and I freeze, afraid to turn my head and look at the foot of the stairs, in case I see the body lying there in a pool of blood.

Dennis is staring at me and I realize I'm breathing loudly, gulping air, counting to ten and exhaling through my mouth. Rescue breathing. *Get a hold of yourself, Lucy.*

I look around the room, trying to focus on something tangible. The fridge is covered with dozens of novelty magnets shaped like fruit, flags and sports team logos—all holding work schedules, school timetables, coupons and prescription renewals. I lean across the table to get a closer look; I recognize the medication—it's the mother's anti-depressants. It takes all the self-control I can muster to stop myself from arranging the chaos of magnets and giving it some order. Tidying, organizing and straightening always help soothe my anxiety and seeing this mess on the fridge is triggering me, hard. I need to look away so I focus on counting the cracks in the ceiling, aware of Dennis watching me, wide-eyed.

A few minutes later a furious young girl stomps down the stairs and into the kitchen. She's wearing an oversized t-shirt and plaid pyjama bottoms and has last night's makeup smeared under her eyes. Her mother stands behind her, arms folded, glaring at the back of her daughter's head.

"Good morning…" I begin. I pause, raising my eyebrow and waiting for someone to fill in the blank.

"Julia," the mother says.

"Good morning Julia. I'm Detective Constable Gauthier, and I'm investigating an incident at the Taiga facility. What can you tell me about it?" Julia's eyes dart around, flicking between me and her mother and her brother, finally coming to rest on the baggie of pills in the middle of the table.

"Nothing," she whispers.

"You know nothing about it," I repeat, starting to get irritated. It's been a long night. "Nothing about a dead man, who he might have been, or his missing vehicle, or his wallet… or these pills?"

Julia shakes her head. "There's no truck here," she says, her voice smug. I knew girls just like Julia; if I'd stayed in the East Village long enough I'd probably have turned out just like her.

"I hear you," I say, noting she'd said it was a truck. "No truck here. I see that. So, if I were to get a warrant to search this house," I continue. "I wouldn't find anything. No ID, no wallet, nothing…" Julia's face goes pale and I know I'm right again. "Where's his wallet, Julia? Don't make me get a warrant and have to tear your mother's house apart. Never know what else we might find."

Julia's face flushes but she stands her ground. She's a tough girl. Her mother's eyes narrow and she reaches over and snatches a faux leather handbag with huge gold initials all over it from a hook by the back door. Julia grabs for it, but she's too late. Her mother dumps it onto the table and all the contents spill out: lipstick, hairbrush, change purse, wallet, makeup kit, and another wallet. A man's wallet.

I pick it up and flip it open. It belongs to a Maurice Cobb. The photo on the driver's license identifies him as the dead man in the lawn chair. The wallet contains several credit cards, some bankcards, just over a hundred dollars in cash, and a security ID card from Taiga.

"Who took the truck Julia?" I ask. "Your boyfriend?" Julia shakes her head, her jaw set. She isn't going to give him up. "What's his name?"

I look at Dennis. He stares at his sister, chewing his nails to the quick. It's obvious Julia won't crack and after a minute their mother sighs heavily. "Andre," she says. "His name is Andre Dumont. He lives on Elm Street."

I pick up the wallet and the baggie of pills and stand, considering for a moment. "I'm going to forget I was here. But I don't ever want to see either of you two again," I finally say to Dennis and Julia. "I don't want to hear your names, or ever see a piece of paper with your name on it come across my desk. If I do, I'll suddenly recall this morning." I shake the baggie and wallet in front of them. "Do you get my meaning?"

They both nod but I don't believe them. Their mother grabs my arm as I go out the door.

"Thank you," she whispers, her eyes full of tears. "Thank you."

I walk back to my car. I know I haven't rescued anyone. This is the East Village. Not many get out and nobody gets saved. Maybe her kids will end up okay, but the odds are against them. I'm not sure I've even done them a favour by letting them off but I can't face the extra paperwork. I just want to get home to bed.

FOUR

DOREEN SITS AT the table near the front window of the Green Bean coffee shop, waiting for Phil to bring her coffee. He'd seen her come in pushing her walker and told her to take a seat. She likes to sit in the front window with the view across the street to the canal and watch the people come and go. This afternoon, the coffee shop is full of students from the high school down the street and Doreen also notices the regular group of *working girls* from the East Village. Doreen doesn't mind them; they're just women who work hard for their money—a lot harder than she'd ever had to, that's for sure. But she doesn't have any patience for the men who sometimes join them. Pimps and hustlers. Bad men with hungry eyes.

One of them comes in the front door leading a young girl with long brown hair, wearing tight jeans, a short denim jacket and too much makeup. He makes a big show of sitting her at a table and asking her what she'd like. *Something sweet*, he says with a wink, *Like you.*

She recognizes the girl; Doreen never forgets a face. She lives down the street from her, across from the parkette with its rusty swing set and the broken teeter-totter shaped like a duck. Her name is Tiffany, which Doreen knows dooms her to a certain kind of life, especially if she grows up in the East Village. So many Tiffanys and

Britneys, Brandis and Candis-with-an-i, destined to be strippers, or worse.

Tiffany now sits at the wooden table and primps her hair as she waits for the man to return to the table. Doreen watches as he sits next to the girl, closer than is appropriate, his thigh brushing hers. He keeps touching her hand and leaning in close to whisper compliments in her ear, making her giggle and blush in embarrassment.

Doreen doesn't like where this is going and she resolves to keep an eye on the situation.

FIVE

"SIX, SEVEN, EIGHT... Nine," I inhale and dig deep for one last rep. "Ten," I grunt on the exhale then I let the weight slip from my sweaty palm. Several heads in the gym turn to look at me. Dropping weights is strongly discouraged, but I just don't have anything left and have to let it go. I sit on the bench, my muscles trembling with exhaustion, unable to move. It's lucky the gym is quiet and no one's breathing down my neck trying to get onto the chest press machine. I can sit for a moment and catch my breath.

I haven't slept well. I never do when I'm on night shift, and thanks to the last hours of my shift this morning I was wired and I barely managed to doze off. My anxiety has been off the charts lately anyway and I had to take something extra just to try and get some rest. The adrenaline rush of finding Maurice Cobb's body was one trigger, but I know it was the interview I'd had with Dennis Sharp's family that had gotten under my skin and into my brain.

My racing pulse and the lump in my throat tells me that it's back: The anxiety that's terrorized me for years, that medication and years of therapy have managed to get locked into its cage. It's *just anxiety*, everyone says. A crippling, terrifying, destructive monster that sets my pulse racing and makes me want to run in a blind panic to escape. Just anxiety.

I know what triggered my feelings of foreboding and impending doom: returning to the East Village. Every time I have to go there on a call I'll feel my heart race and my breathing get shallow, but I've learned how to manage it. Slow, deep breathing, regular sleep, vigorous exercise and my daily dose of SSRIs have kept me functioning on a day-to-day basis for years. But something about that family, that all too familiar house, so close to the one I keep trying to forget, forced me to crack open my emergency medication and the Lorazepam had helped take the edge off.

Being in that house brought back things I don't like to let into the light. Things from my past, things about myself, that I've spent years keeping in the dark. I've learned the hard way there's no point in bringing them out and turning them over; I've spent years doing that with my shrink and in the end they still just have to go back into the box with the lid shut tight. Sometimes the pressure builds up in there and I'm afraid the lid will blow right off.

And sometimes I let it.

If I don't let off steam, I don't know what I'll do. It's like a valve and if I don't release the pressure, ideally in approved ways like at the gym, I'll have a panic attack, or worse. I feel the intense impulse building before it erupts. I'm irritable, my thoughts race and I have palpitations and pressure in my head. The anxiety becomes too much and I have to do something. Adrenalin and cortisol flood my body and I can feel it coming on. I'm not always able to assess when to confront and when to walk away and when it comes to fight or flight, I choose fight.

Lately I've been walking along the canal at night. I don't go out into the streets looking to make them safe for the public. I need it to keep people safe from me. I do it because I want to find trouble; I'm looking for it.

I've seen the gangs meeting up, dealing, fighting. They are minding their business, like I'm minding mine. But if someone tries it on with me, I'll fight. And I will win.

I stretch my back, do some neck rotations to loosen the kinks in my spine and check my posture in the mirrored gym wall. Not great, so I make a mental note to do more to work on my posterior chain. I can use some development on my glutes, hamstrings and deltoids. I can also use a haircut, I realize. My shoulder length red hair has no style. And, maybe I also need to do something about the dark circles under my eyes, plainly visible against my pale skin covered with freckles. I stare at my reflection for a moment feeling the familiar disassociation, as if I don't recognize myself. *Who am I?* There are many days I don't even know.

A polite cough startles me and I quickly get up off the bench, wipe it down and move toward the leg press. I ignore my inner voice as it begs me to head for the showers and adjust the position of the seat to allow for my short legs. At only five feet five inches, I know I'm not the ideal height for a police officer, but human rights legislation didn't allow them to discriminate when I'd applied. Anyway, my daily workouts make sure I'm strong enough to take down any suspect if it ever comes to it.

But the real reason I work out hard all the time is to manage my anxiety, to divert and channel the torrent of panic that constantly threatens to overwhelm and drown me. Along with my SSRIs and weekly visits to my therapist, I've found hard physical exercise is what works best to keep my demons at bay. I go to the gym most days, to lift weights and do some cardio. I hate cardio.

I know I'm not the only one on the force with mental health issues; far from it, from what I've seen and heard. Other officers self-medicate with alcohol, drugs and sex, or with whatever else floats their boat. I'm not going to judge them. Many of them share their problems, but I will never give them a chance to judge me. Nobody needs to know my business.

"One, two, three," I count out loud. Then I'll do some squats and lunges before rewarding myself with a sauna. I know how it would play out if I ever shared my issues with anyone. There might be forgiveness and pretended understanding for anxiety and depression in one of the older guys who'd seen some things in their day. But I hold no illusions that generosity would extend to me: a young female who'd quickly risen to Detective Constable. Not a chance. The old guys would be all over it: criticizing my weakness, how it proved I wasn't capable of oversight of the team and couldn't handle the pressure. How I wasn't as strong as a man.

I've overheard them for the five years I've been on the force; their speculation about my personal life, their jibes and jokes whenever Pride month came around: "Are you going to the Parade?" I keep a tight lid on my personal life; I'm not about to give them a stick to hit me with.

Cooper led the campaign; he's one of the old guard. He's a creep who once asked me in the station if I was a *vagitarian,* thinking he was a real funny guy. But nobody laughed, at least not when I was in the room.

Cooper's reputation is notorious throughout the entire Niagara Regional police force and I've heard rumours about him for years, everything from laziness and incompetence to conspiracy and corruption. I have it on good authority that Cooper is crooked, but like everyone else I don't want to know. We all turn a blind eye. I've learned how to keep my mouth shut and my nose out.

He's had five disciplinary hearings involving aggressive behaviour, discreditable conduct and unreasonable use of force. He'd been sent to retraining, charged with insubordination, forced to attend anger management counselling, and he'd even been demoted at one point from First-Class to Second-Class Constable. They'd docked at least four hundred hours of his pay in the past ten years, but since he'd never been found guilty of a criminal offense the tribunal couldn't dismiss him and he was still on the force. When I'm feeling cynical I put it down to the old white guys, protecting their own, and maybe that's true. Those old white guys have never done anything for me.

Last year Cooper was jumped one night as he was coming out of a bar. He was beaten badly and he had to take a few months off to recover, which was a huge relief to the rest of us. They never did find out who did it, but they left him with a limp—a permanent reminder of the beating. I was on patrol that night and remember it clearly—the cool mist coming off the lake, the roads gleaming wet and the streetlights haloed. I'd been driving past and saw him going into a biker bar in a shady part of town. A good cop would never go in there, unless he was meeting someone he shouldn't. But Cooper wasn't a good cop.

I saw where he'd parked his car—around the corner next to an abandoned hardware store. It was out of sight, poorly lit. A bad choice, any police officer would tell you. Of course it would never occur to Cooper he was at risk, or that someone might be waiting for him.

I finish on the leg press and walk over to the wall, leaning against it and letting it take my weight. I'm tired. Tired from the workout. Tired of my job. Tired of my life. And I know I'm too young to feel this way, but I can't summon the energy to think of a solution.

Planting my feet shoulder width apart, I slide down into a wall sit. I check in the mirror to make sure my knees are bent at ninety degrees then turn my mind off. It's so tempting to look at the clock, to watch the seconds tick past until I reach two minutes. But I've learned that just makes the time go slower.

There is no way I'll tell anyone about my anxiety disorder. Why give anyone the chance to believe my mental illness is the unique defining factor about me? It isn't, not even close. Even though sometimes I feel it is.

My hamstring goes into a severe cramp and I stand up to stretch it out. That doesn't help, and the pain intensifies so I lift my leg onto a bench and lean into the stretch, massaging the hamstring as best I can. Gradually the muscle spasm releases as I hold the stretch and breathe deeply.

I have bouts of sleeplessness over the fact that I didn't disclose my anxiety and depression when I'd first applied for the police force. The medication I'm on didn't show up in my urine tests and they don't even have the right to ask about my mental health in the first place, so why should I volunteer that information? I knew they'd have rejected my application, despite their public statements about non-discrimination and inclusiveness. And lying on the application would immediately have disqualified me if they ever found out, so I'd lose either way. And I was surely damned if they ever learned the truth about my past, about what's in my sealed juvenile file.

My shrink says my anxiety is caused by childhood trauma, but unfortunately labelling it and identifying it doesn't make it stop. It's a constant, grinding tension I control through meds, and meditation, and exercise, and more meds. I've been seeing her for years and I never tell her what I really do. I wouldn't want to disappoint her, not when we've made so much progress.

She's seen the cuts on my hands when I come in for my sessions. I tell her I've been hitting the bag at the gym too hard. If she sees my lie she never lets on. I hit a guy. I hit a wall. I hit two guys. I put someone in hospital. They deserved it.

For the life of me sometimes I'm not even sure why I'd joined the police force, given my background. Sometimes I like to think it was for the stability of the job; I need security and order in my life. A steady paycheque, qualify for a mortgage, have a good pension. And there are rules to follow, clear ideas about *right and wrong*, and there are obvious *good guys* and *bad guys*. Or at least I'd thought so when I first joined.

The nature of the job fits my disorder so well. I'm always uneasy but my anxiety helps me keep an eye on things, making sure everything is under control. Order is important to me; it keeps the madness at bay. The chaos of my mind and especially of my past fades into the background when I face mayhem every day in my job. And my constant dread that something bad is going to happen is justified, rationalized and reinforced. Because something bad always happens.

The muscle spasm finishes my workout for the day. I've had enough and head toward the sauna. Today was leg and chest day; I'll be back tomorrow for back and arms. Maybe tomorrow I'll do some cardio. Not likely, but maybe.

SIX

THE GREEN BEAN is packed and I stand to one side as Phil makes my usual Americano. I really need a coffee and he's moving so slowly I'm already past impatient and moving into irritated. It's the last shift of my night rotation and I'm going in two hours early because I don't know what else to do with myself. I've done my workout, cleaned my house, done my laundry and after pacing for an hour I gave up and decided to go into work.

"Excuse me, Lucy?" Phil says. "Could you do me a favour? I'm swamped here."

He takes my silence as acceptance and slides a coffee and cinnamon roll across the counter to me. "Please take these over to the lady at the window table." I take the mug and plate from him and he beckons me closer, dropping his voice to a whisper. "Be careful. She bites."

The woman is dressed in old clothes and I can see her sweater has a stain on the front. An old brown overcoat is tossed across the back of the chair next to her, revealing its torn lining and she wears a crocheted purple and white wooly hat that mostly covers her flyaway white hair.

Her lips are narrow and turned down so it comes as a surprise when she gives me a big smile as I put down her coffee, showing teeth so white and large I know they have to be dentures.

"Thanks," she says, her voice as gravelly as a cement mixer. "I appreciate it. I can't really manage on my own." She indicates the walker parked next to the table.

"*Americano!*" Phil shouts as he places my paper cup on the counter and gives me a smile.

"Would you like to join me?" the old lady asks.

I would not. But I'm not sure how I can refuse. Also, it's the only empty seat in the house.

"Sure." I manage a smile. "Be right back." I grab my coffee, top it up with cream and sugar and join the woman just as she is carefully cutting her cinnamon bun in half and placing a piece on a paper napkin.

"Here," she says, sliding the napkin across the table to me. "These buns are huge." Phil had just warned me about her but here she is offering me half her cinnamon bun.

I extend my hand across the table. "I'm Lucy," I say.

The old lady gives me a big smile as she shakes my hand. "I'm Doreen."

"Do you live around here?" I try to make conversation, which is not one of my strengths and as I ask the question I realize how stupid it is. The woman wouldn't likely be travelling any great distance with a walker. And, based on her shabby clothes it isn't tough to figure out she's from the East Village, just a couple of blocks away, across the Clarence Street lift bridge.

The East Village is the dirty secret in the region. Once it was a thriving working class neighbourhood, but now it's mostly boarded up houses and empty lots, left behind when people moved away after the refinery shut down.

"For over fifty years," Doreen nods. Her bright eyes appraise me. "You look very familiar to me."

I smile and immediately feel the tension rise up my back. "I'm in here a lot," I shrug it off. "I just live over by the hospital, on Forest Drive." Normally I protect my privacy and would never reveal where

I live, but this small talk with a complete stranger is hard work. I don't know what else to say. I try to mask my awkwardness by taking another bite of the bun and chewing slowly.

"I've seen you in here before," she nods, studying me through narrowed eyes. "Are you from around here?"

"You mean from the East Village? No, I'm from Wainfleet," I lie. I feel the old woman's eyes are on me and it makes me uncomfortable. It feels like she ever misses a thing.

Doreen shakes her head. "I never forget a face.'"

"Fifty years." Her persistence is making me even more uncomfortable and I change the subject. "You must have seen a lot of changes around here in that time."

"It used to be such a nice place, this town. Back when the refinery was open. Not like now. Crime. Drugs. It's not safe." Doreen looks over at the table by the door.

I follow her gaze and we both watch as a man flirts with a young girl. I recognize what's happening; the pimp is grooming her so he could turn her out. I also recognize him. His name is Mark Sempe and he's well known to police in the region. He's also well known to me, even though I try most days to forget it.

"There was a stabbing just the other day," Doreen continues. "Right over there." She points to the bus shelter across the street and down a few blocks.

The shelter is still sealed off with yellow caution tape and I can see a few floral tributes lying in front of it, as well as an old stuffed teddy bear. I've seen this before and know how it will play out: For the next few days the police tape will remain wrapped around the bus shelter, and there will be more police cruisers in the neighbourhood than usual. Then everything will go back to normal: The yellow tape will come down. The shelter will be cleaned and any blood washed away by whatever company the town has a service contract with. The tributes and teddy bear will be taken away on trash day.

"You need to be careful," I say to her. "Maybe stay close to home, especially at night."

Doreen bursts out laughing, cackling loud enough that people turn to look. "I didn't get to be my age by being careful," she says. "Don't worry about me. Anyway, there's nowhere to go at night. My dancing days are behind me." She pats her walker and winks. "Arthritis."

"Ouch," I say, finishing my coffee. "Can you take anything for it?"

Doreen nods. "Doctor's afraid I'll get addicted to opiates." She cackles again. "I told him I'm half dead already, what's the risk?"

My phone rings and I answer it as Doreen cackles at her own joke.

It's Decker, calling from the station.

"I thought you would want to know that your suicide, Maurice Cobb, has a record. Assault against his ex-wife. Conditional discharge. Currently on probation."

"I'm on my way in now," I say, waving goodbye to the sharp-eyed Doreen and wondering if was true she never forgot a face.

I feel the anxiety start to flutter in my chest as I walk to my car, thinking of what Doreen said. That she knew me. But how could that be possible?

I toss the rest of my coffee into the trash bin, realizing that drinking it would be the worst thing for me right now. Caffeine will only contribute to the mounting feeling of panic surging in my chest. The idea of sitting through the evening briefing, then spending the next eight hours in a patrol car is making it worse. What I want to do is run. Or punch a bag until I'm exhausted, until the feelings of agitation and anxiety fade away. I reach my car and I'm considering taking some rescue medication when I hear a scream, coming from the canal.

"Help! Someone's in the water!"

It's like the answer to my prayer and I tear across the street toward the canal where a couple is standing by the rail. The woman is on her cell phone and I can hear her shouting to the 911 Operator as I vault the low fence and race to meet them by the water's edge.

"We're at Promenade Park," the woman is shouting into her phone. "By the canal. Someone's in the water!"

The man has pulled the lifebuoy off the stand and is holding the red and white ring across his chest, looking panicked and unsure what he should do with it.

"I'm a police officer," I shout as I approach. I'm briefly aware of his wide eyes staring as I sprint by him, grabbing the lifebuoy from his hands. I reach the concrete edge and kick off my shoes as I scan the current for the drowning victim.

Fifteen feet from the edge a hand rises up from the water, right next to the weir canal. The water is turbulent and the hand disappears the moment I see it, but I keep my eye on the spot as I stride jump into the water, holding the lifebuoy close to my chest.

I hit the cold water and go under for a second, but scissor my legs together to thrust myself back up to the surface and I start to swim to where I'd seen the arm. I can't see anything in the dark roiling water and hesitate, not sure if I should try and dive under, hoping it's not too late.

I hear sirens approaching. The ambulance and fire department are close. But I doubt they'll be in time if I don't find him. I'm spinning around in a panic, looking for something, anything that will help me find the person when a shoulder rises up out of the water. Hope flares in my chest and I dive, grabbing for whatever I can reach. Luckily I'm just able to catch hold of the fabric on his sleeve and I grip it tight, pulling the victim toward me, up and out of the water.

It's a man. I roll him over in the water, ready to tow him out, to resuscitate him until the paramedics can take over when I realize I'm too late. The sight of his bloated face and white eyes tell me he's been dead for a while and I let go in revulsion. The movement I saw must have been his body caught in the turbulence from the weir and maybe if I hadn't been on the verge of an anxiety attack I would have thought twice before I'd jumped in after him.

I get hold of myself and taking hold of his sleeve I start to swim to the side of the canal to wait for the paramedics.

"Pull on the rope," I shout to the couple who are both recording the rescue on their cell phones. Neither reacts and I realize I should make sure the victim's bloated face is hidden, so I turn him over, face down, and start to swim again. They stop for a moment as they understand what it means. But then they start to video again.

"Pull on the damn rope," I shout again, louder. The man slips his phone into his pocket and starts to haul me in, hand over hand. I'm holding the dead man by his jacket, ensuring he's face down in the water and by the time we reach the side of the canal the paramedics are on the scene. They take over the recovery, help me out of the water and sit me in the back of the ambulance while they check me over.

"I'm f-fine," I say through chattering teeth. "I'm a p-police officer. I'll be okay."

The paramedic raises a skeptical brow. "You may be a police officer, but you can still get hypothermia. Your lips are blue."

"I just need a hot shower," I argue. "I've got to get to work. My shift starts at seven."

"Looks like you started early today," she laughs. "Does this count as overtime?" She puts away the blood pressure cuff. "Are you okay to drive?"

I nod and climb out of the ambulance. If I wasn't freezing cold and wet I'd have waited around for the Coroner, but a hot shower and change of clothes is more important right now. I should just about make the evening briefing, though Decker's probably wondering what's taking me so long.

I guess I asked for it. I wanted something to help with my anxiety and there's nothing like a rescue to do just that. It's one of the reasons I joined the police force in the first place.

SEVEN

I'VE MADE AN appointment to meet Maurice Cobb's ex-wife and give her the news. I wonder how she'll react to learning her abusive ex-husband has killed himself. I hope she doesn't cry and get emotional; I didn't do well in empathy training.

When I arrive at Womyn Collective Flower Farm it's almost dark, but I can see a few women are still out in the fields cutting blossoms and placing them in buckets, then loading them onto a small tractor. A bell rings and the tractor, loaded with sunflowers and dahlias makes its way along the rows heading back to the barn, the women trailing behind. Womyn provides both shelter and employment for abused women from all across the Niagara region. The residents make jams, soaps and herbal vinegars, run a pick your own flower farm and a thriving florist business.

Womyn didn't exist when I was a child, when my mother could have used the refuge. If it had maybe my life would have turned out differently.

I park next to the barn that houses the Womyn shop and production facility, but the sign is turned to Closed, so I walk up to the main house. It's a sprawling old red brick Victorian farmhouse and I can see money has been spent on painting and restoring the building; that must mean business is doing well. I ring the bell, look up at the security camera and wait.

A voice comes through the intercom, and I hold up my ID to the camera, in case my being in uniform isn't proof enough of who I am. "I'm Detective Constable Gauthier. I have an appointment."

The security is a recent addition at Womyn, added after the abusive husband of a resident had broken in, looking for his wife. Sophie Tuinstra, the founder of Womyn, had held a shotgun on the guy until the police arrived and I was surprised she hadn't shot him. There's nothing Sophie wouldn't do to protect the women and children in her care.

The door opens and a woman escorts me into the front sitting room, which is furnished with a sofa, a pair of wing chairs and a coffee table that holds a lush flower arrangement. Another massive one stands on a sideboard, an example of the floral design work Womyn is famous for.

The floors are worn pine planks, and covered with hand-woven area rugs in bright colours. They're probably also made here, another example of the kind of handcrafted products the Womyn made: rugs, table runners, tea towels and napkins.

A thin, dark haired woman sits in one of the wing chairs. She's nervous and her hand keeps plucking at the armrest of the chair.

"I'm Detective Constable Gauthier," I say as I take a seat. "Are you Geraldine Bennett?" Cobb's wife has gone back to her maiden name after their divorce. The woman nods.

"I'm sorry, but I have some bad news for you," I say. "Regarding your ex-husband Maurice Cobb." The woman's eyes flicker. I'm not sure if it's in anticipation of the news or just a reaction to hearing his name.

"Is he dead?" she whispers.

"Yes. I'm afraid so." I sit for a moment, letting the news settle. She takes a deep breath. "Good," she says after a moment. Geraldine Bennett is clearly not going to shed a tear over her ex-husband. She isn't a hypocrite, pretending to be sad. I like that.

"We found him this morning, at the Taiga facility," I begin. "Do you know why he might have been there?"

Geraldine Bennett shakes her head. "No idea. I haven't heard anything about him in over a year, thankfully." She seems suddenly to be very tired. Her shoulders slump and she bends over, holding her head in her hands.

"Are you all right?" I ask after a moment. "Can I get you something? A glass of water?"

She raises her head and meets my eye. "I can't believe he's dead," she says, her face breaking into a smile. "You're certain? He's really dead?"

I pull out my notebook, relieved this isn't going to be as difficult as I'd thought.

"May I ask you some questions about Mr. Cobb?"

She shrugs. "I honestly don't know much. It's been… difficult." I can imagine. I'd read his file when I got to the station: He'd broken her jaw. Was charged with assault, pleaded guilty. There were several other incidents on record: five calls to the marital residence; several of them from neighbours who'd heard her screaming. Maurice Cobb was not a good man.

"Do you know where he worked?" The questions are routine; we already have his home address from the driver's license I'll be going by there next as part of the investigation.

"No," she replies. "As far as I know he wasn't working anywhere." Her lip twists in scorn. "That way he didn't have to pay child support."

"How many children do you have?"

"Two. They don't live here… at the shelter," she adds after a moment. "They've been living with my mother." I don't need to ask why. It would be much more comfortable living with their grandmother. Bennett didn't have that option—she was staying at Womyn for her safety, to protect her from Cobb.

"What was his last place of employment you're aware of?"

Gathering information about a victim, even though it might prove to be a suicide, is part of the job. Investigators aren't supposed to draw any conclusions. That's the ultimate call of the medical examiner or Coroner. Our job is to learn as much as we can about the victim. Did he suffer from depression? Was there suicidal ideation? Had they made any long-term plans? What was their lifestyle? Any drugs, gambling, debt, or alcohol issues? What was going on in their life when they died?

She hesitates for a moment before answering. "He used to work in the pharmaceutical industry. At Advik Therapeutics. But he left last year."

"What did he do there?"

"Research. He was a molecular biologist."

That tells me Cobb was highly educated. I struggle to put that together with the man who apparently was working as a security guard at Taiga when he died. What had happened to him?

"Do you have any idea why he left his position at Advik?"

She shakes her head and I wonder why she looks so frightened.

EIGHT

COBB'S APARTMENT IS a low-rise walk up, over a store on Nickel Street. It's in the damn East Village, of course. I've worked so hard to get out of here, and it seems like every day I keep getting drawn back.

The apartment is managed by the Patels, a couple who own the Indian grocery store below it. Mrs. Patel orders her husband to escort me upstairs and unlock the door to Cobb's unit. Even though I don't speak Urdu, I'm sure I hear her tell him to not let me out of his sight, given how he shadows me through the apartment.

Mr. Patel explains that they'd rented the apartment furnished, so none of the furniture belongs to Cobb; just the clothes in the closet and the few books and papers piled on the kitchen table are his. Not much of a legacy. I go through the drawers in the bedside table and gather it all together with the paperwork on the table then I start to go through it systematically, putting things to either the left or right hand side once I've read them over. Left is of no interest; right is to take back to the station for further scrutiny.

"You can leave me to this," I say over my shoulder after a few minutes of feeling him fidgeting behind me. "I'll be a while." His eyes dart back and forth between the pile of papers on the table and the open door that promises escape. Which is less appealing to him, I wonder: The prospect of spending the next hour watching me sift through Cobb's stuff or facing his wife's wrath if he leaves me alone in the apartment. In the end he leaves me to it and returns to the shop.

It takes less than an hour to go through Cobb's lottery tickets, a thick divorce file, two sets of termination papers, several unpaid parking tickets, bank statements that show he was in overdraft, and lots overdue bills, including one from the truck dealership where he'd financed a brand new Ford F-150. According to one letter, he was behind on his payments and they were threatening repossession. It adds up to a picture of a guy in deep financial trouble, who'd lost his job and his family, and was working at a job far below his qualifications. It doesn't take my Psychology degree to tell me suicide isn't unlikely, given these circumstances.

Near the bottom of the pile of papers I find several pay stubs made out to Maurice Cobb. They're from Pelham Woods—the long-term care facility up on the escarpment. Looks like Cobb had a second job, and no surprise. It's pretty clear he needed money and one minimum-wage job wasn't going to cut it.

There's also a cell phone bill, but no phone had been found at the scene, nor had one turned up when I'd found Cobb's wallet in Julia Sharp's purse. Maybe the phone had gone off in his truck when it was stolen. Even though I have little hope the truck will ever be found, uniform are out looking for Julia Sharp's boyfriend Andre Dumont. When we catch up with him, he'll just deny stealing it anyway, despite what Julia's mother said.

It occurs to me that maybe the truck wasn't stolen after all. Maybe it was repossessed by the dealer, as they were threatening to do. Based on the letter, dated just a couple of months ago, it was imminent. I make a note to follow up when I'm back at the station.

I also find a thick file and a journal full of scribbled notes that I have a hard time deciphering. It looks like some kind of test data, as well as chemical formulas and lots of math equations. Whatever it is, it's way over my head. I decide to take it with me and find someone who can help me decode it and see if it's in any way relevant.

Most times the night shift of a duty patrol officer is a circus, especially from after the bars let out when I get to spend hours dealing with the worst of the region's population: Assault, vandalism, public intoxication, traffic infractions, DUIs, drug dealing and domestic abuse. But at least the time goes quickly. Tonight is no different and I'm grateful to head off shift as the sun is coming up.

I'm exhausted, but as I put my key into my front door lock it sticks and I'm hit with a wave of anxiety so intense I have a feeling of displacement, as if I'm out of my own body. My knees go weak and I cling to the doorframe. Is this even my home? All the houses in the street look the same. The panic starts to race through me. Have I actually gone to the wrong house?

I turn the key again and this time the lock opens and to my relief I'm able to push the door open. I'm tired, that's all it is. Just tired after a long shift. All I need is a long shower and to go to bed.

I head into the kitchen, pour myself a drink and lean up against the sliding glass doors to the deck. I catch my neighbour's look of disapproval seeing me holding a glass of wine first thing in the morning. I raise the glass in a toast to him and he turns away. Screw him. I just finished a ten-hour night shift and this bottle of Sauvignon Blanc isn't going to drink itself.

Then I realize something is off. I put down the glass and look around the kitchen. Nothing seems out of place, but I can't shake the feeling that someone has been here. Or maybe it's just my anxiety, humming along like it always does. My constant companion, my evil shadow.

I take another drink of wine and walk around the kitchen island, looking carefully at the room. Then I wander into the living room and stand by the window, wondering if I'm imagining things. The house is clean, as always. Part of my anxiety management is constant tidying, cleaning, and making sure everything is in its place. And everything is. The bookshelves? No, they're fine. The television remotes? No—they are neatly lined up as I'd left them. Something catches my eye. A slip of paper is sticking out of the drawer in the coffee table. I didn't leave it like that. There's no way my condition would ever allow it.

Someone has been in my place. I know it in my gut. Who? And what were they looking for? I go over to the drawer and pull it open. Someone has been going through my papers and documents. Everything seems to still be here, but it's out of order.

The early morning light is still weak so I get my flashlight and go out the sliding doors onto the deck. I walk through the backyard then all around the house, checking under each window before I move on to the front yard, where I crouch on the lawn. The new angle of sight reveals a set of tracks through the morning dew. I can tell they've been made by narrow tires, like from a stroller. Or a bike. I get out my phone and quickly take some pictures of the tracks before the sun melts the dew and erases them.

I look closely at the front door and see scratches around the lock. That's why my key didn't feel right when I'd first tried it. Someone has broken into my home. Whoever it was had come here after I'd left for work last night, likely after dark sometime to make sure they weren't seen.

My heart is racing as adrenaline floods my body. My anxiety is back, this time with good reason. I'm not just imagining it and it's not because I'm tired. Someone definitely broke into my home, but what were they looking for?

NINE

AFTER MY DAY off, I'm rested and my anxiety is back to low-normal range. Once roll call, the briefing and duty assignments are over, I drive out to Pelham Woods to see what I can find out about Maurice Cobb. It's a large facility, with a retirement wing where senior citizens can rent apartments as well as several secure wings for residents with various forms of dementia or brain injury.

I haven't been here since I was in high school when I was dragged along to visit my dying grandfather. I hated those visits in the airless room with the dim light, watching the silent tears streaming down my parents' faces as the old man lay in bed waiting to die. His eyes wide open, he'd lie day after day, with his head facing the window, staring as dawn became dusk then became dark. I feel the familiar knot forming in my chest and I breathe deeply, trying to relax and fight the anxiety welling up in me.

I take a quick walk through the large, airy ground floor atrium. The building has been taken over by new owners and completely renovated since I was last here. The first thing I notice is a massive flower arrangement on a table near the front entrance. It has to be at least four feet tall and is overflowing with twigs and fruit, flowers and greenery. The fragrance of the lilies lures me in for a closer sniff and I notice a stack of business cards and brochures next to the flowers, advertising Womyn Flower Farm and their design business.

The main lobby is laid out as an old fashioned streetscape, complete with faux streetlamps. Next to a hand painted sign that reads Administration, an office door is open. A woman is sitting at a desk, surrounded by piles of papers and files. The lanyard around her neck identifies her as Susan Armstrong, Human Resources. I introduce myself and show her my ID.

"I'm here inquiring about one of your employees," I tell her. "Maurice Cobb." The flash of alarm in the woman's eyes is unmistakeable. "He's no longer an employee," she says. "His employment was terminated last week."

"Why, may I ask?"

She looks uncomfortable and hesitates long enough for me to know she's about to lie to me. "There were some complaints. From patients." It seems unlikely that the patients in a dementia care ward would be in a state to complain about anything, but I don't challenge her.

"What was his role here?"

"He was in security, an overnight position," she says, pretending to study some papers on her desk. "He manned the front entrance after hours, and did hourly walk-throughs to check all the wards and exits, that sort of thing."

"What was his last day of employment?"

"I'd have to look." She looks irritated. "Why do you need it? Has he done something?"

"He's dead."

"Dead!" She recoils in shock and her eyes fill with tears. "When? How?"

"Yesterday. We're investigating the circumstances now." I'm surprised at her reaction; Cobb didn't seem like a likeable guy. "Were you two friendly?"

She looks embarrassed. "No, not at all. I'm just... hormonal I guess." She points to her abdomen. "Pregnant. Four months." She spins her office chair around then rolls it to a filing cabinet in the corner. "I even cry over coffee commercials. But I do remember Mr. Cobb; that was a sad situation. He was so eager to have the job. Seemed so happy when he started working here. It was a complete shock when he had to be let go." She quickly finds Cobb's file and hands it to me. "It's all in there," she says. "I'll make you a copy."

I glance over the two pages she has given me. It isn't much. The first sheet of paper is Cobb's application for employment. On the form he'd filled in his address and personal information. In the previous employment boxes he'd listed his job at Taiga, and two other minimum-wage positions in retail. There was no mention of his research position at Advik Therapeutics, nor any indication he had any post-secondary education, much less a PhD in chemistry.

Why had Cobb not provided his true employment history? Was he embarrassed about the circumstances behind his leaving his research position? Did he not want them to ask any questions, so he wouldn't have to tell any lies?

The second sheet is an incident report, written up the day Cobb was fired. Cobb had been suspected of attempting to steal medications; Pelham Woods had dismissed him immediately and a Dr. Chowdhury had signed off on the document. On an impulse I walk back toward the administrative offices and ask Ms. Armstrong where I can find Dr. Chowdhury.

The elevator doors open onto the second floor and it's clear that only the lobby has been renovated. This floor, the same one my grandfather was on, looks identical to how it did all those years ago, with the worn floral carpet and the chipped ceramic tile by the nursing desk. I remember how much I hated it here, how I resented all of those visits. My grandfather never thought of me as part of the family in the first place. And he didn't even recognize his own son by the end.

The floor is laid out in the shape of a letter T, with the nursing desk in middle of the three wings. The center and right wings are for regular patients and the left for palliative care. I avert my eyes from the left, from where my grandfather spent his final weeks, in a dark quiet room, lost inside his own head. He'd taken years to die; first losing his memories, then his personality, then the ability to walk, talk or swallow. My palms are clammy and my mouth dry as I focus on the task at hand and shut the memories back in their box.

I find Dr. Chowdhury at the nursing desk in conversation with a nurse so I hang back and watch as the staff go around the lounge, giving out plastic cups of juice or tea to the residents. In most cases they have to put the cup into their hands and gently squeeze their fingers to remind them how to hold it. Most of the patients just sit, holding the cup and not taking a sip until one of the attendants comes by and encourages them to raise it to their mouth and have a drink. Finally the nurse picks up the files and leaves and I'm able to approach.

"Dr. Chowdhury?" He turns and the smile instantly leaves his face and his expression becomes guarded. I'm used to this. Most people are suspicious of the police, and with good reason. We don't usually come with good news. "I'm Detective Constable Gauthier, with Niagara Regional Police. I'd like to ask you a few questions please."

He leads me into a small consulting room adjacent to the front desk. From the computer on the table and the locked drawers it looks like this is where they keep the patient medications and records.

"It's about a former employee of Pelham Woods. Maurice Cobb."

Chowdhury looks irritated. "What about him?" I hear a noise, coming from the patient lounge. The doctor turns his head then decides it's nothing and turns back to me.

"Can you tell me about the reason for his dismissal?"

"Why is it of interest?" It's clear he doesn't want to answer. "What's he done now?"

"He's been found dead." Chowdhury doesn't react to the news. It's as if he didn't hear me. He keeps turning toward the lounge, distracted by some noise that I don't understand, like a dog hearing an inaudible high pitched whistle.

Then there's a crash and a scream and we both run out of the consulting room. A man is tearing around the patient lounge, grabbing sofa cushions and stuffed dolls and flinging them at the other patients. He's shouting incoherently and howling as tears stream down his cheeks. The snack trolley has been pushed over and all of the tea, coffee and cranberry juice is spilled everywhere.

One of the care workers is trying to calm the man, her hand reaching out to try and take hold of his arm and restrain him.

"Donald," she keeps saying his name in a calm, firm voice, trying to get him to focus on her. "Donald, stop it." He turns and starts to shout at her.

"Stop it," he screams, his eyes bulging. Spittle flies from his lips as he works himself into a frenzy. "*StopItDonaldStopItDonaldstopit-stopitstopit.*" Then he runs headlong into the glass door that leads into the dining room. There's a sickening crack as he collides, as his head snaps back and he falls to the floor in a crumpled heap. The tempered glass door fractures into thousands of small particles and stays frozen in place for a split second, holding the shape of Donald's head before it shatters and rains down onto him, covering his body like crystals of ice.

TEN

DR. CHOWDHURY RUSHES over to the unconscious patient and bends to examine him. I stand back as staff moves quickly to clean up the mess and restore the room to order. The nurse isn't even concerned with the patient lying on the floor. Her head is bent over the patient files and she's double-checking something, probably making sure his medications are correct and no mistakes have been made, like a missed dose. It looks to me like she's covering her ass.

The nurse is skinny and dark haired and the only remarkable thing about her is that her uniform looks as if it's been worn for a few shifts since it was last washed. She glances up from the files and notices me watching her, then she goes back to the files, making a point of turning her back so I can't see her face or what she's looking at.

The rest of the patients in the lounge are unfazed by what just happened. Most of them remain asleep in their wheelchairs, unaware of any possible danger they were in. Sitting on one of the loveseats is an elderly woman with a walker parked beside her. It's Doreen.

"That was exciting," she says when I come over to say hello. "I almost didn't recognize you in your uniform." Her eyes sparkle and she's clearly enjoying herself. She's sitting next to a woman who's smiling happily but looks vacant.

"Good to see you Doreen," I say. I'm about to sit down when Doreen yelps.

"No!" she says. "Not there." I look at the suspicious stains on the upholstered seat and pull up a wooden chair instead. "Some of them leak," Doreen says, tipping her head toward the other residents. Both Doreen and her friend are sitting on vinyl chairs. Much easier to keep sanitary I'm sure.

"I'm here most days," she says. "Visiting my old friend Nadia Efimov." Her voice rises slightly as she pats her friend's knee. The woman turns her head and nods with interest. "Not usually this much excitement around here though."

"Efimov," I say, trying to remember why I know the name. "Are you related to Rose?" The white haired woman stares at me and blinks twice. Maybe she doesn't understand English?

Doreen laughs while the other woman continues to stare at me. "You know Rose?" she asks. "This is her mother."

"I worked at Thorny Rose when I was in school," I say. "Years ago. And of course I met her again recently, with everything that happened there…" Doreen nods. Of course she knows the story; it was in all the papers and news broadcasts for weeks.

The elevator doors open and a pair of attendants in hospital scrubs emerge, pushing a gurney. They go over to the patient and lift him onto a stretcher, then roll him out the way they've come. The doctor is following them to the elevator and I leave Doreen to intercept him. His expression becomes anxious when it's clear he's going to have to talk to me instead of following the patient.

"What was that about?" I ask. "Does it happen often?"

"Oh no!" he exclaims. "A psychotic break like that is rare. Very rare." We walk together away from the elevators. "In advanced stages of dementia, many people develop BPSD," he says.

"What's that?"

"BPSD is an acronym for Behavioral and Psychological Symptoms of Dementia," he says. "That can be anything from agitation and anxiety and wandering, all the way to delusions and hallucinations."

What I'd just witnessed looked far more serious than agitation, but I don't argue. "Is he on medication?"

Chowdhury nods. "All of our patients are. It helps us manage symptoms and keep the patient comfortable and safe."

"Safe," I echo. "This medication is an anti-psychotic?" Dr. Chowdhury looks irritated and defensive. "I thought those made people passive and sleepy. Not violent."

"As I said," he snaps. "This is very rare. I'm going to look into his medication, and make whatever adjustments are needed."

We've made our way back to the consulting room. "Can you share the reason for Maurice Cobb's dismissal?"

"Oh, yes," he seems eager to change the subject. "He was seen, in this very room, actually."

"And you assumed..."

"That he was stealing medication of course," he says. "There's no reason for him to ever be in here, especially at night. We dispense many opiates like morphine, Oxycodone, Fentanyl. Any of them could be sold." Or used. Maybe Cobb had addiction issues on top of the rest of his problems. Or possibly it was the cause of the rest of his problems.

"But nothing was missing?"

"No, because he was interrupted."

"Can you please give me a quick explanation as to how the medications are stored and dispensed?"

"Yes, I suppose so," he glances at his watch to underline how busy and important he is.

Dr. Chowdhury points to a metal cabinet with multiple small drawers, each with a lock. "The medications are all stored in these cabinets, replenished as needed by the pharmacy, when the nurse sees the quantities are low. Every day the medication cart," he points to it, sitting in the corner, "is audited by the nursing team and all narcotics and controlled substances are spot-checked and counted. There's a drug record book that's filled in with all the medication that is dispensed to patients during the day. This room is always locked when unoccupied and as you can see it's in full view of the nursing desk."

"And as a member of the security team, did Cobb have a key?"

"Certainly not. He would have no reason to. He was not on the medical staff," Chowdhury says. "The nurses do, of course. As do I."

"So, Cobb would have to break into the cabinet to steal the drugs," I say. "And that would certainly be quickly discovered, given your system." Chowdhury shrugs, disinterested, but I continue. "The damage to the lock would have been evident as soon as the nurse on duty went to get whatever she needed." It would be a one-time deal and he'd be the most obvious suspect if the break-in happened overnight. Not a great business plan for someone who wanted to sell drugs.

Dr. Chowdhury nods. "Yes, but..." He stops and gathers his thoughts. "I've found that in cases of addiction, people aren't always thinking of the consequences, or if they'll get caught."

"So you're now saying he was an addict?"

Dr. Chowdhury exhales, exasperated. "I don't even know the man. I have no idea why he wanted to steal the drugs."

"What about the patient medical files?" Maybe Cobb had been in the room for some other reason.

"They are kept on the computer," he points to the monitor on the desktop, "and hard copies are in these file drawers." The filing cabinet doesn't have locks.

"You don't feel the need to lock these? For patient privacy?"

"As I said," Dr. Chowdhury is defensive. "The room itself is always kept locked. And the medication is double-locked, as per Ministry guidelines." He looks pointedly at me. "Is there anything else? Anyway, don't you need some kind of a warrant for this?"

"I'm only asking you a few questions Dr. Chowdhury. What would make you think I need a warrant for that?"

"Then we're done here," he says as he heads for the elevator.

ELEVEN

SIOBHAN FINN IS Director of Public Relations at Taiga—an unusual choice for management to send to meet with a police officer investigating the death of one of their employees. I guess they're concerned about the spin when word gets out about his death. And that word is starting to look interesting: Maurice Cobb, the guy who was fired from Pelham Woods, purportedly for attempting to steal opiates, also worked at Taiga, the largest cannabis producer in the region. I can't see any connection between Pelham Woods and Taiga, but that doesn't mean the public and media won't create one. Or that it's not there.

She hands me a folder. "I've pulled his file for you to take a look at. Is there anything specific you'd like to know?"

"His employment history would be a start. The nature of his duties. Anything you can tell me about his life."

"I wouldn't know anything about his personal life," she says. "Mr. Cobb wasn't an employee of Taiga. Our security is outsourced to a private firm."

"But he had a security ID from here," I say as her phone rings.

"Excuse me please," Finn says as she glances at it and rolls her eyes. "I'll be a few minutes. In the meantime, would you like to speak with the guard on duty? He may be able to help, just as a start."

"Sure, that would be great." I walk over to the security desk, where a skinny young man sits, pretending to study the video monitors. I'd noticed him checking me out when I came in; I recognized the uniform envy. I know his type: a guy who'd gone to the local police college, maybe even got a diploma in criminology, but for some reason he never got hired onto the force, so he ended up working as a security guard.

I introduce myself and he eagerly stands up and shakes my hand. "I'm Ron Vandermeer," as if I might remember his name and give him a nod when talking to the Chief of Police, a man I've never met in my almost five years on the force.

"I'm here inquiring about Maurice Cobb. Did you know him?"

"Not really. I talked to him in passing a couple of times, like when we changed shifts." Siobhan Finn finishes her call and rejoins us, and I notice Vandermeer shrinks back when she approaches. It's obvious she intimidates him.

"What exactly did Mr. Cobb do, as part of his duties?" I ask. "Can you walk me through a typical shift?"

"Sure, I guess," Vandermeer says, once Finn has nodded her permission. He beckons me behind the security desk and shows me a bank of monitors. "Mostly we sit here and keep an eye on these. We monitor the alarm systems and video surveillance cameras."

"Do you ever leave your post here? To do a walk through?"

"We do foot patrol every hour," he says, sliding a book across the desk to me. "We need to make sure the buildings and equipment are secure, and all the access points are controlled. Prevent losses and damage. Observe and report irregularities, security breaches. Make sure there are no trespassers." He sounds like he's reading his own job description. "It's all logged here."

"Who's here after hours?" I glance at the log.

"Just us. The security guards," he says. "The growers, technicians and office staff are all gone by six at the latest."

"And if someone needs to get in after hours what happens?" I ask. "Say a staff member forgot something, for instance."

"They'd call in from the main gate. We talk to them on the intercom and make sure they're here on legitimate business. And of course the same again at the door here." He points to the video feed of both the front gate and the door.

"And the entire perimeter of the property is fenced?" I ask. "There's no other access into the site?"

"Absolutely secure." He nods. "All of it. Almost a million square feet under glass greenhouses. Offices, warehouses, all surrounded by a ten foot fence, topped with razor wire all around the forty acres."

"Not absolutely secure. That's where Maurice Cobb died," I say, pointing at the monitor. "There's a big hole cut in the fence. And signs that local kids have been partying there for some time." He looks down, embarrassed. "I'll make sure we look into it," he mumbles.

I point to his ID badge, which is just like Maurice Cobb's. "Are you an employee here, Mr. Vandermeer?"

"Yes!" He nods eagerly, then stops. "I mean, no. Not exactly. I'm assigned here, but I'm on a contract, with Limestone Security…"

"Would you like a tour?" Finn interrupts. "I can take you around the facility, give you an idea of what we do here." It's obvious she's making a show about how happy they are to cooperate with police and I follow her through a pair of sliding glass doors into a long hallway, but all I can think about is that Cooper's private security company has a contract with Taiga. Talk about a small world.

"Taiga will soon have over two million square feet of green-house space," Finn begins, in very practised PR mode. "We also have an additional fifty thousand square feet of drying and processing rooms, and a state of the art laboratory."

"Did you say *two million* square feet?"

"Absolutely," she laughs. "We need to expand our production capacity since the market demand is growing. Faster than we can keep up, in fact."

Finn walks me through some double doors and into a rigid plastic vestibule outside a greenhouse.

"We'll need to wash our hands and put on protective clothing," she says, handing me a pair of booties and a smock.

I'm confused. "Since when are cannabis plants dangerous?"

"It's to protect the plants, not you," Finn laughs. "We have hundreds of million dollars of value in plants growing here and we need to make sure to minimize, or eliminate, any risk of virus or insect infestation getting in." She puts on her smock and booties then hands me a shower cap. "Yeah, I know," she says apologetically. "They look terrible, but it's policy."

Once we're both dressed she unlocks the door using her pass-key and we enter a huge greenhouse, full of bushy three-foot tall cannabis plants all growing in large black plastic pots. I can see two workers, both dressed exactly like Finn and me, complete with shower caps, smocks and booties. It's impossible to see if they are men or women.

"This definitely is all state of the art," I say with genuine admiration. I've busted lots of local grows in my time on the force, and I've been in quite a few in the days before I'd even thought of being a police officer. Some of them had reasonably professional set-ups, but none of them had the capacity to grow more than a few pounds of weed a year.

"High Tech. Almost like you don't need any humans involved in the process at all," I add.

"Well, that's definitely not true," Finn says. "Growing cannabis is extremely labour intensive, especially during harvest. And we need highly skilled human eyes on the plants every day, pruning, and checking for signs of disease or nutritional deficiency. But, anything we can automate, we do—to minimize error."

"How many strains do you grow here?"

"Twenty five different strains are grown at this facility. We have three full crops a year, and harvest around twelve thousand pounds of cannabis flowers." I try to do the math as best I can in my head. A pound of weed on the street is worth around twenty-three hundred dollars, times twelve thousand..I give up and get out my phone while the Finn is busy swiping her passkey at yet another door. The calculator tells me twelve thousand pounds of cannabis is equal to around twenty seven million dollars… *no that can't be right.* I do the math again and it is.

Finn's phone rings again and she holds up her hand in apology as she answers. She walks a few feet away for privacy and I'm able to look around. At the far end of the greenhouse, a crew is working behind a screened-off area. One of them is a tall Jamaican man, wearing a yellow, green and red striped Rastacap under his shower cap. He and his two co-workers are laying irrigation hose in a section of the greenhouse that's lined out with new plants. He notices me watching him and quickly turns his back to me, so I'm not able to see his face. He must have said something to the other two because they quickly head behind the screen, as if they also don't want to be seen. Or did I imagine it?

Siobhan Finn finishes her call and glances at her watch. The tour must be over, I realize.

"How many staff do you have here?" I ask, deliberately not taking the hint.

"We have over three hundred full time employees at Taiga."

"And do you employ additional agricultural workers at busy times? Like for harvesting?"

"Definitely," she says. "If we don't have enough staff, the crop won't be harvested in time. The quality will suffer as a result of even a few days' delay and we'll lose a lot of money."

I wonder what the men are doing. They seemed to be hiding, trying to avoid being noticed. Are they are illegal? "Do you hire any migrant workers?"

"Temporary Foreign Workers," Finn corrects me. "Not yet. We've decided not to participate in that program."

I'm surprised. Most large farmers in the area bring in migrant workers. "Why not?"

"The cannabis industry is very specialized," she says. "Typical temporary agricultural workers don't have the skills we need. Any mistake could cause a contaminated crop, which is potentially costly. It's just not worth the risk."

I glance back toward the Jamaican man, but he has disappeared. There's no reason to assume he's a migrant, I realize. But why did he seem so furtive?

TWELVE

ON THE WAY back to the station I put in a call to Decker when my car radio comes to life. ***Ten Forty Five Fatality. Green Bean Cafe. Fourteen Colborne Street. Ambulance is on the scene. Code Two.*** I hang up and pull out onto the street. I can talk to him later.

Decker beats me to the coffee shop. I pull up next to his car near the ambulance and fire engine, making sure to block as much public access to the cafe. It'll inconvenience people, but our priority is to secure the scene and ensure that the first responders are able to get the victim to hospital if needed.

I go inside and see the body of a man lying on the floor next to a table. Paramedics are no longer working on him. One ambulance attendant stands next to the door talking into her radio as two paramedics push past her and roll in a stretcher so they can remove the body.

I recognize the dead man. It's Mark Sempe—the pimp I saw grooming the young girl just a few days ago.

Phil is behind the counter, his face pale with shock.

"How are you?" I ask. He doesn't seem to recognize me. "Phil? Are you okay?" He snaps out of it and blinks.

"Yeah, I'm fine," he mumbles. "Americano?" He has gone into autopilot.

I shake my head. "No, thanks Phil. I'm okay."

I look around the cafe. People have clearly left in a hurry and their coffee cups and half-eaten muffins litter the tables. Only a few patrons remain, including Doreen. There's no way the death of some pimp would drive her out of the coffee shop.

Decker is speaking with one couple and pulls out his notebook to start taking their statements. When the paramedic finishes her call I go over to speak with her.

"So, what happened?"

"It looks like an overdose," she says. "We gave him Naxalone. Performed CPR, but he was gone. We couldn't save him." I thank her and watch as she follows the stretcher out to the waiting ambulance.

Decker is speaking with the young girl who'd been Sempe's prey. She's shaking and crying, barely coherent. Decker introduces her as Tiffany.

"He was so happy today," she sobs. "He was talking about our plans, what we were going to do. He was so up, in such a good mood." I bet. Euphoria is a sign of overdose.

"How else did he seem to you?" I ask. "Confused? Tired?"

"He was a bit tired. He was working late last night." Decker and I exchange a look.

"What does he do?" This will be interesting. I wonder how far the pimp's grooming of her has gone. Does she have any idea what her boyfriend was really up to?

"He owns a club in the city," she says. "And he's a music producer." So, not too far then. That's good. Lucky for her that he died before he put her out to work.

"So, you think he was working late," Decker asks. "That's why he was so sleepy?"

Tiffany nods. "I just let him doze off... I was on my phone anyway," she says. "It was cute, how he was sleeping. I took a video. I was going to post it on Instagram."

I look out the cafe window into the parking lot and watch the ambulance attendant close the back doors and prepare to drive off as an unmarked police car pull up and a large red-faced man awkwardly climbs out. Cooper. As usual, he's late to the party. He slams the door and limps over to the fire truck. He's had a noticeable limp ever since he took that beating, but I'm sure he puts it on for sympathy.

"Constable Decker is going to drive you home now," I interrupt Tiffany's story. I want to get her away before Cooper comes in, for her sake. "You're upset. If we have any more questions we'll call, okay? He'll take your contact information." She follows Decker out the side door.

I'm surprised at the loathing that roils up inside me when I see him making his way into the coffee shop. I hate myself for it, but the idea of bumping into Cooper, having to speak with him—even now while responding to an emergency call, turns my stomach. I know he'll say something patronizing, or belittling or openly offensive, something I'm supposed to pretend is a joke, or just let wash over me in the *go along to get along* culture of our workplace. I can't do it. I'm not in the mood to make nice and I can't trust myself to not let my feelings show. So I decide to hide.

Maybe it's not the most adult choice, I admit. I motion to Phil, who's rushing around trying to clear the messy tables.

"I'll have that *Americano* now, please," I say then point to Doreen, who's moved back to her usual table in the window. "And a refill for that lady." I want to get away from Cooper's line of sight. He wouldn't typically waste his time talking to me anyway, but it's better to be safe than sorry.

Doreen is reading the paper and when I put the coffee down in front of her she looks up in surprise. "Thank you Lucy," she says. "I barely got to drink my first cup, what with all the fuss."

"I can imagine." It isn't every day that a notorious local pimp dies on the floor next to you. "You weren't at your usual table today," I observe.

"No… it was taken when I got here," Doreen shakes her head

in irritation. "So I had to sit next to *them*." She purses her lips. "It wasn't very comfortable."

"What did you see?"

"As little as possible," Doreen says. "I was minding my own business. Phil brought me my coffee, like usual," she begins. I can tell Doreen wants to tell her story.

"But he forgot the sugar. So I got up to get another sugar, and my walker accidentally bumped their table, and his coffee spilled. You should have heard him swearing at me." She shakes her head in disgust. "I went over to Phil and ordered him another one, brought it over and gave it to him. Asshole never even said thanks."

I shake my head, picturing Doreen having to navigate her walker through the crowded shop to get him a new coffee, then Sempe swearing at her.

"About half an hour later," Doreen continued, "I'm back at my table, I hear the girl scream and look up and he's on the floor, thrashing around." She watches me over the lip of her coffee mug. "Did he have a heart attack do you think?"

I shrug. "Couldn't say. The coroner will let us know." I don't need to tell Doreen it's a suspected overdose. She has enough to worry about just living in the East Village.

I smile at Doreen. "You don't seem to bothered about what happened," I say. "Good that you aren't letting it get to you."

"When you get to be my age, you've seen a few things," Doreen shrugs. I follow her gaze and see she's looking through the window at Cooper. He's leaning against the door of a patrol car, talking with the officer at the wheel. "We all die," she says, staring at Cooper. "And we'll all be safer without him around."

For a second I don't know who Doreen is referring to—the dead pimp or Cooper. "The problem is," she says. "There are always more like him."

I leave Doreen to finish her coffee and newspaper and head back out to my patrol car. I assume Decker has gone back to traffic stops on Killaley so I drive out in the opposite direction, towards Wainfleet and the conservation areas by the old flooded quarries. I can usually issue a few parking tickets along the bridge there, where fisherman always leave their cars in the clearly posted no parking areas. As long as I keep my quotas up management will keep me in their good books. I don't like it, but I understand this is how the game is played. In less than ten minutes I've issued four tickets and I'm quick enough to drive off before any of them can get back to shore to argue with me.

Then I turn back into town and head over to the bar Mark Sempe used to run. I park on the street out front and look it over. It doesn't open until the evening, and I'm sure they won't stay closed tonight just because one of the owners died. It's a dump, but it's what passes for a club in a small town like ours. People with better taste and more money will drive over to Niagara Falls and hit the casino or one of the nightclubs there. Sempe has interest in a few of those too, as well as at least one in Toronto. I know this because I used to work for him, years ago. I doubt he'd ever recognize me. Of course we can't test that theory now because he's dead.

I was only seventeen when I graduated high school and was accepted to University of Toronto on a partial academic scholarship. But the minute I arrived in the city I started getting into trouble: drinking underage, partying with an older crowd, light drug use. My grades slipped, because it's tough to get up for class if you've been dancing until four o'clock in the morning at some club, high on ecstasy.

I'd needed a part time job to help pay my way through school; my parents didn't have any money and the scholarship only covered about half my expenses. One of my roommates got me a job in the bar where she worked; it was owned by Mark Sempe and some of his shady partners. The tips were good and I got to eat for free, so that helped with expenses. But the hours were long, and between doing split shifts and working until the bar closed after one o'clock in the morning, it wasn't long before I was on academic probation and at risk of losing my scholarship.

I kept it up for months thanks to a lot of help from drugs that were everywhere at the bar. Cocaine to keep me up, alcohol to relax me when the shift was over, then more cocaine to give me a boost so I could get to class. It made me feel strong, invincible even. Nothing like myself at all, and I thought that was a great thing because I didn't really like who I was.

One of the other bartenders taught me how to short pour most drinks, sell the extra shots for cash, and pocket the money. I'd learned a few ways to skim by not ringing in drinks, and hiding the money I charged the customer in the cash drawer or my tip jar.

Sempe was tipped off that something was going on, so he did a mid-shift bar drawer audit and found the extra cash in my till, the money that I'd skimmed but hadn't managed to pull out in time.

Sempe was about to call the police and have me charged with theft when I admitted I was only seventeen. I was two years under-age and had been serving liquor in his establishment for months. If he called the police he'd lose his liquor license and be out of business. So he let me go and I ran.

I'd spent the rest of the school year hiding in my dorm room, never going out for fear of running into someone I knew from those days. It helped me pull up my grades so I at least got through my year, though not with honours. I lost my scholarship, but I didn't care. The next year I transferred my credits to the local university and finished my degree there.

I'd felt so ashamed of having blown it, having to come back to Niagara with my tail between my legs. I never told anyone what had happened; my parents just thought I'd been homesick and were happy to have me back. They made up my old room, asked no questions, and I lived at home until I graduated.

So many nights I've lain awake, wondering if there is something wrong with me, something dark, some missing moral link that allowed to me get drawn into that bar scene. Maybe it was the same thing that took over the night my stepfather died.

Was that why I'd become a police officer? To make up for the bad stuff, so that I'd always be forced to look at right and wrong, every day of my life, and make sure I made the right choices? I feel my blood run cold as an idea springs into my mind. Maybe that's my nature, the terrifying thing inside I'm always fighting, the thing that causes my panic attacks, and my constant anxiety. Maybe it isn't a struggle to keep my secret as I've always thought. Maybe it's a battle to keep my real nature from coming out.

THIRTEEN

"SIR," I ENTER Staff Sergeant Bruni's office and close the door as he indicates. This is not good; I can feel it.

"How are you doing, Constable Gauthier?" is his opening, as he motions for me to take a seat across from him.

"Fine, Sir," I reply, feeling uneasy. "Thank you, Sir."

He leans back in his chair and smiles. "I need you to reign it in."

"I'm sorry Sir? I don't follow."

"You were investigating the fatality this morning at Green Bean Cafe."

"No, Sir," I say. "Decker and I responded to the call. When we arrived the scene was no longer active." I don't mention chatting with Doreen. "Decker drove one of the witnesses home; she was upset. I got a coffee and left."

Fucking Cooper. He'd seen me there and decided to complain. About what, who even knows? Bruni looks at me steadily. I know he's in a tough spot; he doesn't like Cooper either, but he needs to keep the peace.

"With all due respect, Sir. Cooper is a dickhead," I blurt and regret it the minute the words leave my mouth. Bruni's eyebrows rise in surprise. He stares at me then bursts out laughing.

"You are correct, Constable Gauthier," he says, wiping his eyes.

"But you never heard it from me. And he's at least two decades senior to you."

I sigh. "He reported me? For showing up to a call?" Bruni shrugs and I understand it's more than that. It's because I'm a new Detective Constable, and a female. And that I have a degree in Psychology. Cooper had joined the force right out of high school, back when you could actually do that, when you didn't even need a degree to be promoted within the police force; you just needed to serve your time. Cooper had no patience for anyone with an education; he thought we were all soft. And God help you if you were a diversity hire, or as in my case, a female.

Bruni clears his throat and my heart leaps into my throat. I just know that whatever he's going to say is not good.

"Gauthier," he says. "I have some concerns."

"Concerns?" My voice comes out as a squeak.

"Police work is teamwork. It's the most important thing about the job."

"No I in team, Sir?" I try to joke to lighten the mood, but Bruni doesn't smile.

"I'm not sure if you're much of a team player. You hold yourself apart," Bruni continues. "You're solitary."

"I don't understand where you're going with this. Sir." But I do get it: it's the old guard looking out for themselves again. This is what being honest and letting him know how I feel about Cooper gets me. Probably Bruni and Cooper go way back and I've just hit my nose on the blue wall of silence; I forgot cops—especially young female cops like me, don't rat on other cops or even criticize other cops.

"Don't get me wrong," Bruni goes on, but I'm only half-listening. "You're a great police officer. You're smart, and you have excellent instincts and analytic abilities, which you've proven many times since you joined the force. But being alone in a patrol car... it doesn't really demonstrate you're able work well on a team. I need you to show me you can."

It's impossible for me to not feel defensive, but it won't do me any good to let Bruni see how angry I am. I feel the hot flush of shame creep up my neck and across my cheeks and I know, even though I won't admit it, that Bruni is right.

I am solitary. I don't get close to people. It makes it easier to control things, so I can feel safe and manage my anxiety. And, if I don't let people get too close they aren't going to ask questions and I won't have to lie.

"Sir." I acknowledge him, keeping my eyes down. I'm afraid to say anything else in case my voice betrays my emotions.

"What else have you been working on?" Bruni asks, changing the subject. I sense a trap, but I'm not sure if it's just my paranoia or if Bruni is setting me up for another dressing down.

"I'm working the Cobb case, Sir."

He makes a face. "I get it, Constable Gauthier. You're trying to prove yourself. You just got your DC and now you want to make your mark. But…"

"But?"

"We don't need you wasting resources on a death that is clearly a suicide."

"Resources?"

"Your time," Constable. "Your time is a Division resource. You could be working on other things."

"Like what? With due respect, Sir."

"We have the stabbing death… and the shooting on Port Street last week. And the body that was found floating in the canal." *You mean the one I found,* I almost correct him, but I manage to catch myself in time.

"We've been following up on all of those, Sir." I feel a flush on my neck. My heart starts to race. "We've done several interviews, you'll find them all in the reports. And we're waiting on forensic results and on the autopsies."

Bruni smirks. "So, you're saying you've got time on your hands?"

What's this about? Is Bruni about to assign me some pointless work in the archives?

"I'm not trying to trap you Constable," he says, reading my mind. "You're doing good work. I'm happy with you. Carry on."

That's it? I exhale. I thought he was going to tear me a new one, but maybe the planets are aligned in my favour.

"What have you found about the Cobb case?"

"I'm just doing the standard preliminary investigation in the case of a suspicious death. Just looking into his background, state of mind. Textbook stuff, Sir."

Bruni smiles at me. "Okay. But to be clear, you may have passed the exam but you're not a detective. Yet. And from what I understand about the Cobb case there's nothing to detect." I nod. "If there were," he continues, "the case would be assigned to Major Crime and it would be the Homicide Unit's job." He must see the disappointment in my eyes and he looks down at his paperwork. "With your support, of course." That's uniform's job, supporting the investigative divisions in whatever way is required. But it isn't where I want to remain.

In my first few years on the force I'd been relegated to lots of foot patrol, parking and by-law violations, school visits like every other fourth or third class constable. It took me almost five years to work my way up to first class Constable and I've just written the OPC exam and passed in the top tenth percentile.

"Regarding that, Sir…" I say. Bruni raises his head. "I'd like to be considered for promotion," I say. I may be a Detective Constable but I'm still in uniform until I can get a placement.

He smiles. "Not a surprise," he says. "I can see you're ambitious. You don't see yourself ending up like Decker, with all due respect to him. He's a fine Constable."

"No, Sir." The last thing I want is to remain in uniform, riding a patrol car, for the next twenty-five or thirty years.

"Where do you think you might want to be assigned, Constable?"

"I've been giving it a lot of thought, Sir. I'd like to work in Major Crime. Homicide."

Bruni looks disappointed. "I had thought, or hoped," he begins after a moment, "that with your experience in community policing and your post-secondary degree, you might want to consider Crime Stoppers. Or maybe an assignment to the Regional Community Mobilization Bureau." I feel my rage rise. More *pink collar* policing, perfect for the ladies. Is he fucking kidding?

"There's a lot of responsibility in that area, and the potential for career growth," Bruni continues. "Working with our community partners and the Media on Youth Services, Schools and Community Mobilization..."

"No," I cut him off. "Thank you, Sir." I know if that's where I'm going to end up I'll leave the force. Community policing means I'd be spending all my time back in the East Village and there is no way that's going to happen. "I've given it a lot of thought, Sir. Major Crimes is where my interest is."

I see the expression on Bruni's face and temper my tone. "I understand you and the Inspector plan how to best use the resources on the force, to achieve service goals and objectives." I'm desperately looking through my mind for any bureaucratic jargon that will help me plead my case. "And that the force needs to assign detectives and officers as needed. But I feel my skills would better serve the force if I were assigned elsewhere. Sir."

Bruni shakes his head. Then he smiles. "Okay, understood," he says. "And Constable Gauthier?" he says as I rise to leave.

"Yes, Sir?"

"Stay out of Cooper's way."

FOURTEEN

I'M SITTING ON the couch, too tired to even think. I don't even remember the drive home. Not good, I know. Driving while preoccupied or distracted is an offense, as I tell people daily, but it's been happening to me a lot lately. Between not sleeping well, the stresses of the job, and the extreme fatigue I'm pushing my body into every day at the gym, something has to give. The little pep talk Bruni gave me today didn't help matters either.

Keep it together, I tell myself. *Keep it together*. It's become my mantra, repeated often out of fear of allowing myself to slip into depression again. Deep, slow breath. *Focus on the moment. This too shall pass. Keep it together.* When is my next shrink appointment? I make a mental note to check my calendar.

I can clean my house, and I do it every day. My cupboards are organized and my drawers perfection. I'm never behind on my laundry and my dishes are always washed. But I can't open my mail. It piles up in a basket on the hall table for weeks at a time until I can face it. Classic avoidance behaviour.

I can function at work; that's never an issue. As soon as I get into the station and put on my uniform, I'm good. I know who I am. I'm protected. I feel safe and in control.

But when I get in the door at home, I lose sight of who that person is. Of who I am. I'll sit in a chair and stare out the window for hours, paralyzed, unable to move. I zone out. I'm not thinking. I'm staring at nothing. I'll suddenly realize it's dark and I've been sitting for hours and then I come to as if I've had a blackout. I wonder if this is what crazy feels like. Maybe I'm going nuts. Finally, after all this time.

Are you depressed? I hear my shrink's voice.

I'm fine, I tell her, every time. And she can only take my word for it.

Are you drinking?

Sometimes, I lie. The truth is *often* and *a lot. I take my meds. I eat right, I exercise,* I tell her. She notes it all in her book.

One thing I do manage is to get to work on time for every shift. And I make sure to go to the gym every day. Apart from that, I spend a lot of time staring out the window, or watching whatever I can find on television. I haven't been able to read a book in months; I just can't focus on the words, or retain what I've read on the page, or even in the previous paragraph.

I stare out the sliding patio doors at the wasteland of my tiny back yard. I bought the townhouse three years ago and have done nothing outside. When I took possession there'd been a flower garden out there, but not much of it has survived my care.

I really should eat something. Forcing myself to stand and walk over to the fridge, I open the door without any expectation of finding anything edible. I lost interest in grocery shopping and cooking ages ago. The only thing I find I'm able to do is clean. My townhouse is spotless, tidy, and empty—especially my fridge, I realize.

There's some leftover Thai takeout that's only two days old so it probably won't kill me. I spread the cardboard containers across the counter, pile some onto a plate and stick it into the microwave. While it's heating I open a bottle of wine and pour a glass, then reach into my gym bag and extract the file I removed from Cobb's apartment.

I eat my dinner perched on a stool, studying the papers spread in front of me. They make no more sense than they did when I'd first gone through them and I have to admit they never will. I don't have a medical or science background. There's only one thing I can think to do, and that's make the call I've been avoiding for months. I take a deep breath and pick up my phone, scrolling to find the contact I've held my finger over hundreds of times, about to delete, but have never been able to.

I let the phone ring three times before I hang up. Half an hour later the phone rings. It's Maja. I take a deep breath and pick up.

"Hi," I say.

"Hi," she says. A moment passes. "I'm glad you called."

"It's been too long," is what I say. But a hundred other things run through my head. *How long have you been back? Have you missed me? Why haven't you called? Have you forgotten me? Do you have someone else now, someone you love better?*

"Yes."

"I need your help," I begin. I hear Maja's sharp intake of breath. "It's a work thing," I'm quick to say. "Do you think you could come over? Or... I could come over there. If that's better for you." I need to keep it professional between us now.

"I'll come over," Maja says after a moment.

Twenty minutes later there's a knock and I hesitate before answering it. I've been hoping for this for months, and dreading it, and now I'm afraid. I open the door and there is Maja, with a bottle of wine in her hand and a nervous expression on her face. I feel my heart crack.

"Come in," I say. "Sorry, the place is a mess."

"Not possible," Maja teases and I laugh, like always, as I get two glasses out of the cupboard.

We go over to the living room sofa. I've spread out Cobb's notes on the coffee table and Maja starts to look through them. I hand her a glass of wine, relieved we won't have to make small talk and catch up. There is so much to say and even more that's better left unsaid.

"This is it?" Maja asks. "The work thing you need help with?"

I nod. "It's a case I'm working on. I don't understand any of it and I thought, I hoped, that with your background you could translate it."

"Maybe," she shrugs. She takes a gulp of wine and starts to read the papers while I sit, notebook open on my lap, waiting to record whatever Maja comes up with.

"It's a bunch of test data and research notes," she says. That much I've already figured out.

"About what?"

"Dementia. Statistics about the disease," she holds up a paper. "This shows how the economic burden is increasing worldwide." She holds up another. "This graphs the expected increase in mortality rate over the next fifteen years, and the projected costs attributable to the care of dementia patients between now and 2050." Maja's eyes widen as she looks at the graph. "Three hundred and fifty billion dollars in North America alone."

"Yikes."

Maja shrugs. "Dementia is a terminal illness, with very high patient care costs. It's palliative care on a massive scale."

"It's a terminal illness... ?" I echo.

"Sure. People don't think of it that way, but it's true. And all we're able to do is manage the symptoms and offer some relief from psychosis or pain."

"What else is there?" I point to the notebook with the cryptic scribbles in it.

Maja opens it. "Data," she says, flipping through the pages. "It looks like test results, and comparisons and analyses of those results. Maybe whoever wrote this," she holds up the notebook, "was involved in developing some new drugs or treatments. Why don't you ask them?"

"He's dead."

Maja nods. "That'll do it." She drinks her wine and reads

through the rest of the papers, while I do my best to be patient. I look at the top of my friend's head, bent over in the gleam of the lamp and wish I could stroke her hair, wish I could sit next to her again and hold her. But that's over now and we have to figure out a way to move forward, despite everything.

I blink back my tears. Maja wanted it all and I was always holding back. I couldn't tell her the truth. I couldn't share who I really am. My guilt and shame wouldn't allow it. So it had ended between us. Or maybe it was more accurate to say it couldn't really begin.

We finish the bottle of wine and I open a second one. I even manage to put out a plate of the cheese, some olives and some crackers I found in the cupboard. Miraculously they aren't stale. Maja finally puts the papers in a neat pile and leans back on the sofa.

"This guy was a researcher, who seems to have been developing a new drug to treat dementia. There are really only two drugs commonly in use today: Risperidone and Haloperidol, for people with severe Alzheimer's or other forms of dementia." I nod for Maja to continue. "They are prescribed for patients in distress, from delusions or hallucinations."

"Okay…" I'm writing notes, trying to keep up. "So they are just for management, to keep the patients comfortable."

"And docile."

Donald at Pelham Woods definitely hadn't been docile. Maybe they need to change his meds.

"I don't know who this dead guy was," Maja says. "But if he was anywhere close to coming up with a cure for this disease, he was going to become very rich." I think of Maurice Cobb, getting fired from his jobs. Living in a shabby apartment. Sitting in his folding lawn chair, waiting for the sunrise while his life trickled into the soil. He never made it to rich.

"But, like most diseases," Maja says. "The real money is in the treatment, not the cure. Keep them alive so you keep the money coming in."

"I'd forgotten how cynical you are," I laugh. "And, I have another favour to ask."

Maja looks resigned. "What?"

I hand over some of the pills Dennis Sharp had found on Cobb's body. Just a few; I'd entered the rest into evidence. I just know that nobody will bother to figure out what they are, especially now they've decided it was a suicide. But something is telling me they could be very important. "Can you get these analysed somehow? Tell me what they are?"

Maja gives me a look. "Are they some kind of controlled substance? Illegal?"

"I don't know." I throw up my hands. "They are connected somehow to this," I gesture to Cobb's papers. "I think."

Maja sighs and puts the pills into her handbag. "I better not get pulled over on the way home."

FIFTEEN

DOREEN GETS NADIA settled in her wheelchair in the rooftop therapy garden and sits beside her on a bench. She lights a cigarette and inhales with deep satisfaction. The garden is in an enclosed courtyard, just off the patient lounge. It's sheltered from the wind and every warm day they come out here so Doreen can sneak a cigarette behind the bushes.

A head pops over the top of a shrub. It's one of the care workers. "You can't smoke here."

"Fuck off," Doreen snarls and the head disappears. She knows that'll be the end of it. Every time a new worker finds her smoking they go through this routine. They always give up in the end.

She smokes and watches a small crew from the Womyn Farm work in the garden, pulling up the dead annual flowers and laying out hundreds of tulip and daffodil bulbs, ready for planting. Doreen recognizes Sophie among them.

Nadia is dozing, but Doreen can see she's fitful and agitated. Normally she's quiet and placid once asleep but today her friend's face is contorted in pain.

Where is that damn nurse? Clearly Nadia needs some relief. When was her last pain medication administered? Nadia is on a Fentanyl patch, and that should do the trick. But it isn't working today, that much is clear.

Doreen looks around the garden, hoping to see another care worker in the grounds. If she hadn't scared that one off, she could have asked her to fetch the nurse. For Doreen to go on her walker in search of her isn't an option, especially if it means leaving Nadia unattended. She hears voices nearby, from just behind where the path curves behind some shrubs. She leans to one side on the bench and can see through the branches. It's the nurse—the skinny bitch who always looks like she needs a wash. And she's with that cop, the creep.

Doreen strains to listen to what's being said, sorry that she can't hear as well as she used to. She can't make out what the cop is saying, but he's angry. His finger is pointed at the nurse's face and she looks frightened. Then he grabs her arm and shakes her, making a final point before he walks away. The nurse takes a few seconds to calm down before she follows him back inside.

"Nurse!" Doreen calls as she goes down the path. "Nurse!" But the woman ignores her.

"Bitch," Doreen mutters as she grabs hold of her walker. She'll have to go inside and get some help.

Sophie hears her yelling and comes over, wiping the dirt off her hands.

"Hi Doreen," she says. "Everything okay?"

"No. That fucking nurse has gone deaf. She ignored me just now when I was trying to call her."

Sophie nods. "I saw," she says. "Mueller's a bitch. Everyone hates her." Doreen makes a mental note of her name. "Anything I can do?"

"Can you help me get Nadia back inside? I think we've had enough fresh air for today."

Sophie pushes Nadia's wheelchair and holds the door for Doreen, then helps them get settled back in the patient lounge before going back to work in the garden. In the process Nadia wakes up and starts moaning and writhing, her frail body twisting around in the wheelchair. She needs something for the pain, immediately.

Doreen looks around and sees the nurse standing as she usually does near her medical cart by the nursing station.

"Nurse," Doreen calls. "Nurse! Please."

The nurse continues to ignore her as she stands at the cart, charting something as Nadia lies back in her chair, moaning in pain. "Nurse!" Doreen shouts at the top of her lungs. Let the bitch try and ignore that.

The nurse raises her head and glares at Doreen. "Now that I have your attention," she yells. "If you don't get over here right now I'm going to shove that clipboard up your ass."

The nurse slams down the clipboard and walks over to Doreen. She stands over her with her arms folded. "What is it?"

"Mrs. Efimov is in a lot of pain," Doreen says. "As you can see for yourself, if you'd bother to actually check on your patients."

"She's not due to have her Fentanyl patch changed yet," she says, shooting Doreen a dirty look. "All I can do is give her some Oxycodone if needed."

"I'd say it's *needed* now, wouldn't you?" The nurse rolls her eyes and storms back to the cart to prepare the pain medication.

What is wrong with that woman? Doreen shakes her head. For someone in a caring profession she doesn't seem to give a damn about her patients.

Once the nurse finally gives Nadia some medication she lays back and sighs and Doreen is able to relax. She sits back and looks around at the dozens of residents in the lounge, all in various stages of decay as they inch their way toward death. Some are in severe pain, like Nadia with her arthritis on top of her dementia. Others are physically fine; they stride up and down the halls like caged tigers, but their minds are gone. It'll take them years to die, since their bodies seem determined to keep on going. Some are still very strong; she's witnessed a few times recently when it took three care workers to subdue one of them.

It seems like things have been getting worse at Pelham Woods over the last year, with more patients acting out and having aggressive outbursts. And the nursing staff are a lot less keen to give out pain relief, like just now with Nadia. When Doreen walks the halls she can hear patients in their rooms, moaning in pain. That should not be happening.

Doreen watches the nurse out of the corner of her eye. Katrina, her nametag says. Thanks to Sophie she now knows Katrina's last name is Mueller. She already knew Katrina Mueller is the worst nurse she's ever seen; the slowest to respond if a patient rings a bell, whether they need toileting or pain relief, or even to answer the phone if it rings while she's near the nursing station. Doreen's heart always sinks when she comes for a visit and sees Katrina Mueller is on duty.

Doreen keeps an eye on Mueller as Nadia dozes. She sees her look over her shoulder and check if anyone is in the nursing station before she slips into the room where the medications are kept. Doreen leans over as far as she can, to try and see what she's doing in there but her angle of view is wrong and she can only see part of the room. A few minutes later Mueller comes back out with her hand in her pocket. She looks flushed as she walks quickly back to the medicine cart. Doreen decides to sit in another chair the next time she comes to visit, one with a better view.

SIXTEEN

I'M SURPRISED TO find the President of Advik Therapeutics waiting for me in the lobby when I arrive. Amit Joshi is a large man, both tall and wide, and he wears a brilliant turquoise blue suit and a gold silk shirt, with a matching tie and pocket square in a vibrant paisley print. For a man of his enormous size he doesn't seem shy about drawing attention to himself. He has rings on several of his fingers and wears a large, and very expensive-looking, gold watch. Evidently Advik Therapeutics is successful, if the way its President dresses is any indication.

"Amit Joshi," he says enveloping my hand in his, then wrapping the second hand on top and pumping my arm up and down. I'm surprised; most people aren't that friendly with police detectives who drop by their office. That puts me on my guard.

"Detective Constable Lucy Gauthier," I say, returning his smile. Joshi's an easy man to like, I decide as he ushers me through the doors toward his office. He talks the entire way, waving his hands into each area, describing what they do and the history of the company. As we go down the hall I take in what I can of the open concept office area, where several people are bent over their computers or telephones. We pass a couple of closed doors, one marked Private and the other Lab.

Once I'm seated across from Amit Joshi at his enormous wooden desk he offers me a drink. He's so hospitable and eager I begin to feel uncomfortable.

"Would you like some water? Or a coffee? It's fresh and delicious," he says as he pours himself a cup from a *cafetiere* on the sideboard.

"Coffee would be great," I say, grateful to see he has real cream in a jug, not just milk or those horrible UHT creamers. Joshi fusses around, making sure I'm comfortable and happy and it gets to the point I wonder if he's forgotten the purpose of my visit.

I turn to accept the coffee from Joshi and almost spill it in shock. Hanging behind the door is a human skeleton.

"What is that?" I ask, stupidly.

Joshi laughs. I realize this is probably a joke he plays often.

"It's a skeleton," he says.

"It looks... *real.*" The bones are yellowed and stained like ivory, not white like the skeletons I remember in my university labs.

"It is," he says. "Genuine human."

"How..." I falter and don't know what to ask. *Why* would be a good place to start.

Joshi leans back in his chair and smiles in pride. "I am descended from the oldest family of skeleton-providers in Calcutta," he says. "I'm very proud to say."

"Now much of the worldwide skeleton trade is plastic," he continues. "Though there are still providers of human bones, of course. It's very much a niche market, as you can imagine. My family diversified some time ago, but I keep this as a tribute. To remember where my family came from."

"Diversified?" I ask. "What else does your family do?"

"I'm an entrepreneur," Joshi says, not answering the question. "I have many businesses. Cyber security, software. I have shares in Taiga. And I own a chain of retirement homes and long-term care facilities."

"Pelham Woods?" I venture.

"Yes, that's one of mine," he says with pride. "We got in that market at exactly the right time. The population is aging, and so many baby boomers will need a place to stay, as they find they can no longer manage on their own."

He's made money from the dead and the nearly dead. "Interesting," I say as I get my notebook out and lay it on my knee, ready to take notes. "Now I wonder if you can please tell me about Maurice Cobb."

The smile falls from Joshi's face. "Maurice Cobb," he repeats. "Yes." He leans back in his chair, his eyes not meeting mine. An awkward moment passes as he stares into the middle distance.

"He used to work here," I prod.

"Of course," he says vaguely. "Yes, I may remember Mr. Cobb. I'm not really sure I knew him. He was a researcher. I believe…"

"And when did he leave the company?"

"I'm not sure." I can tell he is lying. "Maybe two years ago? I don't really know. I'd have to check."

So far that's two lies he's told me: pretending he doesn't know what Cobb did, or when he'd left his job. I have to wonder why.

"Was Mr. Cobb a good employee? Why did he leave Advik Therapeutics?"

His smile is stiff. "May I ask why you are inquiring? Is he in some trouble?"

"He's dead, Mr. Joshi." I study his face for a reaction and find none. "We're looking into his background as part of the investigation."

Joshi ponders for a minute then picks up the phone on his desk. "Angela," he says. "Can you please bring in the file for Maurice Cobb?" The fact that the person on the other end of the line didn't ask any questions is interesting. As is the fact that the employment file of a barely remembered former employee is so close to hand. I understand that despite what Joshi just said, Cobb has not been forgotten.

We sip our coffee, which is indeed delicious, and wait for Angela to bring in the file. Within minutes she lays it on Joshi's desk and leaves without glancing at me.

Joshi opens the file and flips through it, but does not offer it to me.

"He left Advik in November of last year," he says.

"So, less than a year ago," I say as I write. "And how long had he worked for you?"

"Eight years," Joshi says, keeping his eyes on the file.

"How many employees do you have here at Advik, Mr. Joshi?"

"Eighteen," he says. I nod.

"Forgive me, Mr. Joshi," I begin. "You had a man working for you for eight years, who left your employ less than a year ago, and you claim you don't really remember him? I find that hard to believe."

Joshi spreads his hands and shrugs. "What can I say? I'm very busy."

"Perhaps there is someone else here at Advik, someone who worked directly with him, who might be able to answer some questions?"

Joshi pretends to consider it for a moment. "I'm not sure if there is anyone who could help you," he says. "We've had some turnover recently. A lot of new people have come onboard. They wouldn't remember Maurice Cobb."

I don't buy it, and it's certainly intriguing that Joshi is going to so much trouble to prevaricate. All it's doing is making me more suspicious. He'd have done better to give me some useless facts and send me on my way. Now he's just made me curious.

I give him a big smile. "What did Mr. Cobb do here?" I ask.

"Research," Joshi says. "He was working on product development."

"New pharmaceuticals?"

"Yes."

"And why did he leave Advik?"

"His employment was terminated," Joshi says. I raise my eyebrow and meet his eye. I wait and watch him struggle for a moment then he breaks. People always do. Nobody is ever able to stand sitting in silence, especially in the presence of a police officer with an open notebook. "He stole research data and sold it to one of our competitors."

"Corporate espionage."

"Exactly." I can now see his rage, no longer hidden under his jovial bluster. That's better for me. Angry people are less careful.

"I was forced to hire private security after it happened," he says.

"We should speak with them as well. What company is it?" I ask, my pen poised over my notebook.

"Limestone Security." *Great. Just perfect.* I make a note to have Decker follow up with them. The less I have to do with Cooper and his security company the better, especially after my conversation with Sergeant Bruni. I may not be a genius but I'm smart enough to know not to poke a bear.

"And after Cobb left your company, do you have any idea where he went, or what happened to your data?"

"None," he says tersely. "I suggest you contact his wife. She worked with him on the project."

"His wife?" I'm stunned, recalling the timid woman I'd met at Womyn. "She was an employee of Advik as well?"

Joshi nods. "She conducted research and clinical trials on several of our exploratory drugs. However I can't tell you anything about her either. She left the company at the same time as her husband."

I nod. That won't be a problem; I know where to find her. The question is, why hadn't Geraldine Bennett told me she'd worked at Advik with her husband?

SEVENTEEN

SOPHIE IS DRIVING the tractor when I arrive at the Womyn collective and she leaves the rest of the crew working in the field and comes to meet me.

"Hi," she says, giving me a hug. "I heard you were just here the other day. And you didn't stop and have a drink with me?"

"I was working," I say. "I didn't really have the time."

"You're all busy and important?" Sophie teases. "Now that you're a detective and all." She steps back for a second with a puzzled expression. "But you're still in uniform. What's going on?" She looks like she wants to go fight someone at the department on my behalf.

"Relax. I just passed the exam five minutes ago," I say with a laugh. "It takes a while to get assigned to a detective unit. For now I'm officially a Detective Constable, but I still do my patrol shifts. It's all good." Sophie doesn't look like she believes me.

"I'm here to speak with Geraldine Bennett again." Sophie looks suspicious. She's run Womyn shelter for years and is very protective of the women under her care. She is also very wary of the police, who more often than not have let those same women down, which is how many of them ended up coming to her for help in the first place. She's like a mother bear defending her cubs; there's nothing she won't do to ensure the women are safe from the men who hurt them. I've heard her lie under oath and I have no doubt she'd kill if she felt she had to.

"Okay…" Sophie hesitates. "What's going on?"

I don't have to tell her but there's no reason not to. "Her husband was found dead, which you know." Sophie nods. "When I first spoke with Geraldine she withheld some pertinent information."

"Withheld?" Sophie is defensive. "She was probably just upset."

"I wouldn't call her *upset*," I say with a wry smile. "She was relieved."

Sophie's lips curl in a smile. "I bet she was."

"What does she do here," I ask. "At the collective?" The women who live at the shelter all work together to keep the operation running, in exchange for their board and lodging. Some of them brought skills with them when they came; others learn new skills during their stay at the farm that allow them to be independent when they leave, once they're safe from their abusers.

"She's a designer," Sophie says. "Our best, actually. Geraldine took a training course after she arrived and has been practically doing all of our weddings and corporate work single-handed ever since. She's helped me build our floral design business into what it is now, beyond just the cut-your-own and the fresh bouquets at the market we've always done." I'm impressed. The Womyn floral arrangements I've seen are stunning. They're always unique; lush and fragrant with fruit, flowers and berries from the Niagara region.

"She's probably in the shop," Sophie says, pointing to the barn. "Why don't you take a seat in the cafe?" She follows me into the shop where bunches of dried herbs hang from the rafters and the shelves lining the barn's walls are filled with jams and jellies, lotions and handmade soaps. A large oak harvest table in the middle of the barn holds a display of herbal vinegar and oils, packaged with ribbon and raffia and the Womyn label. The aroma of lavender drifts through the barn.

"How's business?" I ask.

"Better," Sophie says.

Earlier this year Sophie had been accused of manufacturing illegal cannabis products in her kitchens. But when the police had carried out their search warrant there was no evidence of illegal activity. It's just possible she's innocent. Or possibly someone tipped her off before the raid.

"Glad it all worked out." There's nothing more I can say.

"She's not in here, obviously," Sophie says, heading back out the door. "I'll go find her. Be right back."

I pour myself a coffee from the self-serve counter, leave some change in the honesty jar then sit down to wait for Geraldine Bennett. I'm almost finished my drink when Sophie comes back into the cafe.

"Sorry about the wait," she says. "She's in the barn, working on a wedding order for tomorrow." She leads me across the gravel driveway to the barn where the floral design business of the Womyn collective is run. One half of the building is crammed with bunches of florist greens and buckets of flowers. Two large tables are in the middle of space, full of arrangements destined for the wedding reception. Another table holds a long bridal bouquet, propped up on a stand to allow the designer to work on the trail of blossoms.

Three women work together to assemble the table arrangements. Each holds a short red handled knife and they're cutting stems of crab apples, viburnum branches and leathery greens and fitting them into the green floral foam that fills the containers. Another of the women cuts stems of lilies and roses and inserts them, as they build the arrangements up. The third woman comes along at the end, and inserts vines and trailing blossoms, arranging them naturalistically and with flair, transforming each individual arrangement into something unique and lovely.

The last woman is Geraldine Bennett. She looks even thinner and more exhausted than she did when we'd first met. I'd have thought that relief at the death of her abuser would have looked better on her.

It's obvious she's irritated at the interruption when Sophie waves her over, but she puts down the flowers and folds her knife and heads over. Sophie takes her place at the table and continues the design assembly line. The women are no doubt working to a deadline, and a wedding reception won't wait.

"Geraldine," Sophie calls. "Can I use your knife? I lost mine somewhere."

Bennett pulls the knife back out of her apron pocket and tosses it to Sophie. I catch a glimpse of a Swiss Army knife, with the distinctive red handle and gold cross. All the women working on the floral designs seem to be using them. I guess they keep a good edge and are easy to sharpen, and they aren't too large for a woman's hand.

Geraldine pulls out a chair and sits with me, but stays well back from the table, as if she might need to run out at any moment. I'm pretty sure Sophie is listening in as well; she might consider me a friend, but I'm still a police officer, and Sophie is vigilant about the women in her care.

"Thank you for speaking with me again Ms. Bennett," I begin. The way the other woman sits there passively intrigues me. Most people would attempt some small talk to fill the silence when sitting across from a police officer, but she's silent. It's also interesting that she hasn't asked any questions about Maurice Cobb's death or our investigation into it. Even if she doesn't care, it's human nature to be curious.

I hand over a photocopy of the suicide note found next to Cobb's body.

"I wonder if you could confirm this is your ex-husband's handwriting for me." We already know the note is likely genuine, based on comparisons with the documents I'd brought back from Cobb's apartment. I'm just curious about the reaction I might get from his ex-wife.

Geraldine Bennett barely glances at the note. "Yes, it's his," she says.

I nod and pretend to make a notation in my book then fold the paper and put it into my pocket. Still the other woman doesn't ask any questions. She hadn't asked any when she'd first found out her ex-husband was dead; nor has she inquired about how he'd died or where his body was found. Now she's just been shown a suicide note and evidently has no curiosity about that either. I wonder if maybe that's a typical response from a woman who'd suffered years of abuse, like some kind of disassociation.

"I understand his employment at Advik Therapeutics was terminated because he was accused of corporate espionage," I say. "Is that correct?" Geraldine Bennett slowly raises her eyes to meet mine. She is frightened.

"Yes," she whispers.

"And you were also employed there, at that same time?" She nods. "Were you also implicated in the theft?"

I watch as she struggles for a moment, perhaps trying to come up with the right ratio of truth to believable lie. I know that people seldom tell the whole truth, and it's my job to get to the heart of it.

Bennett bends her head, revealing the grey roots of her hair. "He wasn't a thief," she finally says. "My ex-husband was a lot of things, a lot of bad things. But he didn't steal from Advik." The specificity of the denial is interesting. Had Cobb stolen from somewhere else?

"Amit Joshi was clear that was the reason they let him go."

"Joshi," she snorts and her lip twists in scorn. "He's a liar. And a phoney."

"Really?" I don't disagree with her assessment, based on my initial meeting with Amit Joshi. "Why do you say that?"

"He acts like he's the big genius behind the businesses. It's not even his."

"Whose is it?"

"Advik is his wife Zahira's company. She's the brains. He's just… the noise."

"And what role does Zahira Joshi play at Advik?"

Bennett shrugs. "I'm not sure she has an official role there. Not a public one at any event. She's got a doctorate in chemistry."

"So do you think she had anything to do with your husband losing his job at Advik?"

"I doubt it," she says. "She wasn't in the office much. Or in the lab. It was all Amit Joshi. He accused my ex-husband of theft so they could fire him. And ruin his reputation."

"And why would he do that?"

Bennett looks away, her jaw set. "He'd helped Advik develop a drug that failed several clinical trials. The drug wasn't safe. It needed more research. Advik was pushing it through anyway. They lied about the test data, so he reported them."

"He was a whistleblower?" Bennett nods. "What kind of drug was it? What was it designed to treat?"

"Dementia. It was meant to help manage the symptoms."

"And it didn't work?"

"It did show lots of early promise," she says. "It even seemed to reverse or slow brain degradation and the loss of certain mental faculties. Test patients were able to reason and plan again, which are key indicators in treatments for Alzheimer's or other forms of dementia."

"And then what?"

"It led to psychotic breaks and violent aggression." I flash on Donald, flinging himself into the glass door.

"When was the last time you saw your ex-husband Ms. Bennett?"

"Two weeks ago," she admits after a long pause. "At Pelham Woods. I was delivering a bouquet for their front lobby. We donate one every week, as a promotion and they display it next to a pile of our brochures. It brings us a lot of business. Mostly funerals."

"He was working there?"

"I saw him wearing a security guard uniform," she says, her voice so quiet I have to lean in closer to hear her. "I-I couldn't believe it. I was so frightened I just ran out and hid in the delivery van. I couldn't let him see me." I nod, encouraging her to continue. "I didn't understand what he was doing there." Her eyes narrow. "But I figured it out. He must have been asking around, and he found out where I live, what I do for work."

"So you believe he was working at Pelham Woods to get access to you?" I try to hide my skepticism.

"I know him." She keeps her eyes on the floor and doesn't look at me as she speaks. She's wringing her hands and rubbing a spot on her arm. I'd read in the file that Bennett had sustained a spiral fracture on her left wrist. That's the kind of fracture you get when someone twists your arm, hard. "I know his obsessive tendencies," she whispers. "The way he holds onto things, never lets anything go." She raises her eyes to mine again. "I'm still afraid of him, even though I know he's dead. He hurt me, for years. I haven't been able to sleep in months. Maybe years. I have to take sleeping pills just to avoid the nightmares."

"And apart from that incident, you've had no contact with him since the divorce?"

"Not since the restraining order, after he put me into hospital. I knew I was safe here, at Womyn. But if he figured out I'd be making deliveries at Pelham Woods… that I was on my own. He could get to me anytime. I was terrified. "

EIGHTEEN

I'M DRIVING BACK to the station when my phone rings. It's Maja. I feel my heart flutter with anxiety and I pull over to the side of the road before I answer.

"Hi you," I say, like I always used to answer Maja's calls. I feel the tears spring to my eyes when I hear her response.

"Hi yourself," Maja says, as she always did. I feel a catch in my throat and I'm unable to speak for a moment.

"So," Maja continues and I'm grateful for the chance to collect myself. "I've got the results back on those mystery pills you gave me the other night."

"What did you find out?" I ask, eager to take my mind off what had gone wrong between Maja and me.

"They're an organic chemical compound, typical of a butryphenone-type. It seems to be related to a heterocyclic compound in a thiazine class…"

"I have no idea what you are saying," I interrupt. "Can you tell me what drug it is?"

"That's not how this works," Maja says with a laugh. "If the pills had an imprint on them I could tell you… but they don't. Best I can do is a chemical analysis and then we can guess what they are used for."

"Imprint? What do you mean, like a label?"

Maja laughs. "Yes, Lucy. You know this! Every pill that's federally approved, prescription or over the counter has an imprint on it. Those letters, numbers or logos?"

"Right," I feel embarrassed. I should have known that right away, it was Police 101. "So, what's your best guess, based on your chemical analysis?"

"They might be a dopamine receptor," Maja says. "When I read through his notebook I saw that he was studying 5-HT receptors and dopamine and serotonin neurotransmitters…"

"In English, please."

"They could be something to treat movement disorders."

"Like what?"

"Ataxia, dystonia, tremors, tics, Parkinson's or Tourette's," she lists off possibilities. "Similar neurological problems."

"Okay," I sigh. This seems like a dead end. Maybe Cobb had received a medical diagnosis that, on top of his other problems, led to his decision to end his life. Maybe he just couldn't deal with it. Of course, the question then is why did he have the pills in a plastic baggie, not in a prescription container like one would get from a pharmacy. That made no sense.

"Anything else it could be?" I ask, my suspicions growing.

"An antipsychotic?" Maja guesses. "Something for treating dementia, given all his research on the disease."

"So whatever pills these are, they weren't legal. Could they have been experimental? Something he was developing?"

"Sure," Maja says. "If he had access to a lab." I think for a moment. Why would Cobb have the pills, assuming they were ones he'd been developing? He hadn't worked at Advik for almost a year. It made no sense that he'd have stolen them a year ago and carried them around all this time. Or were they some other drug, maybe something that he'd stolen from Pelham Woods?

I arrive at the station and check in then go join the meeting in the briefing room. Sergeant Bruni had called me and suggested I come in and sit in on the update from the Homicide Unit, in case I have anything to add on the Cobb case.

"I did put everything into my reports, Sir," I'd told him on the phone. "Is there anything...?" Not that I wasn't keen to be invited; I just felt paranoid, like somehow I was being set up. Was Bruni subtly telling me the reports aren't adequate? This was one of the many tricks my anxiety plays on me, making me double and triple think everything I do or hear. It's exhausting.

"It's fine, Gauthier," he'd said, cutting me off mid-explanation. "See you here."

I slip into a seat at the back of the room and look around. Some of the faces are familiar; I've seen them around the region at various crime scenes. The Homicide Unit is made up of Detectives from all over the region; I'm assigned to District 6, and there are almost seven hundred sworn officers in the force, so odds are most of the faces won't be familiar to me. I'm the only female in the room.

A serious tall black man I recognize as Detective Sergeant Quinn Agu is standing in front of a white board that holds photos of several victims, one of which is Maurice Cobb. Agu intimidates me, and I know I'm not alone. He has a deep, resonant voice that sounds just like Darth Vadar and a physical presence that makes everyone give him space. I've never seen him smile. Part of me doubts he ever has.

"This is Detective Constable Gauthier," Agu says by way of introduction to the rest of the Homicide team, none of whom seem the slightest bit interested in me. "In case some of you don't already know, she's with Division 6. She's one of the first responders when Maurice Cobb's body was found."

He turns back to his notes. "We've had an identification now on the victim found floating in the canal last weekend," he read. "His name is Leon Flores, and he was a journalist." I hear a low rumble of exclamation around the room. Agu holds up his hand. "We were able to match his fingerprints to a minor charge he had twenty years ago. The pathologist says there are multiple contusions on his skull and evidence of blunt force trauma, bruising on his upper body, and cause of death is drowning. It appears he was likely beaten unconscious then thrown into the water."

One of the other Detectives raises his hand. It's DC Vogel, the youngest member of the Homicide Unit. "Was he a local man, Sir?" Vogel is one of the chattiest, most talkative men I've ever met. When I see him coming I've learned to pick up my phone and pretend to be on a call or to leave the room. Looking busy doesn't help; he'll just stand by my desk and talk away, oblivious.

"No," Agu answers. "He was from Toronto. I don't know what he was doing in town."

I raise my hand. "What sort of stories did he typically report on, Sir?"

Agu looks impatient. "I have no idea," he says. I put down my hand quickly, embarrassed. Was that a stupid question? Agu switches topics to the next case: the shooting on Port Street, as I pull out my phone and Google Flores' name. If there are any stories online that he's written it might provide a clue about what he was investigating.

Within a minute I've found that Leon Flores worked for The Standard, and that he'd won awards for his reporting on labour issues during the teachers' strike and corruption in regional waste disposal. As quietly as I can, I slip out the door into the hall and put in a call to Jane Fairfield, the features editor at The Standard, whose name I've found online.

I identify myself, and give her the news about Flores' death.

"Oh, my God…" Jane Fairfield says when she hears the news. "Are you sure?'

"Yes, Ma'am," I say. "We are treating it as a suspicious death."

"I'll have someone from the paper out there right away," she says, clearly thinking like a news editor.

"Excuse me, Ms. Fairfield," I interrupt before she can hang up the phone. "That's great, but I need some information from you. Can you please tell me what Mr. Flores was working on?"

"He's working on a series about migrant workers in the fruit and wine industry," she says after a moment. "How they are treated, social conditions, government regulations, health and safety, legal and illegal workers... the whole thing." She pauses and I hear her take a deep breath. "He was working undercover," she adds. "Posing as a migrant worker on several farms in the area."

"Do you have a list of those farms? Or any more information you can share with us, like where he was staying?"

I can hear the editor typing on her computer as she is speaking to me. I wonder if she's looking for the information I requested or if she's drafting the news story about the murder of their prize-winning investigative reporter.

"His plan was to stay in worker housing, when it was provided," she says after a minute. "He also rented a place. A shack he called it, out by the lake. Here it is: Lakeview Cottages, Lowbanks. I can email you a list of the farms he was working at. Will that help?"

I give Fairfield my email address and hang up, then slip back into the briefing room just as they are getting to the update on Maurice Cobb.

Agu noticed I'd left the room and raises his eyebrow when I take my seat. "Thank you for joining us, Detective Constable Gauthier." His disapproval is clear. "As I was saying, the autopsy results on Maurice Cobb are conclusive. He had large quantities of alcohol in his bloodstream as well as sedatives. The slashes on his arms are consistent with suicide, as is the note found at the scene. However, the absence of hesitation cuts, as well as the fact that no weapon was found at the scene, indicate this is possibly a suspicious death."

He looks directly at me. "Do you have anything to add, DC Gauthier?"

I stand. "Sir," I begin. "I've been looking into his finances and conducting some interviews into the case, with his former employers and his ex-wife. It would appear his state of mind would support the idea of suicide. His life was a mess," I say. "He was deeply in debt and the dealer was threatening repossession of his vehicle… Maybe that's where the truck has gone," I feel a rush of excitement as the idea pops into my mind. "Maybe it wasn't stolen at all, Sir. But I still don't have any ideas on the blade…"

"Thank you, Gauthier," Agu interrupts me, holding up his hand. He starts to wrap up the meeting.

"Sir?" I put up my hand, interrupting him. I can feel the impatience in the room as the rest of the Detectives are eager to go for their coffee breaks. I'm sure Agu is doing his best not to roll his eyes, but he nods for me to proceed.

"I just got off the phone with Leon Flores' editor at The Standard," I begin, reading from my notes. "He was working undercover, doing an investigative piece about migrant workers here in the region." Several heads turn in my direction, and hear some whispers among the other detectives. "I have the address of where he was staying here, and she's sending me a list of farms he was looking into. My I have your permission to carry out some inquiries?" Agu says nothing; his dark eyes study me. Then he smiles.

NINETEEN

IT'S IMPOSSIBLE TO find a parking spot in front of Pelham Woods, thanks to the two large cube vans blocking the way, both parked directly in front of the No Parking Tow-Away Zone sign. I go into the lobby and I'm surprised to find it full of people with walkie-talkies, headset microphones and clipboards. Across the floor run dozens of thick electrical cables powering tall standing lights that have been set up along one wall, as well as some monitors, cameras and computer equipment. It appears they're making a movie at Pelham Woods.

The elevator door opens and immediately I'm blocked from stepping off by a young woman wearing a headset. She holds up her hand, her expression serious and self-important. I glare at her until she finally realizes she's facing a uniformed police officer. She looks shocked and drops her hand and steps aside.

"I'm sorry," she whispers. "We're shooting." I give her a half smile and stay behind her until she hears someone shout.

"Cut", the voice says. "Reset."

The woman extends her hand to me. "I apologize for that," she says. "I'm Allison Rapp, the producer. Can I help you?"

"What are you producing?" I ask.

"A promotional video for Pelham Woods," she says. "We'll be here the next couple of days getting shots of the facility, all the recreational activities, dining room, fitness facility, the works." She hesitates for a moment. "Is there a problem, officer?"

I shake my head. "No problem. Getting anything of interest?" I ask, noting they aren't shooting in the left wing. There's nothing of promotional interest there I expect. What they're creating is a video of old people smiling and enjoying quality of life, playing bingo and doing line dancing—basically nothing like the reality of Pelham Woods.

"Oh yes," Allison Rapp says. "It'll be very relatable. Everyone has elderly parents or grandparents. And we've got some great shots and interviews already."

Relatable. So many old people spending their last days here, in dark, quiet rooms, lost somewhere inside their own heads. I can definitely relate.

"Where are you shooting now?" I ask, eager to get past the producer and do my own interview.

"The dining room," she says. "We're getting the patients being served lunch."

"Lunch?" I glance at my watch. "It's not even eleven o'clock."

"Pretend lunch," she laughs. "It's staged, mostly with residents from the retirement home playing patients for the shoot. The real patients are in the lounge." The real patients are mostly in wheelchairs and completely unresponsive, hardly good candidates for starring in the promotional video.

"How long is that going to take?" I ask as the dining room door opens again and three women emerge. The first one is tall and has her hair tied back in a tight bun. She holds the door so the others can follow. The next is Nadia Efimov, and last is Doreen, pushing her walker. All three women look to be dressed in their finest outfits, no doubt for the filming. Doreen spots me right away and the three of them make their way toward me at a snail's pace.

Suddenly there's a scream from the patient lounge. I push past the video production team and run. Turning the corner at the nursing station I see a crowd in the middle of the patient lounge, huddled around the man in pyjamas. He's shrieking gibberish and holding a knife against the neck of a woman in a wheelchair. She lies back, her throat exposed and eyes wide open, but from the blank expression in her eyes I doubt she's even aware of what's going on.

A PSW stands near the man holding, out his hand and trying to pacify him.

"Give it to me, Alan," he says in a calm, quiet voice. "Give me that right now." The patient stops screaming. He hesitates and turns to the PSW, eyeing him suspiciously. Then he jerks the knife away from the woman's throat and holds it out in front of him, threatening anyone who comes close.

My heart starts to race and I feel tunnel vision closing in. I can't breathe, my mouth is dry and I can feel my hands shaking. I stare at the knife and I just want to run.

Then I realize it's a butter knife without any point or edge and I move fast, pushing past the care worker. I grab his arm and wrench the knife away from him. Alan struggles and tries to fight me, but I'm far too strong for him and I easily shove him backward. He flops down onto the sofa behind him, blinking like an owl. The PSW rushes over and stands nearby, in case he needs to be restrained again.

Dr. Chowdhury appears behind me. "Thank you," he says, accepting the knife from me. I step back and pull out my phone.

"What are you doing?" he sounds panicked.

"I'm calling this in."

"Surely that's not necessary," Chowdhury blusters. "This man is unwell. It's not a criminal situation. There was no intent to harm."

"That's not what it looked like to me," I argue. "He could have killed that woman."

"With this knife? Hardly."

"Doctor, this is the second violent incident I've witnessed here in as many days," I say. "You assured me when we met that these episodes were extremely rare." Chowdhury flushes and his eyes dart back and forth.

I notice out of the corner of my eye that the cameraman and audio guy are right behind me, and the camera is still rolling. It wouldn't surprise me if they've captured the whole thing.

"Dr. Chowdhury," I begin. "I thought antipsychotics tend to make patients passive and docile. And dementia destroys the ability to reason, to a great degree." Chowdhury nods but looks wary. "So I don't understand why or how Alan was able to take a knife, presumably from the dining room and hide it, then pull it out and use it to threaten that other patient. That takes the ability to calculate, to plan. Why is he able to do that when, from what I can see, the rest of the residents are…" I stop. What are they? Catatonic? Inert? Vegetables?

"It's just part of the disease I'm sorry to say. Only a very small percent ever become violent."

"Doctor, your patients are off the charts. This is not normal."

"It's just an anomaly," he protests. "Dementia is such an unpredictable disease." He glances at the skeptical expression on my face and stops talking.

"In my experience I'd say dementia is very predictable," I say. "Every step of the way down."

Dr. Chowdhury starts to argue then he just gives up. He turns on the cameraman. "Put that away, immediately," he demands. "And make sure you erase any footage you have of this… incident."

The cameraman smiles and shrugs. "Sure, no problem," he says as he slings the camera off his shoulder and goes off to join the producer by the elevators. When the door opens they all pile in, presumably looking for something else to film.

Chowdhury turns back to me. "I don't have an explanation," he says, raking his hand through his thick hair. He's clearly frustrated and I sense he's nervous.

"I do," a small voice says at my side. I turn and see it's Nadia

Efimov. She's standing between the tall woman and Doreen, who's leaning on her walker.

"You have an explanation?" I prompt her.

Chowdhury sighs in exasperation and takes hold of her arm. She flinches and it looks to me like he gives it a hard squeeze.

"Mrs. Efimov," he snaps. "Please, take a seat in the lounge." She blinks as he shoves her toward the rest of the patients. Doreen glares at him and gently guides her friend away.

"They're putting something in the water," Nadia protests as she's led into the lounge. "Everybody knows it's true."

TWENTY

I MAKE THE call and report the incident. While I'm on the phone the nurse approaches Dr. Chowdhury and points out some notation on her clipboard. He looks irritated then pulls out his pen and initials a few spots. It's the same woman from the other day, and she's still wearing a wrinkled uniform. Her nametag says Katrina. She's a thin middle-aged woman, with fading short brown hair and glasses. There's nothing remarkable about her at all; she's nondescript, in the very definition of the word. An ordinary sort of woman who'd pass through a crowd unnoticed and through life unremembered.

Dr. Chowdhury waits for me to finish my call before pointedly looking at his watch again. "Are we done here?" he asks. "I have rounds." I'm about to suggest my accompanying him just to rattle his cage, but decide against it. He can wait. I should remain on hand for when other officers show up in response to my call.

"Thank you Doctor," I say. "I'll catch up with you another time. Soon." I catch the look of relief in his eyes turn to alarm and I smile with satisfaction. I have to admit I don't like Dr. Chowdhury, or trust him.

He heads for the elevator and I turn to catch up with Doreen and the two other women in the lounge. They've just settled themselves on either side of Nadia Efimov and Doreen is fussing with a cushion, placing it behind her friend's back so she's more comfortable.

"May I join you?" I ask and sit down without waiting for an answer. It's something police detectives all learn to do early in our careers.

"Of course," Doreen says. She turns to the tall woman, who is looking at the back of a wing chair. "This is my friend Lucy," Doreen continues and the woman nods her head, still looking in exactly the wrong direction. It's disconcerting.

"Of course you know Nadia," Doreen says, patting her friend on the knee. "And this is Anna Kozlowski," she indicates the tall woman, who smiles at the chair.

"You know Nadia?" Anna Kozlowski asks the chair in a heavy Slavic accent.

"We've met," I say. "I know her daughter Rose. I used to work at Thorny Rose, when I was in school." The woman nods, still looking away.

"Anna lives right across the road from the restaurant," Doreen says. "She's got macular degeneration. She can only see out of the sides of her eyes." That explains her orientation; I'd thought she was nuts.

"I see everything," the woman snaps. I doubt that, but I'm not about to argue.

"So do I," Nadia Efimov says. "But they never believe you, no matter how many times you tell them."

A snort of laughter right behind makes me jump and I turn to see Katrina the nurse, eavesdropping. She reaches past me and hands a small plastic cup to Nadia, then stands watching to make sure Nadia swallows the pill before giving her some juice to wash it down. It must be medication time.

"What do you see, Mrs. Efimov?" I prod. It's unlikely, but maybe she did see something worth considering. The nurse is still standing there listening but when she notices me looking she hurries away.

Nadia shakes her head in irritation and won't say any more. From Doreen's expression I understand there's no point in pressing her. Nadia Efimov is in the dementia ward for a reason. How reliable a witness could she be to anything?

"We three girls have been friends for our whole lives," Doreen begins. "For over seventy years now. I'm godmother to both of their children." Anna Kozlowski nods, still staring at the back of the chair as Nadia closes her eyes and starts to doze off. "We went to school together." Anna Kozlowski is smiling. "We'd go to dances and parties," Doreen continues. "Driving in cars, going to the beach... so many good memories." She looks at Nadia, who is quietly snoring in her chair. "For some of us anyway."

Doreen's eyes narrow as she looks toward the nursing station where I can hear a loud male voice. It's Cooper.

"Excuse me, ladies," I say as I rise to meet him. "The cavalry has arrived."

I take a deep breath and walk over to Cooper, wondering why he'd be responding to the call I'd made.

"Gauthier," he says with a nod. "What's going on?"

"There was a violent incident with a patient," I say as I bite my tongue. I was about to refer to him as Sir when I remember he no longer outranks me, so fuck him. Cooper is just a Detective Constable, like me.

"Everything under control?" he looks irritated, as usual.

"Yes, it seems to be." He flashes me another look and I struggle to keep my expression neutral. It won't help anything if Cooper sees how much I detest him.

He sighs and makes a big show of pulling out his notebook and jotting something down. Then he limps over and starts to speak with the surly nurse. I watch out of the corner of my eye, while pretending to look at my phone. They certainly look chummy. Maybe they're friends.

Katrina Mueller is nodding and agreeing with whatever Cooper is saying to her. She doesn't look happy. Cooper dismisses her, closes his notebook and ambles through the patient lounge. I watch as he swaggers past the patients, checking everyone out and letting them know by his demeanor that the situation is under control, now that he's arrived. When he walks past Doreen he's brought up short. She's glaring at him with an expression of pure hatred. Cooper flinches and breaks stride, pausing slightly before he turns away from Doreen and makes his way back to the nursing station.

"Everything's quiet now," he says with authority. I don't bother to respond. He looks like he's considering something. "No need for you to report this," he says as he heads for the elevator. "I'll take care of it when I get back to the station."

"Fine," I shrug. He probably needs to make it look like he'd been doing something, to keep up his quotas. He can have this call.

TWENTY ONE

I WATCH AS Doreen and Anna Kozlowski leave their friend dozing in the lounge and walk together toward the elevator. Anna keeps one hand on Doreen's walker as a guide to help her navigate. I catch up with them as the door opens.

"Did you have a nice visit?" I ask.

They both smile. "Too much for me," Anna says. "All the filming took too long. Usually we only stay an hour at most."

"How are you getting home?" I realize that neither of them drives and Pelham Woods is too far out of town to be on any bus route. "Can I give you a lift?" I offer. "I'm going back to town."

"You bet!" Doreen agrees immediately. "But, Anna doesn't live in town. She's out on Concession 6, near Ridge Road. Is that all right?"

"Not a problem," I smile. "We're here to serve and protect."

I help them both into the back seat of the patrol car and drive up the escarpment, passing empty vineyards where fat bunches of dark grapes had hung only weeks ago.

Anna Kozlowski gives directions as we wind through the country roads, but I only pretend to listen. I remember Doreen had said Anna lived across from Thorny Rose. Not only had I worked there years ago, I'd made several trips out there earlier in the summer when there'd been a series of deaths and a poisoning at the restaurant.

I pull into Anna's driveway and stop the car next to a hand-made wooden sign with a painted address: 4351 Concession 6. Anna Kozlowski's home is an old farmhouse and from what I can tell it's in very poor repair. Maintaining a home is a lot of work, especially for an elderly woman with eyesight problems.

"How big is your farm?" I ask. I can see rows of fruit trees in the distance behind the barn.

"Just fifty acres now," Anna says. "My son runs the farm. I'm too old to work."

"What do you grow? Apples?"

Anna nods. "Mostly, for eating and cider. And some pears too." I open the door for her and she starts to climb out, brushing off my help. She manages easily to climb her front steps and enter the house; years of practice would probably let her do it in her sleep. Doreen waves out the window, even though it's unlikely Anna can see her as she unlocks her front door and slips inside.

I'm looking across the road at the Thorny Rose sign. It's one of the best restaurants in the entire Niagara region. Maja and I had come here for our anniversary last year, when the roses were in full bloom and the entire garden lush and fragrant with blossom. I feel my throat tighten as I climb back into the car.

"Rose is my goddaughter," Doreen says, apparently unaware she's repeating herself. "She owns that restaurant."

"It's a great place," I smile, grateful for the distraction. "How is Rose?" I ask. I've seen her a few times around town, at the farmers' market or the marina. But we haven't spoken in months.

"She's fine," Doreen says. "The crap about her husband wasn't good for business, but she's a smart girl. She'll be okay." The story had been in all the papers, local and national, for weeks after it happened. It's gone quiet for now, but people never forget, especially in small towns.

Doreen gives me her address in the East Village and I aim the car back toward town, my heart sinking. I know Rodney Street all too well.

"That other cop," Doreen begins after a moment. "The guy who showed up at Pelham Woods. Is he your partner?"

"*Cooper*?!" I laugh. "No way." I almost say *God forbid,* but don't need to let a civilian in on station politics. "We don't really have partners," I say. "There isn't enough budget or manpower here to put two officers in the same car, so we mostly work alone. We'll call for backup if we need it."

"You don't get lonely, being on your own all day?"

"No, I enjoy my own company," I say. In fact, I prefer it. People are a lot of work.

"He's a bad egg that one."

I try to play it cool. "Cooper? What do you mean?"

"I saw him beat up a kid," she says, her jaw tight in anger. "The kid's epileptic. He had a seizure and that cop threw him on the ground, beat him up and then tasered him." She shakes her head. "I saw that cop punch him in the head, with a closed fist, after they'd already handcuffed him." I have no trouble imagining Cooper doing it. "It was in all the papers—didn't you see it? The family are suing the police now."

Doreen is staring out the window, lost in thought. "You should have seen that cop's face when he was punching that poor young man. Hateful. Somebody needs to teach that guy a lesson."

I doubt Cooper is capable of learning anything at this point. "Do you have children Doreen?" I ask, changing the subject.

"I had a son," she says after a moment. "He died."

TWENTY TWO

THE DISTRICT 6 Police Station is a short, squat, red brick building that looks like it might be a sub-station for the local electricity company. The other stations in the region all have new modern buildings of glass and steel, with up to date offices, technology and facilities. But this building, with only one story and just a few windows along two sides, is the stepchild of the entire region's police station buildings. It's unimpressive, underfunded and understaffed.

Decker meets me when I come into the station and walks me through the security doors. "The autopsy results are in on that sudden death at the Green Bean," he says. "No surprise."

"Overdose?" I ask.

He nods. "Fentanyl and heroin. What's interesting is that he took it orally."

I stare at him. "That's weird, isn't it? I don't think I've ever even heard of taking heroin that way."

Decker shrugs. "Different strokes I suppose. He could have taken it up his ass for all I care."

"So, that's it?" I ask. "Close the investigation?"

"I'd say so," he agrees. "The department isn't going to be interested in spending money or time to look any further into the death of a known pimp, drug dealer, and all around dickhead like Mark Sempe." Decker pushes open the doors into the cafeteria and goes over to the coffee machine. "He's dead," he says. "That's one less of them out there."

Even though I'd never say it aloud, I agree. The world is better off without pimps like Mark Sempe in it. The way he'd been grooming that girl disgusted me. And she would've been just one in a long list of young women he'd put out onto the streets. And that was apart from the problems he'd caused through his dealing and whatever else he was involved with. It's tough to care about him being dead.

When I'd grown up in the East Village there were lots of guys just like him, even in my own family. Like my uncle, dead of an overdose on our living room couch from sampling his own wares. Up and down our street there were drug dealers, addicts and alcoholics, wife beaters and drunks. I'd heard things were better before the refinery closed down; I wouldn't know. That was way before my time.

"What about Cobb?" I ask. "Are his results in?"

"Suicide." Decker hands me a coffee. "Coroner says he can't question the lengthwise cuts on his arms, even though there weren't even any hesitation cuts."

"So, either he was definite about killing himself, or someone did it for him."

Decker makes a face. "There aren't any indications that anyone else was even involved."

"The blade walked away by itself?"

"I know." Decker rubs his face. He looks tired. The deep lines around his eyes make me wonder how old he is. In the bright autumn sunlight that streams through the vertical blinds he looks at least sixty. Ready to retire. Past caring.

"Maybe whoever took the truck took the knife. Or one of the kids."

"Took it as some kind of trophy?"

"Maybe it was a cool knife? I don't know!" I make a mental note to see if it's at all likely Cobb had a special knife of some kind, one that a kid might want to steal.

"Apart from the missing knife, it looks like suicide to me too. The guy's life was a mess. His wife left him, for good reason, and he'd lost his job. Again. Was working as a security guard, and he even got fired from that."

"I hear you," Decker agrees. "The guy was lost. It's obviously suicide."

"What did you learn about him from Limestone Security, by the way? Anything of interest?"

"Not really. They placed Cobb at a couple of part time jobs…"

"Taiga and Pelham among them?"

Decker nods. "He barely registered on their radar. Their records show they placed him, but that's about it. The clerk remembers he was really keen to get the job at Pelham Woods. Kept asking her about getting a job there." Decker laughs. "I'm pretty sure Cobb thought the idea of working night shifts at a nursing home sounded like a sweet deal. Great chance to catch up on his sleep."

"Limestone Security is Cooper's retirement plan, right? How's business doing?" The sooner Cooper retires the happier a lot of us will be, but I don't say it out loud. I haven't forgotten the bollocking Bruni gave me.

"Great. He's got tons of work. You interested? I could put in a good word for you."

"No way," I say, smart enough not mention how much I despise Cooper. "I don't know how you do it. Just thinking of doing all that overtime exhausts me." I'm surprised Decker has the energy himself. He's not young and I know he's lazy, a guy who'll do the minimum requirement.

"So, back to Maurice Cobb," I change the subject. "He goes out to a nice secluded spot—with a great view," I add with a smile at Decker. "And he drinks a lot, smokes a lot, prepares himself and then slits his wrists."

"But?" he asks.

"Exactly," I say. "But. It doesn't feel right. Something else is going on. Those pills he had on them are some off-brand anti-psychotic drugs."

"How do you know that?" Decker demands, sitting upright and glaring at me. "What are you looking into the pills for, Gauthier?"

I hesitate, unsure of how much to share with Decker, or why he's so upset about my inquiry. "I had a friend test them," I say, hoping he won't care, as he doesn't about most things. But for some reason this has gotten him worked up. "It was the fastest way to find out what they were," I explain. "I didn't think Sergeant Bruni would even bother, since it was being filed as a suicide."

"Anti-psychotic? Not your typical recreational drug," Decker says without interest. "So they weren't for him to get high, or to sell to anyone else." He shrugs, happy to dismiss it. "Big deal. I still doubt there's anything there."

"I'm thinking they are something experimental, maybe something he'd been working on at his last job. He had all those notes and charts and research at his place. It's like he was still doing some investigation, or maybe trying to prove something."

Decker snorts, dismissing my speculation. "You're working too hard Gauthier. Trying to make this more complicated than it is. What would he have been trying to prove?"

I drive west along Lakeshore Road, heading out to Lowbanks to look into the rental cottage where Leon Flores was staying. The place is a popular rental area in summer, with some of the cottages and cabins having the luxury of a private beach. The whole area empties out after Labour Day and now most of the rental cabins are already shuttered and locked up for the winter, their electricity shut off and their pipes drained so they won't freeze when the cold weather comes.

I have to make a hard left into the sandy overgrown driveway when I almost miss the turn into the rental cottages, then leave the patrol car in what looks like a parking area and walk toward the building marked Office.

I knock, but there's no answer, which is unsurprising. I try the handle and the door is locked. A quick scan of the area shows me there are ten cabins of various sizes, with five of them lining the beach and the other five about a hundred yards away to the north of the water. There's a meadow behind the second set of cabins, giving the area a bit of a natural feel and providing a noise and privacy buffer between them and the road.

All of the cabins are made of weathered wood siding, and all have large porches and wooden decks. I imagine that there would be patio furniture, barbeques and picnic tables set out during the summer rental season. But now all of that has been put away, secured inside the shuttered cabins.

I'm pulling out my notebook to write down the number painted on the Office sign, when someone calls out. "Can I help you?" A woman is coming toward me along the driveway. "I saw your car," she says. "I just live across the road."

I glance at the house she's pointing to, across Lakeshore Road. It's a classic red brick Ontario farmhouse, with a wraparound porch lined with hanging baskets all still overflowing with colourful flowers.

"I'm the manager here," she says when she finally reaches me. "I'm Roberta Jackson." She's a tall, handsome woman wearing a floral African head wrap.

"I'm looking for information on Leon Flores," I say. "I understand he was staying here." I do not mention we've found his body, but the woman is sharp.

"Is he dead?" she asks. "I thought he might be because I haven't seen him in over a week. He usually checks in, tells me when he'll be away."

"I'm afraid so, Ms. Jackson. He drowned, in the Canal." Roberta Jackson looks surprised then suspicious.

"So someone killed him." She shakes her head. "Nobody goes swimming in the Welland Canal, especially in autumn." I shiver, remembering how cold the water had been when I'd jumped in after Flores' body.

I nod. "We are treating it as a suspicious death."

"He was a nice man," she says. "I'm sorry. How can I help you?"

"Can you tell me when he moved in? Where he lived?"

"Of course," she says. "I'll take you there now." She starts walking along the sandy track toward the beach and I follow her. "He moved in about a month ago; I'd have to check the receipts to give you the exact date.

"I told him we were closing down for the season. We normally close up after Labour Day. But he was willing to pay cash in advance, for two months." She shrugs. "I thought why not? I was going to be around doing some renovations on cottage 9 anyway. He seemed like a good guy. I told him there's no heat, the places aren't winterized. He said he didn't care."

"Did he tell you why he needed to be here?"

She hesitates. "Not really. He said he was doing research. I thought maybe he was some kind of a writer. Said he liked the quiet and privacy." We arrive at Cabin 3, the only one that isn't closed up for the season. There's one plastic chair and a small table next to the door. From the deck he'd have had an unimpeded view of Lake Erie, for miles in either direction.

Roberta Jackson unlocks the cabin and lets me go in first. It's a tiny place, just one bedroom off a central kitchen and living room. Which makes sense, since most of the summer guests' time would be spent out on the deck or down on the beach. The front room is tiled, a practical choice as people would always be tracking in sand from the beach. The furniture is spare and old, but everything is covered with clean matching slipcovers so even though nothing originally matched it all goes together.

"We rent furnished, obviously," she says. "And provide all the bedding and dishes. He just had to buy his own food." She picks up a dirty plate that had been left on the table, next to a pair of binoculars. "I even cleaned for him, just once a week. He paid me extra for that. I also changed his bedding. He wasn't so good with the dishes." She puts the plate into the sink and runs water over it.

"When was the last time you were in here, to clean?" I ask.

She thinks for a moment. "It would have been five or six days ago, I'd have to check. I usually cleaned for him on Tuesdays. That's my day off."

I'm confused. "I thought you worked here."

"Oh, I do," she laughs. "But that doesn't pay the bills, does it? I also clean house for some families in town. Feels like that's all I do. Clean my own house, my rental cottages, and for other folks in town."

"I clean a lot too," I say. I do not add it's one of my ways of self-medicating my anxiety disorder. Wouldn't do to have Roberta Jackson lose faith in the police department, assuming she has any.

"It was easier to look after his place than most," Roberta continues. "He was away every day, for hours. And since he wasn't here to party or play on the beach he didn't track sand into the place. Basically, Mr. Flores ate a bit, drank a few beers sitting on the deck, slept in the bed, and worked on his computer."

"Computer?" I look around. "Where is it?"

"He always had it on the table," Roberta says. "It was a laptop."

It's gone now, I note. And in his personal effects, found on his body after I'd pulled him out of the Canal, there'd been no wallet, no phone and no keys. Since the cabin had been securely locked, with no evidence of a break in when I just arrived with Roberta, it was safe to assume whoever had killed him had used the stolen keys to get in and had taken the laptop.

"You live across the road," I say. "I guess you saw him come and go?"

She nods. "Sometimes, if I was home. He had an old red Ford Fiesta. Piece of junk, I don't even know how it was still on the road."

"Mr. Flores was an investigative journalist," I say. "We understand he was here working on a story about migrant workers."

Roberta's eyes light up. "That makes sense," she says. "I saw him one time, downtown early in the morning. He was standing with a group of pickers, as if he was waiting for the bus to collect them and take them to work." She shakes her head. "I couldn't figure out where his car was."

So Flores had driven to this pick up spot, posing as one of the migrant pickers. A migrant worker couldn't very well show up to work in his own car.

"Where was this pick up spot?"

"Downtown, by the Food Basics grocery store," she says. "It's near the hostel where the migrants live during the season."

"I thought the farmers put them up, gave them room and board at the farms?"

"Some do, I suppose. They still have dorms or barracks in the old barns. But not everybody's got the space now. So they get boarded at the hostel, or one of the old motels in town."

I quickly check through the closet and the single set of drawers in the bedroom while Roberta washes the few dirty dishes and leaves them to dry on the rack. There aren't many items of clothing and what there is looks like the sort of clothes he'd chosen to blend in as a migrant worker: Nothing expensive or new, maybe even purchased from a thrift store.

"Should I clean up in here?" Roberta asks when I came back into the kitchen. "Get all his clothes and stuff together?"

I nod. There's no point getting a forensic team out here. All that's left is a few changes of clothes and some toiletries. I'm sure that whoever took his laptop had been careful enough to not leave fingerprints at the scene. "Yes, we'll notify his next of kin and have them collect it," I say.

Roberta locks the door behind us. "I'll keep it all in the Office," she says, looking around. "So I can get this place winter-ready now? Board it up?" She looks to me for confirmation and I nod. It was lucky for her Flores had paid in advance.

We stand together on the deck for a moment, admiring the view. Flores had a pair of binoculars on the table. What had he been looking at? Sailboats? Shorebirds? Sunsets?

"So, who lives in those places over there?" I ask, pointing to a row of spectacular homes perched up above the dunes. There's no shortage of overbuilt McMansions dotting the Niagara landscape; these all have their patches of sand clearly posted Private.

"Rich people," Roberta laughs. "Every one of those is new. They bought up all the old places, tore them down and built custom."

"Anyone I've heard of?"

"One guy's a lawyer from Toronto," she says. "Two families are from across the border. They live in New York State somewhere. One is an Indian family."

My curiosity is piqued. I can clearly see a huge stone house, sitting prominently high above the dunes. All the trees around it have been cut down and an expansive lawn laid down to the stones that line a private beach.

"Whose house is that one?"

Roberta smirks. "You mean the *Mistake on the Lake*? That's what we all call it. A guy with lots of money and no taste, and he wants everyone to know it."

"Would that be Amit Joshi?" I ask. "The guy who owns Taiga and Advik?"

"And a lot of other real estate around here," she nods. "Yup, that's him." I wonder if that's who Flores had been keeping an eye on with those binoculars.

I head back into town, hoping to find Flores' car in the Food Basics parking lot. Even though the lot is posted saying after hours parking is prohibited and all vehicles will be tagged and towed, they never are. I find the red Ford Fiesta parked around the side of the grocery store, as I'd expected. It isn't even locked, so I have no problem searching inside. But I find nothing. Flores was careful. I call in the vehicle to have it towed to the police impound then sit in the patrol car waiting for the tow truck.

Flores was supposedly investigating migrant workers in the region. Writing a series on how they were treated, on government polices around immigration, on a day in the life of a temporary farm worker. He was posing as a migrant worker. Had he been killed because of that? Did some racist creep attack him?

There's always been this ugly resentment in the East Village, a distrust of the migrants and anger that they're taking jobs from the locals. But the fact is, before any farmer can even bring temporary foreign workers into the country they have to advertise the positions locally. No one ever applies. The locals don't want the jobs. The work is too hard, the hours too long, and the pay too low. It's easier to bitch about foreigners than it is to work twelve hours a day in the blazing heat picking fruit. Hell, the white kids in the East Village won't even take a job in fast food, or at a convenience store. But they sure hate those that do, especially if they aren't Caucasians.

Was this death a hate crime? Did someone kill Flores because they took him for a migrant worker? Maybe he was down by the canal and some drunks decided to take their miserable lives out on him.

Or what if he'd uncovered something illegal during his research, something that required him to be silenced. What do those binoculars have to do with it? Is it a coincidence that Amit Joshi, one of Taiga's owners, lives just down the beach from Flores' cottage? Taiga, where Cobb had worked and where he'd died.

TWENTY THREE

MY PHONE RINGS just as I'm driving into the crime scene and I grab the handset and throw the car into park. It's the Ford dealer who sold Maurice Cobb his new truck. We've been playing phone tag for a few days and I don't want to miss him again.

"I'm not sure why you're calling Detective," he says after the introductions. "I spoke with one of your colleagues a few days ago and gave him all this information."

"My colleague?" I hate sounding stupid and I hate incompetence even more. Decker's laziness again. "I'm sorry, I didn't get the message."

"As I told him," the dealer sounds irritated and I don't blame him. "Maurice Cobb's truck was fully paid off."

"*Paid off?*"

"Yes, in two cash payments over the past two months."

"So it wasn't repossessed?"

"Nope. He owned it free and clear."

I thank him for the call then climb out of the car, slamming the door in anger. I start to walk as fast as I can, trying to work out my frustration.

First of all, why didn't Decker remember to give me this valuable piece of information? Making me waste my time calling the dealer, following this idea up, and all for nothing. Was it some kind of a joke? Knowing Decker it was just carelessness, which doesn't make it any better.

Second, and more important in the grand scheme of things, where did Cobb get the cash to pay off the truck?

I slow down my pace and mull over the possibilities. The only sound I hear is field crickets chirping in the long grass that lines the road.

Cobb didn't have a job. He didn't have anything of value to sell, as far as I know. Except maybe he did—the formulae from Advik Therapeutics. Maybe Amit Joshi wasn't lying about corporate espionage after all.

My boots crunch on the gravel driveway as I walk slowly toward the tall fence, looking carefully into the brush on either side for anything that might have been missed when we'd first discovered Cobb's body. It's been almost a week since Cobb died, and the crime scene investigators had of course been over the site, but I'm afraid that something might have been overlooked. But since it looks obviously like a suicide, and human nature being what it is—lazy and impatient, I think it's worth another look.

I slip through the hole in the fence, noting that the security team at Taiga hasn't bothered to repair it yet. That's surprising, given my visit earlier when I'd called them out on their less than perfectly secure perimeter. I walk over to the spot Cobb's lawnchair had sat. Apart from the heavily trampled grass there's no indication he'd even been there. Rain has washed away all traces of his blood, and the feet of the investigating officers have obliterated the rest. Which may have been exactly what Cobb had wanted when he'd come here to die.

What kind of a man was Maurice Cobb? Obviously he was an intelligent one since he had a PhD and had worked in pharmaceutical research. One who'd lost both his job and his family through his own actions. He was also an abusive husband and, given his non-payment of child support, an indifferent father. Maybe even a bad one. I wonder if he'd hurt his children as well as his wife? It wouldn't surprise me; there are no shortages of bad fathers.

I sigh and raise my head to admire the view. In the distance the lake is a deep indigo blue, with white caps racing across the water, chased by the sharp wind. Up here on the escarpment the air is still and the sun is warm, especially in this sheltered spot. It's peaceful and quiet. Tall clumps of goldenrod and milkweed bloom all around the clearing, covered with bees and Monarch butterflies. No wonder Cobb had chosen this spot to die.

Down by the lake is an isolated house, built in the clearing in a forest of red maples and beech trees. It's on a Firelane that leads down to a small private beach. I'm filled with a rush of envy, thinking of the lucky people who live there, in seclusion and privacy. What would that have been like? To not have to hear the people next door as they brawled and cried, or drank too much and smashed things. That was the soundtrack of my childhood. Or not having neighbours nearby to call the cops on you, when things ignited in your home. Too many times the police had come to my house, about my uncle or when my stepfather beat my mother. Not that it ever went anywhere with the cops, just like the many calls I'd read in Bennett's file. Everyone thought my stepfather was a good guy. He was loads of fun down at the Legion. Geraldine Bennett's situation resonated deeply with me; it was all too familiar.

Once he gave my mother a five-finger necklace and kept her in a chokehold against the wall until she passed out. I stood on the stairs seeing her face go red, then a dull grey as she slumped to the floor. The entire time he was choking her he stared up at me, ignoring her gasps and her hands feebly clawing and trying to free herself. He was daring me to do something, to say something, to give him an excuse to come after me next. But I was too afraid to move.

The only time I'd dared to call 911 he'd charmed the cops who came to the house and chatted with them guy to guy. My mother had just stood there, mute and tearful. As they were leaving I'd heard them say it was *just another East Village domestic.* Then he beat my mother again and pissed on her after he'd knocked her unconscious.

He used to tell me it was lucky I was smart because I wasn't pretty. But he was a *great guy.* Everyone loved him. He'd loan people money, when we didn't have enough for groceries then he'd hit my mother for complaining. He'd help anyone fix their car or their front step but couldn't lift a finger to do any repairs at our house. He was a great guy. Always had a funny story to tell.

I was lucky I was able to get out. Because of what happened I was able to escape the East Village, and I'd moved to Wainfleet for a better life with my new family. From what I'd seen at Dennis Sharp's house things aren't any different in the East Village now, twenty years later. Kids who live there still do the same things they've always done: theft, drugs, petty vandalism and breaking probation.

Those kids had been here in this clearing the night Cobb died. Did they take the knife? Did they take the truck? They'd taken the pills and cannabis, but Dennis had handed them over to me. If I hadn't come to his house that morning, would he have tried to sell them? Probably. He was only ten or eleven years old, but they start young in the East Village.

I look around the clearing again, though I know now there's nothing left to find. I start walking in ever-widening circles, starting with the spot Cobb had died. I make it to the outside of the clearing when my phone rings.

It's Decker.

"We've found Andre Dumont," he says. "He's at Drifter's on Nickel Street."

TWENTY FOUR

DRIFTERS TAVERN IS quiet at this time of the afternoon. But it's Friday, and the start of a weekend, which guarantees the place will be packed after ten o'clock once the band starts. And I know there'll be at least a couple of calls out here, after fights in the parking lot and brawls inside the bar.

The music is loud, the lights low and the drinks cheap, so Drifters is packed most nights. And in the afternoons it's always a safe bet we'll be able to find certain persons of interest there, either playing pool or at one of the many arcade games that line the back wall.

I park behind Decker on the street and get into his car. He looks even more tired.

"You look done in," I say. "How long have you been working today?"

"Going on twelve hours." He checks his watch. "I'm beat."

"Don't you need any downtime?"

"I want to pay off my mortgage before I retire," he says. "My divorce cost me a lot. Need to make up for that." I get it. Divorce is commonplace in the force. Still, Decker isn't that young. Maybe he shouldn't be pushing himself so hard. I guess he must really need the money.

"He's been in there about an hour," Decker says. "Tremblay

recognized him and called it in. I thought you'd like to be here to do the honours."

I smile as I get out of the car and follow Decker and Tremblay into the bar. I do indeed like it. There's an adrenaline rush every time I take down a suspect, and every time I enter a live scene. For an anxious person like me, it feels like a reward for my constant hyper-vigilance. It's like something I've been practicing for my whole life, the way an Olympic athlete must feel when they finally compete for gold. The world finally makes sense, at least for that brief moment.

We find Dumont at a table, sitting with two buddies in front of a pint of beer and a plate of chicken wings. His *what could you possibly want with me* act is pretty good, I have to admit. Dumont seems genuinely confused and surprised. He's probably disappointed he won't get to finish his beer and wings.

"Want me to ask them to wrap them up to go?" I ask, my voice heavy with sarcasm. Dumont is about to say yes when I push him ahead of me out the door. His buddies can finish them off.

At the station it takes a while for him to be processed because Dumont has an outstanding bench warrant for a failure to appear in court over some traffic violations. By the time Decker and I meet him in an interview room he looks exhausted and enraged. The system will do that to you.

"Mr. Dumont," I begin after introducing Decker and myself and explaining we are being videotaped. "We have some questions for you, regarding a missing F-150 Ford Truck, registered to Maurice Cobb."

Dumont shakes his head. "Can't help you," he says.

"So you know nothing about a black F-150, that would have been seen at the Taiga property off Concession 5, six nights ago on September 18th?" He shakes his head again then smiles.

"I wasn't anywhere near Taiga last weekend," he says. "But since I want to co-operate I can tell you I saw a black F-150 at Nickel Beach that night."

Decker and I exchange a look. "What time would that have been?" I ask.

"Around one or two in the morning? Maybe? We were just smoking and having a beer down there. I saw the truck. It had the keys in it. I did not take the truck."

"Just parked there?" Decker asks. "And you expect us to believe the keys were just left in it?"

"It was outside the gates, next to the little shack where you pay to park," Dumont says. "We walked right past it to get onto the beach." I know the spot. Even though it's officially closed at dusk and the entry gate locked, that only prevents people from driving onto it. Runners, dog walkers and late night partiers have no problem accessing the beach.

"What else did you find in the truck? Besides the keys."

Dumont shakes his head. "Nothing," he lies. "I never even went near it."

"You went near enough to see the keys were left in it," I say. "What else did you see?"

"A knife, maybe?" Decker asks. "A murder weapon?"

Dumont looks shocked. Almost as much as when we'd appeared and interrupted his eating chicken wings. But this time I can tell he's afraid. Still, I wasn't falling for it. I tap Decker on the shoulder and motion for him to come with me into the hall.

"We need to do a search of the area around there," I say. "See what turns up."

"What about Dumont?" Decker asks.

"He's got an outstanding bench warrant," I say. "He's not going anywhere."

TWENTY FIVE

THE NEXT MORNING the search team is at Nickel Beach as soon as the sun comes up. I had to call in a favour and the canine unit brought out two new dogs, mostly because they need the training.

Based on what Dumont told us, I have them concentrate the search near where he'd said the truck had been parked. If anything had been tossed from there, like a knife, it would be within a fifty-yard radius, depending on the strength of whoever had thrown it. That includes the beach behind the chain link fence and gate, as well as the gravel parking area, neither of which are likely spots to throw something if you don't want it found. The area directly to the north of the parking lot is an overgrown marsh, which has been designated for natural restoration according to the posted No Entry signs.

"If it's anywhere, it's in there." I point to the swampy patch, thick with Phalaris grass, bulrushes and poison ivy.

"How do you know?" asks the handler. He doesn't look like he's keen on sending the dogs into the muck and I don't blame him.

"That's where I'd throw it."

He lets the dogs loose and I stand back, waiting for what I hope doesn't turn out to be a waste of time.

I look down the beach, which is empty at this time of day. The white sand curves around the bay, unspoiled by cars or umbrellas or tourists. All I can hear is the occasional direction by the handler to his dogs and the scream of gulls.

Nickel Beach is where I'd spent all day, every day in summer until I was eleven years old. My friends and I would leave home and come down here, swimming in the lake and playing in the dunes until the streetlights came on. Most of my friends were like me; their parents worked long hours or they didn't much care where they were all day. So we'd steal whatever change we could from their pockets or collect empty beer bottles and cash them in for money and pool our resources to buy ice cream from the truck that pulled up every day.

I always had good luck picking up my stepfather's empties. He drank most of a case a day and the empties were worth ten cents apiece. On a good day I could buy ice creams for everyone. Though sometimes a good day would quickly turn bad when he found out what I'd done.

A light mist rolls in off the lake and the water is almost still, the waves just barely lapping at the sandy shore. From a distance far up the beach I can just make out the figure of a person walking toward us, pausing now and then to throw a stick into the water for a large black dog to retrieve.

Within ten minutes, before the figure on the beach has even gotten close enough for me to tell if it's a man or a woman, the dogs begin to bark and the handler calls me over. I pick my way carefully through the long grass, trying to avoid tripping over fallen trees and keeping out of the deep ruts full of muck. About ten yards into the thicket, lying on a patch of moss as if on display, is a knife. It's a folding knife with a red handle. I'm sure it has been wiped down, but there's always enough trace blood left behind to test. Soon we'll know if it's a match to Maurice Cobb.

TWENTY SIX

I TAKE A photo and leave the knife for the search team to log and enter into evidence. I'll get the results from the forensic team once they are official, but I already know any blood on the knife will be a match with Cobb's. Which means that this is now a murder investigation. It also means that I'm no longer on the case, since it'll be assigned to the Homicide Unit.

My car radio blares *Ten Forty Five. Fatality. 4351 Concession 6. Code Two.* I recognize the address; I'd just been there a few days ago. It's Anna Kozlowski's farm.

It takes me almost twenty minutes to arrive at the scene, since the Clarence Street Bridge is up and I have to wait for one of the cargo ships to pass along the Welland Canal. I watch a crew working on the bridge, painting out a piece of graffiti sprayed on one of the towers: LIDSVILLE. Years ago the East Village was identified by Niagara Region social services as a *Low Income District*, and the name LIDsville has stuck. LIDsville is a place to pass through, to escape as quickly as you can. It's a place where we were poor, where my stepfather drank, where my mother was never going to save me, and where things would never get better. I smile at the irony that fifteen years later, I'm still stuck in the East Village waiting to get out.

By the time I arrive at the farm the mortuary van is already pulling into the farm entrance, just ahead of the coroner. There's no mistaking the navy blue Subaru as it drives past: It's Maja's car. Clearly it's her on-call duty day and I make a point of leaving my car on the road so she doesn't see me.

Maja and I had first met a few years ago at a crime scene, and now here I am doing my best to avoid seeing her. Even though she's been helping me with the medication it would be too awkward to talk with her today, so I do my best to hide stay out of sight.

I walk toward the barn, where I can see police officers and other personnel gathering in front. Maja has already gone inside to look at the body, so I don't have to see her, for the time being.

"What's happened?" I ask a young constable. I recognize him as a new recruit, a fourth class constable just out of the academy. His nametag says Schultz.

"It's the owner, Anna Kozlowski," he says, reading from his notebook. "Her son found her." My heart sinks. Anna was old; it wasn't exactly a surprise she'd be dead, but still I feel sad.

"How'd she die?" I ask, assuming it must have been a heart attack, or maybe a stroke.

"Probably suffocation," Schultz says. "She was found in one of the apple storage bins. The bins are filled with nitrogen gas," he says in response to my puzzled expression. "It helps to store the fruit long term."

"A storage bin?" I look toward the barn. "How big is it?" I envision a large wooden crate that holds apples. Or maybe an old-fashioned root cellar dug under the barn's foundations.

"It's like a sealed room," he says. "Built inside the barn. Controlled atmosphere storage, very high tech. It regulates the oxygen, carbon dioxide and nitrogen to maximize fruit freshness." I nod for him to continue. "There's only about 1% oxygen inside there. If you go in without breathing apparatus, you aren't coming out."

"How are you so knowledgeable, Constable?"

"I grew up on an apple farm, just over by Pelham."

I shake my head. All I'd learned growing up around here was

how to shoplift, joyride and grow cannabis. But I don't need to share that with the fresh-faced Constable Schultz.

"That sounds dangerous," I say. "How would the farmer get in and out?"

"The storage needs to be fully vented before anyone goes inside," he says. "It's a basic safety rule. If it's not you'd only last a couple of minutes."

"Why would she even be in there?" I say, thinking out loud. I wish I could go into the barn and see for myself, but that wouldn't be appropriate while the Coroner is doing the examination. I'll slip in later and have a look around, ideally before they remove the body.

I hang back, wishing I had some excuse I could use to enter the barn and have a better look at the crime scene. But I know better than to push my luck. It would only irritate the investigators and get me labelled as a nuisance, or worse. One thing I've learned quickly was that the politics of the force is probably more important than my skills and experience, certainly in terms of what will get me promoted onto a Special Investigative Team.

I notice some of the farm workers hanging around the back of the house, rubbernecking. I recognize them as the same guys I'd seen at Taiga: The two smaller guys and the tall Jamaican wearing the Rastacap. Why are they here?

I think of Leon Flores. He'd been working undercover with migrant workers. Had he noticed something strange too? Is that why he'd been killed?

I watch as another Constable leads a middle-aged man out of the barn towards the house. I decide it must be Anna's son, and I walk over to intercept them.

"Please come with me, Mr. Kozlowski," I say taking hold of the man's arm. The other Constable looks surprised then relieved that someone is taking the grieving man off his hands. Possibly he thought that, being a female, I'm just better at this sort of thing. I'm not above using the pervasive sexism in the department to my advantage if it serves me.

I lead him inside and sit him at the kitchen table. "Can I get you a glass of water? Or maybe a cup of tea?" I ask.

"I need a drink," he says pointing toward a cupboard. "There's whiskey in there." I open the cupboard, pull out a bottle of Canadian Club and pour him a healthy shot. He downs it in one and holds out the glass for a refill.

I sit across from him while he nurses his second drink. "I'm very sorry for your loss," I say. He snorts at the platitude. I'm not surprised. Most people default to polite social scripts in these moments, especially if there's emotional pain involved. Much better to keep your distance from all that. "I met your mother the other day," I say gently. He looks up in surprise. "I liked her. She was a good lady."

His eyes well up. "She was the best." He bursts into tears and drops his head onto the table, his shoulders shaking as he sobs. I wait patiently until he calms down. My mind is racing, trying out different scenarios that could possibly explain how Anna Kozlowski had ended up in the apple storage bin.

"When was last time you saw her?" I ask once he'd stopped crying.

"This morning," he says. "I came by to take her and her friend to Pelham Woods."

"Doreen?"

"Yeah. You know Doreen?"

"Sort of," I say. "She and your mother went to visit Nadia Efimov?"

He nods again. "I dropped them off first thing, then picked them up at around eleven," he says. "I left Doreen at the coffee shop downtown and brought my mother home."

"And she had no plans on getting any fruit out of storage?"

He looks at me like I'm insane. "My mother hasn't been in the fruit storage in years. There's absolutely no need for her to ever go in there." He stares intently at me. "She has macular degeneration. She couldn't really even see."

I know. Which raises the question about how she'd ended up in the barn.

TWENTY SEVEN

DOREEN'S HOUSE IS an old frame two story, with aluminum siding and rotted window frames. She has a little front garden of dead grass, with her garbage bins out front, bounded by overgrown privet hedges. There's some old furniture on the front porch so she can sit to watch the world go by.

I hesitate before I knock on the front door. I want to tell her the news in person, rather than have her read it in the paper. I barely know her, but it seems cruel to just leave her learning about it to chance. I take a deep breath and knock. Doreen opens it almost immediately.

"I saw you through the glass," she laughs. "I was wondering when you were going to get around to knocking. Nobody likes to see a police officer on their doorstep, but then I recognized you…" She looks at my expression and the smile on her face fades.

"May I come inside?"

Doreen steps aside and holds the door open so I can enter. "What is it?" she asks. "What's wrong?"

"I have some bad news," I say. "Let's sit down." I guide Doreen toward a worn sofa in the tiny living room. The television is on, and I reach for the remote to mute it. Doreen perches on the edge of the sofa like a bird on a wire and I sit next to her, placing my hand on her knee.

The furniture is an old burgundy coloured sofa with a matching chair, and there are a few throws spread across their arms and back. The throws are either there to hide wear and stains on the upholstery, or for Doreen to wrap herself in on a chilly night while she watches TV. Nicotine has stained the walls to a yellowish brown and the house smells like a dirty ashtray. In fact, there's a full ashtray sitting in front of me on the coffee table. I hadn't realized Doreen was a smoker.

"Okay," Doreen says, doing her best to sound strong. "I'm sitting. Who's died?"

"Anna Kozlowski was found dead earlier today," I say.

"That's impossible," Doreen stares at me, shaking her head. "I was just with her this morning..."

"She was found dead at the farm. In the apple storage."

Doreen's brow furrows. "What do you mean? She never went in there."

I watch Doreen's expression change from shock to anger. Her eyes narrow and her lips press into a tight line as her bony arthritic hands clench into fists.

"Those bastards," she says under her breath. Not the response I'm expecting. "*Fuckers.*"

"Do you know how this might have happened?" I ask. "Do you think someone killed her? Doreen, if you have any information that would help us find out how Anna died, please tell me."

"I need some air," Doreen says as she pushes herself up off the sofa and grabs her walker. She moves toward the kitchen at the back of the house and I follow her out onto a small back deck. It's just high enough to be a trip hazard for anyone coming in the back door from the garden.

I watch as Doreen stares out at her garden, blinking back tears. She reaches into her pocket and pulls out a pack of cigarettes then lights one and inhales. I can see her hands shaking.

The narrow back garden backs onto an alley and a small wooden garage takes up most of the far end. A massive rambler rose covers the garage, encasing it in thorny branches. It probably looks amazing in summer when it's in bloom, but now it looks ominous, as if it's hiding something. From the look of it I doubt the rose has ever been pruned, but a few of the canes have been cut through to allow access to the door.

A massive old cherry tree is growing in front of the ruined fence and a large vegetable garden runs the length of the backyard, but from what I can see there isn't anything growing in it except a few half-dead weeds. It doesn't seem likely that Doreen would be able to tend a garden when she needs a walker just to cross a room.

The fence on the other side of the yard is planted with dozens of roses. Their foliage is still green and a few last blossoms still cling to the tips of the branches, in shades of yellow, pink and white. They climb along the fence, arch wildly into the air, and spring off of flimsy wooden trellises that have been stuck in the ground in an attempt to give them support. It's an out of control, impenetrable thicket of roses, just like the briar patch that grew up around Sleeping Beauty's castle, telling people to keep out.

"You have a nice garden," I finally say. "I love your roses."

Doreen is startled. I think she's forgotten I'm there. "I've planted one for every year I've lived in this house," she says. "Or I used to. I haven't done that in a few years now."

"They look amazing," I say. "That one on your garage is huge."

Doreen nods. "It's old. Planted it twenty five years ago."

"What kind of cherry tree is that one? Sweet or sour?" I'm just making conversation, buying some time while Doreen gets used to the idea that her oldest friend is dead.

"Sour," Doreen says, as she lights another cigarette off the end of her first. "Like me."

I smile, but realize it isn't really a joke. "You ever make jam?"

"Hell no. I tell the neighbours to pick as much as they can," she points at the house next door. "They give me lots of jam every summer that I never eat. Cupboard is full of it." She sits down heavily on one of the plastic chairs. "Whatever they don't pick the raccoons and squirrels take."

"I guess you don't garden as much as you used to."

"Not in years," she sighs. "I used to have a great garden, when I was younger. Vegetables, fruits, all kinds of things. Now there's nobody but me to eat it all, so I don't bother. I'm just too old." I glance at Doreen's face. It looks like she's aged a few years since she first opened the door to me.

I take a seat on the wicker bench across from her. There's a movement next to me and I almost jump straight through the porch roof. A large striped tomcat is stretched out across the cushion. He raises his head and glares at me before going back to sleep.

"He's a handsome boy," I say, my heart pounding. "What's his name?"

"He's not mine."

"Are you sure about that? He seems pretty comfortable."

Doreen shrugs. "He keeps coming around, sneaking inside whenever he gets the chance."

"For how long?"

"About ten years. I call him Old Cat. " She smiles at the tabby as he sleeps peacefully, oblivious to her sorrow. "I need a drink."

"What can I get you?"

"Rye and coke," she says. "Rye's on the counter. Coke's in the fridge. No ice."

I find a reasonably clean glass in the dishrack and pour Doreen a healthy shot. I know enough to make it strong. Doreen won't appreciate a weak drink. Besides, it's medicinal.

I hand it to her and Doreen takes a long drink, followed by a drag on her cigarette. "It's good, thanks," she says.

"Doreen," I begin then I stop myself. "You know, I don't even know your last name."

"McAlpine," Doreen says. "My people came over from Scotland

in 1863 and we've lived here ever since. Descended from United Empire Loyalists." I can hear pride in her voice.

"Mine's Gauthier," I say.

Doreen smiles. "I know, Lucy," she says. "It's on your nametag."

I blush. I'd forgotten I was in uniform. "Doreen," I begin again. "Do you know anything about what happened to Anna?"

Doreen just stares ahead, as if she hasn't heard the question. "Why did you become a police officer, Lucy?" she asks after a moment.

I understand Doreen wants to change the subject, but I'm afraid there's something more behind her question, something I'm not willing to share. Doreen's sharp as a knife and isn't going to be satisfied with a bullshit evasion. "I don't really know," I answer, and that is partly true. "I got my degree in Psychology and Sociology at University, but I didn't want to be a social worker."

"In this place?" Doreen shakes her head. "Hell no. Talk about a thankless, impossible, bullshit job." She squints at me through a cloud of cigarette smoke. "So how did you end up as a police officer? Because growing up around here I can say that's the last thing most of these kids would ever become. Hell would freeze."

I blink. Have I told Doreen I'd come from the East Village? I'm always very careful about what and how much I share with people. Being from the East Village is something I kept close to my chest.

"I'm from Wainfleet," I correct her. I notice Doreen give me a sharp look and I feel my stomach turn over. It's like she knows I'm lying. "It seemed... safe. Secure," I continue, ignoring my anxiety. "I wanted a regular job, with good benefits. And I knew that if I stuck it out for twenty years or go I'd be able to retire and have enough money to do what I wanted."

"You'd put your life on hold for twenty years?" Doreen disapproves. "What if you die? Especially in your line of work. Not everyone gets to live as long as I have. Or Anna did." She looks away, hiding her emotions. Doreen's a tough woman, I know, and a proud one. She hasn't survived this long by letting anyone see her vulnerability.

"Believe me Doreen," I laugh. "I'm about as far away from danger as I can ever be working out here. We don't get much violent crime, and most of that's handled by the Major Crime Units."

"You sound disappointed," Doreen says pointedly. "You want to be close to danger?"

I shake my head. "No. I had enough of that," I say. But I'm half lying. Doreen arches her eyebrow, curious for more, but I realize I've let enough slip. This is a subject I never want to discuss. The truth is my anxiety disorder drives me to seek out sensation and danger, even if I cause it myself. I crave it, and I find it through the kind of antisocial behavior my shrink cautions me against, and through my job. It's potentially dangerous, exciting, sometimes even thrilling— at least it can be when I'm not sitting in a patrol car at a speed trap.

"It's a good job," I continue, mustering as much sincerity as I can. "And I need to live. I've got rent, food, car payment, and massive student debt."

Doreen nods. "Everything goes up all the time. I'm on a fixed income, but with my pension I just about manage. But I don't have a mortgage, or any student debt." Doreen laughs, covering her loose dentures. "And I don't have a vehicle—unless you count my wheels here." She points to her walker. "I think about maybe getting an electric scooter one day," she sounds wistful. "Maybe when my knees give out completely."

"I think the walking is probably good for you."

"That's what the doctor says. It's just so slow... it takes all day to get anywhere. I have to walk to the bus stop, wait for the bus downtown, all the transfers, take care of business, then all the way back home again." She shakes her head. "I guess it keeps me out of trouble."

I nod. I've never given any thought to how hard it is to get around when you are old. "And at night?" I know many of the bus routes didn't run in the evenings. "How do you manage then?"

Doreen laughs. "I haven't been out at night in years. Where is there to go?" She stares out at the garden for a moment before she speaks. "I know why Anna was killed," Doreen says. "She saw something she shouldn't have."

"Anna was practically blind." I I don't want to disagree, but Doreen's accusation makes no sense. "What is it you think she saw?"

"Just like Nadia said," Doreen shakes her head, ignoring the question. "Something is going on there."

"Where?" My head is spinning. Nadia has dementia and Anna had macular degeneration. Whatever either of them thought they might have seen seems highly suspect.

"Pelham Woods." She turns on me. "You need to look into it, right now."

"Look into what? I don't understand."

"The patients," Doreen continues. "They're all going nuts. Every day there's someone else going berserk." I nod, encouraging her to continue. "Nadia has said so, lots of times."

"But, Doreen," I try to be gentle. "Nadia has dementia. Are her stories necessarily reliable?"

"Of course they are," Doreen snaps. "She may lose it every now and then, but she comes around. She knows me and Anna when we visit her. She knows her daughter Rose. And she sees things. Just like Anna did."

"Okay…" I pretend to agree just to get Doreen to calm down. "Okay, I hear you."

I take a deep breath as an idea worms its way into my mind. "Doreen, if Anna did see something, wouldn't she have told you? I mean, you two were best friends, right? Why would she keep that a secret?"

Doreen looks away and I can tell she's struggling with admitting something. "She did. So did Nadia, but I didn't pay attention." Her eyes fill with tears and she reaches for another cigarette. "They're my best friends and I didn't listen to what they were telling me."

"Okay, I'm listening now. What did they say?"

Doreen's lips are pursed and she's clenching her hands in anger. "That nurse. She's up to something, with that cop."

"Cooper?"

Doreen nods. "He keeps dropping by Pelham Woods. He's got no business there. Why's he always coming around?"

"Maybe they are friends?" I have a hard time imagining Cooper has any friends, but still.

"*Friends.* Yeah, sure," Doreen snorts. "They had a big fight the other day," Doreen says. "I've lived in the East Village long enough to know trouble when I see it."

That is something I can't argue with. I've got a lot to think about as I head back to the car. I turn back to Doreen and see her smoking and drinking, deep in thought as she stares at the roses covering her garage.

"Doreen, be careful. If Anna was killed because of what she saw you might be in danger too. You two were always together. You'd have seen the same thing—whatever it may have been."

"I can take care of myself, believe me," she bursts out laughing. "They'll never see me coming."

TWENTY EIGHT

SOPHIE DOESN'T LOOK happy to see me when I come into the barn. She's instructing a couple of women on how she'd prefer to see the display table arranged.

Instead of smiling when she sees me as she usually does, her brow furrows and she looks worried.

"Hi Lucy," she says as she walks over. "What's going on?"

"Sorry Sophie. But I need to speak with Geraldine Bennett. I've got some news."

A shadow passes over Sophie's face. "She's still here," she says. "For now at least."

"Oh, right," I get it. "I guess she doesn't need to stay in the shelter now that her husband isn't a threat."

Sophie rolls her eyes and I'm confused.

"You seem unhappy about that. Isn't it a good thing that's she moving out?" That is the goal of the Womyn Collective, to get abused women on their feet, independent and secure.

Sophie doesn't say anything for a minute. Then she beckons me outside and walks with me toward the house. "She just told me she's setting herself up in business, in town."

"What kind of business?"

"Florist," Sophie says, her voice flat. "She's going into competition with us."

"Brutal." I shake my head. "Where would she get the money to do that?"

Sophie shrugs. "No idea. A private backer?" She turns to me. "After she told me I tried to get her to partner with me, formally, but we couldn't work out a deal that made sense. To *her*, I hasten to add."

"So she wants to keep all the profits to herself," I say. "That's assuming she makes any. Starting a small business is tough. She might end up losing her shirt going up against you."

Sophie shakes her head. "I'm not so sure. She already has the contacts with the bespoke, carriage-trade clients, since she's the one who's been dealing with them for all our weddings and events. She's going to skim the cream. It's going to hurt us." Now I understand why Sophie looks so disappointed. Losing her best designer is bad enough, but to be betrayed by her setting up in direct competition? That's rough.

"That's really low," I say. "Especially given how you helped her out of an abusive situation," I gesture toward the house. "Gave her shelter, security, a job…"

Sophie snorts in disgust. "It's *just business*, she says to me. *Nothing personal*." She holds up her hand for me to wait and goes inside to fetch Geraldine Bennett.

Within a few minutes Bennett comes outside alone, eyeing me suspiciously. Sophie no doubt stayed inside to give us some privacy. And, maybe she isn't feeling so protective of Bennett any longer, and I don't blame her.

"Hi Ms. Bennett," I say. "I just wanted to give you some news in person, regarding your ex-husband's death."

She nods and crosses her arms. "What news?"

"We no longer believe his death was a suicide," I say. "We're treating it as a suspicious death." I watch Bennett carefully for her reactions. The woman has never asked how he'd died, not in either of the two visits I've made to the Womyn farm. Does she really not care? Or does she know more than she's letting on?

"Murder, you mean?" Bennett says after a moment. "You think someone murdered him?"

"It appears that way. It's possible you'll be interviewed again by some detectives from the Homicide Unit."

Her eyes narrow. "Why? I've already told you everything I know."

"It's protocol. They'll be conducting their own investigation."

Bennett snorts. "So now you're interested in Maurice Cobb? I guess it just takes someone to die before the police give a damn. I guess I should just be happy it wasn't me."

She has a point and I'm not about to contradict her. I'm halfway to my car when she calls after me.

"Someone needs to talk to that creep Amit Joshi," she says. "He'd do anything to cover up what he did to my husband at Advik."

I wait in the interview room while the constable on duty goes to get Dumont. Since he couldn't post bond he's being held on his Failure to Appear charge and he's cooling his heels in custody, awaiting his next court date. Even though he's not going anywhere, I need to speak to Dumont as quickly as I can. Now that Cobb's death is clearly a murder the case will be passed over to the Homicide Unit and I'll be left out of the loop.

It isn't personal, it's just the way it goes; a Constable, especially a new Detective Constable like myself, will be relegated to a supporting role in the investigation. If I'm lucky the senior homicide detectives will include me in some way, but there's no guarantee. In fact, it's highly unlikely and I know it.

I'll have to hand over the reports and brief the homicide investigative team, but I really want to have it sewn it up a nice little package for them before I do that. There's always competition for any spots that might open up in Major Crime. Sure, I've passed the exam, but so have lots of other First Class Constables. And if I'm going to stay on the force it isn't going to be in a uniform. I need to do my best to make sure they notice me, and putting this case together definitely will not hurt.

Dumont is escorted in, wearing handcuffs. I offer him water or coffee, to put him at his ease, and explain again that the interview is being videotaped. He nods but doesn't look like he cares much what happens. That's what a night in custody will do to a person. They become sullen and afraid, and they're also probably exhausted since it's tough to get a decent night's sleep in a cell, on a plastic covered foam mattress with just a flimsy blanket and a bright light on all night. Generally speaking, people are a little more co-operative after that, or at least less openly defiant.

"Mr. Dumont," I begin. "We went back to the location you said you'd seen the F-150 parked. The one you say you did not take," I add, opening a file folder and looking through some papers. Dumont eyes me suspiciously. "We had the canine unit search the area." I slide a photo of the knife across the desk. "And they found this knife."

Dumont looks at and shrugs. "I've never seen it before."

"You've never seen it before," I repeat. "Forensic testing tells us that the blood on this knife," I tap the photo to draw Dumont's attention to it, "is that of Maurice Cobb, the man who was found dead at the Taiga property five days ago. He was the owner of the truck you told us you saw at the beach."

I can see the fear in Dumont's eyes. He sits up straight in his chair, his body tense. "I never saw the guy," he says. "And I was never at Taiga. I told you that."

"Right," I agree, looking at my files. "You told me that you'd been at the beach that night, and that's where you saw the truck. With the keys in it."

Dumont nods. "Yes."

"And you never took the truck. You never touched it."

He shakes his head. "Nope. Not me." *Not me* means one of his friends did. It doesn't really matter. I know we'll never find the truck. It's long gone. I don't care about the truck. I'm interested in who killed Maurice Cobb.

"I'd like to believe you Mr. Dumont," I say. "In fact, I do believe you." He looks relieved, but wary. The fact is there's no evidence of Dumont's fingerprints on the knife and I can't think of any reason he'd have tossed it there, when he told me that's where he'd seen the truck parked. He wasn't a bright guy, but he wasn't that stupid. He could have just left it in the truck and the knife would have disappeared along with it. So, that tells me that maybe Dumont is telling the truth. The death of Cobb and the theft of the truck are separate incidents.

"I need you to think very carefully about what you did see that night," I say, meeting Dumont's eye. "Did you see anyone near the truck, maybe when you first saw it? Before you went down to the beach?"

Dumont looks irritated. I know he has something to tell me, but guys like him never want to tell the police anything. Some stupid pride about being a snitch. It's a matter of principle.

"It would help us out a lot," I say. "He had a family. A wife who loved him," I lie. "A couple of kids. It would be a good thing if we could find out who did this to him." I have no problem with lying, if it's in a good cause. Cobb didn't have anyone who loved him from what I can tell, but if there was any chance I can work Dumont I'll take it. "Have you got a kid, Andre?" I already know he does; two, by different women. "You know how much it means, right?"

He nods. He bops his head to some tune only he can hear for a moment as he considers the right thing to do. "I saw a woman driving it," he finally says. "She left the truck then I saw her toss something into the marsh. At first I thought it was the keys. I wondered why she'd throw them away. But when I went closer I saw the keys were in the ignition."

"What did she look like?" I ask.

"Skinny. Old. Short brown hair," he says. "I thought she was a guy at first."

"Would you recognize her again?"

He shakes his head. "Probably not. She was just ordinary looking."

TWENTY NINE

DOREEN SITS ON her front porch and pulls her winter coat tighter against the chill. The light is fading fast as dusk falls; it's only five-thirty in the afternoon and it already feels like evening. There's a slight mist coming in off the lake and she can see a halo around each streetlight as they come on, one by one up and down the street. It's the loneliest time of day.

A souped up car drives past slowly, its loud engine throbbing. Doreen knows that guy; he'd grown up in the East Village. Now he's just another drug dealer and he's got a stable of younger boys who sell for him in town and at the high school. She heard he gave one of the boys a gun. Doreen thinks if she had a gun he'd be the first one she'd use it on.

She stares out into the street as night falls. The mist feels damp but she doesn't want to go inside. She spends enough time in the house. She knows Anna's death wasn't an accident. Doreen knows it's because of what Anna saw at Pelham Woods. When they were visiting Nadia she'd been staring off and then suddenly said, *That's strange. Why is she doing that now?* Doreen had ignored her at the time. But now it feels important.

Nadia kept telling them something is wrong, but she's anxious about so many things that they'd stopped taking her seriously a long time ago. Doreen just put it down to the paranoia caused by dementia, but it's impossible to ignore how she gives the nurse nasty looks and shouts at her whenever she comes near. And she seems to always be in pain lately; even though they've increased her Fentanyl dosage she always needs more.

Doreen knows Lucy doesn't believe her. She's seen that expression on too many faces to not recognize when she's being humoured. She's just a little old lady who everyone ignores. There are a million just like her everywhere, with grey hair, pushing walkers or using canes. Not worth a second look. But her mind is still sharp, even though her body might be giving out. Sharp enough to figure out what's really going on and to put a stop to it.

THIRTY

AS I PREDICTED, as soon as the knife was found to have Cobb's blood on it, the case was taken over by the Homicide Unit and I've been assigned to foot patrol at the Fall Fair. Sergeant Bruni has probably assigned me here since he still hopes I'll accept the assignment to the Community Mobilization team. I understand community outreach is important to the police department. I just don't want to do it. The usual farmers' market has been expanded to include a concert in the evening, a fun fair for the kiddies with rides, and a series of events and displays at the local museum. There are heritage craftspeople and artisans, and vendors selling hand-woven linens, jams and jellies, and wooden carvings. There's also a separate tent for the pet show, poultry show and a livestock competition.

The Fall Fair is a huge deal for the region, attracting tourists from across the province and from over the border and the department makes sure to have a strong police presence. It's also a good public relations opportunity and it gives them a chance to unveil the new million-dollar Mobile Command Unit to the community. It's the pride and joy of the Chief of Police and every chance he can bring it out he does, if only to justify the cost to taxpayers.

The thirty-one foot MCU is essentially an office on wheels and police officers can access the same information and data from it that we can from the station. There are eight video monitors, state of the art technology, a dedicated land line and full access to all of the department's IT systems, and even if the network goes down we have satellite back up. There's a high-definition camera with zoom that's in place at the top of the thirty-foot mast on top of the unit. The MCU was designed for tactical emergency events, like a hostage negotiation or bank robbery, but it's also used at investigative events like the search for a missing person. I can't remember the last time we've ever needed that kind of tactical support in the Niagara region, but then I'm just a lowly Detective Constable. What do I know?

Decker appears and hands me a coffee from the organic roaster in the market.

"Thank you," I say. "It almost makes being here tolerable."

He shakes his head. "You gotta learn to relax Lucy. Take things as they come."

"I'm just frustrated," I say. "And I'm pissed off that Homicide is taking over the case."

Decker looks sympathetic. "You can still support the investigation." I snort. "Just talk to Bruni, see if he'll assign you."

"Maybe I will," I say. But I know I won't bother.

"Where'd you go last night, after we talked to Dumont?" he asks. "You left in a hurry."

"I had to deliver a death notice," I say. "About Anna Kozlowski."

"But I thought her son found her," he says. "Who'd you have to tell?"

"Doreen McAlpine, her old friend. I didn't want her to find out on the news," I explain. "It was unofficial. I just stopped in on my way home."

"McAlpine?" Decker thinks for a moment. "I know that name."

"She lives on Rodney Street, in the East Village. Says she's lived there for sixty years. So, from around the time when you first joined the force," I laugh.

Decker smiles. "She has a son, right?" He has a look in his eye.

"Had. She said he died."

"That fits," Decker says. "Scott McAlpine was always in trouble. I went to school with him."

I'm not surprised. It feels like the whole region had gone to the same high school, with all the country kids getting bussed into town from miles away. "McAlpine was a bad guy," Decker continues. "Ran with a rough crowd in school, then got worse when he dropped out."

"Sounds like a typical East Village story," I say. "What kind of trouble?"

"You name it: trafficking, assault, theft, gangs, weapons." He shakes his head and breaks into a smile. "Why don't we look him up?" he says, stepping into the MCU. "This is outfitted with everything we need, right? Just like the station. So let's give it a trial run." I have no choice but to follow him but I'm not really much interested in the criminal history of Doreen's dead son.

Decker sits at one of the monitors, and types in McAlpine's name. The screen comes to life and after a few more keystrokes Decker has his entire criminal record on display. He whistles and shakes his head.

"Worse that I expected," he says.

I lean in to look over his shoulder. There are charges made, charges dropped, dozens of arrests, convictions, time served, probation orders and restraining orders, for drugs, assault, weapons and theft. Then they all stop, around twenty-five years ago.

"That's when he disappeared," Decker says, pointing to the screen. "I assume he's dead. That's the way these guys usually end up."

I feel him looking at me. "Not many kids seem to escape the East Village," he says and I feel a chill. Does Decker remember me? I was only eleven when I'd left, and they'd changed my name. Does he recognize me?

I can hear my blood pound in my head and my breathing is getting shallow. I have to get away, right now. I down the rest of my coffee. "I'm going to look around," I say, trying to keep my voice steady. "You can take the next shift." I walk into the farmer's market, leaving Decker babysitting the MCU.

I walk blindly through the crowd, grateful for my sunglasses and the uniform cap that hides my face. I breathe deeply, in and out, calming myself and shaking off the dread Decker's comment caused. After a few minutes I'm well enough to look around and effectively do my job.

A group of Latina women stand together by the edge of the stage, where a young man with a guitar is plugging in his amplifier. They're happy and smiling, eager for the show to start. I know they are workers from one of the nearby farms. Workers will often come into town on Sunday, their only day off, and walk around or sit in the park for a change of scene. It's something different from the twelve hours days they spent bent over picking or pruning or training fruit and flowers. At least today they'll have some genuine entertainment to enjoy, thanks to the Fall Fair, rather than what the town usually provides them, which is nothing.

I'm happy to see the women enjoying themselves. Eight months is a long time to be away from home and I bet they don't spend a lot of time laughing on the farm. The harvest is almost finished so they'll be going home soon, to Guatemala or Mexico or somewhere in the Caribbean. It would have been great if I could approach them to ask about Leon Flores, but I don't. I don't speak Spanish and I'm in uniform. They'd rightly be suspicious and I'd get nothing out of them.

I stroll past buskers playing fiddles, guitars and accordions. About fifty yards further along a single guy plays guitar and sings along in a thin nasal tenor, his guitar case open to receive donations. I toss him a dollar coin out of pity. He isn't going to make much money today with that voice.

The crowds are getting thicker as the day's events start up. There are a few concert stages set up throughout the grounds, with jugglers and magicians and sing-alongs for the kids, indie-rock bands for the teens, and an acapella singing competition for the seniors.

About twenty yards ahead of me an old lady is pushing a walker. She's heading into the market. Is it Doreen? She looks familiar, but all old ladies look pretty much alike from the back and I'm not able to get a look at her face. She's so short she keeps disappearing in the crowd. Then I lose sight of her, so I give up and turn into the Womyn Flower Farm booth.

They are set up in their usual spot at the Farmer's Market, and the stall is overflowing with flowers and herb sachets, vinegars and oils. Several women walking through the Fair wearing flower crowns—a Womyn trademark.

They've also set up a selfie booth, with a selection of elaborate, insanely creative flower hats that people can put on and take a selfie. There's already a line forming and Sophie and Geraldine Bennett are helping people ham it up for the cameras. There's a sign outside the booth, explaining the modest two-dollar fee goes to support victims of domestic violence. A donation jar sits on the table, already stuffed with bills and I make a note to ask one of the Auxiliary Police to stand at the booth for the day and keep an eye on the cash.

Rose Efimov from Thorny Rose is behind the counter, helping out with sales. She's ringing up purchases, bagging them and handing them over to customers and generally keeping a low profile. Poor Rose. Her business took a big hit when the scandal broke this summer and now she just has to live with the lingering suspicions of people. Small town people who liked to gossip and to speculate. Bored people with nothing else to do.

I approach the booth. "Hi Rose," I say, getting her attention. "How are you doing?"

Rose smiles, keeping her head down under her sunhat. She's already in the shade under the pop-up tent, so the hat is probably a disguise. She must be fed up with people whispering and pointing at her.

"I'm doing okay, Lucy. Thanks for asking." She looks tired.

"I was just out near your place yesterday," I say then I instantly regret it. Anna Kozlowski had been a friend of Rose's mother. Her sudden death won't have been good news. Rose's smile fades.

"Yeah," she says. "For Anna, right?" I nod. "I don't have a clue how I can tell my mother she's gone."

"Maybe you just... shouldn't?" I say, remembering how bad Nadia Efimov's cognitive health was. "Does she need to know, really?"

Rose considers the suggestion for a moment. "You're probably right," she says. "At this point it doesn't matter at all."

Rose's gaze shifts to someone over my shoulder and I turn to see Amit Joshi strutting through the market, like a ship in full sail. Trailing behind him are three small children and an older woman in a turquoise sari. Joshi wears one of his colourful suits; this time he's in a pumpkin silk with an expensive sheen. I smirk, thinking the colour, along with Joshi's size, isn't the best choice at the Fall Fair. He looks like an enormous grinning Jack O'Lantern. Joshi sees Rose and makes his way toward her, ignoring me. I stand to one side and make a point of listening in.

"Hi Amit," Rose says, now in full restaurant-proprietor mode. "Are these your children? They're beautiful."

Joshi smiles with pride. "Yes, and this is my mother. We're taking the kids out on some rides. And perhaps later some ice cream." The kids started to jump up and down in anticipation.

"How are... things?" he asks. I imagine Joshi must have been one of Thorny Rose's best customers. A rich guy like him, who clearly enjoys the finer things in life, would likely have been there every week for dinner. But the awkward way he speaks to Rose tells me that he's not been back in a while. Probably staying away since the scandal hit.

"Things are really good, thank you," Rose says. I suspect she's lying. "We have a new menu for autumn and some excellent new wines on the list. You really should come out for dinner soon."

Joshi grins. "You know, I definitely will. Soon," he says. "The doctor has me on a special diet," he says as pats his ample stomach. "Says I need to lose some weight."

A tall slender woman places her hand on his arm.

"Hi Zahira," Rose says to her. "How are you?"

Joshi's wife smiles and has a brief exchange with Rose, but her voice is soft and quiet, so I can't hear what's said. After my conversation with Geraldine Bennett I'd Googled her and found she's a scientist with a doctorate in Chemistry and she'd launched Advik before she married Amit Joshi. But now it appears that he never even mentions her contribution, likely because of his massive ego.

She's beautiful and perfectly groomed in Western style, not like her mother in law in a sari. Everything about Joshi's wife is elegant, expensive and tasteful. Understated. Basically she's the opposite of her husband.

I can see the family starting to leave the booth.

"Well, when you want to cheat on your diet, come out. I'll look after you very well," Rose says to Joshi with a wink. "I'll do you a nice elk sirloin with chanterelles, truffles and yellowfoot mushrooms."

Joshi makes a big show of moaning in anticipation. "That sounds delicious," he says, ushering his wife away. "I'm sure I'll be out soon." Rose watches as he turns to follow his mother and children. From her expression it's clear she knows he's lying.

I look out over the market and see it's getting very busy. The street is filled with people. Families are pushing strollers with balloons tied to the handles, the children's faces painted to look like fierce tigers or Spiderman. There's a group of elderly men and women wearing matching red vests making their way over to the makeshift stage. They are the Seniors Pop Choir, and they entertain at every community event, singing current hit singles and classic favourites. If you've never seen a group of octogenarians deliver a mashup of Daydream Believer and Mr. Brightside, you haven't lived.

There's already a crowd gathering in front of the stage in anticipation and it's creating a traffic jam. I watch as the Auxiliary police do their best to ensure people are able to get past. Many of the crowd members are elderly themselves, and lots of walkers and wheelchairs are parked in front. One grey head catches my eye before it disappears into the crowd. Again I'm sure it's Doreen, but I'm not going to follow her. I have to head back to the MCU and relieve Decker.

Before I leave I glance over at the selfie booth and my blood runs cold. Maja is there, trying on a huge hat adorned with sunflowers. She's with a young blonde woman who is vamping in a fascinator made from orchids. They are laughing and taking selfies. Then the blonde woman kisses Maja and I have to turn away. I can't breathe and it feels like there's a hole in my chest where my heart used to be.

THIRTY ONE

WHEN I LOOK back Maja and the blonde are walking away, arm in arm. I blink back my tears and take a deep breath. There's nothing I can do about it. I was the one who made the choice to call it off. What did I think, Maja was just going to wait around? That she wasn't going to find someone else?

I just wasn't able to give Maja what she asked for: the truth. To be honest about who I am, about my past, about where I've come from. I'd told her some of it, what I'd hoped would be enough. But Maja knew I was holding myself back; hiding the truth of who I am. And I couldn't go any further, so the choice was made.

I look back at the Womyn booth and I'm surprised to see Cooper, leaning across the counter, his red face right up in Rose's. Whatever he's saying to her, it isn't good. Rose is recoiling and drawing back, but she isn't afraid of him. If anything, she looks defiant and angry, daring him to do whatever he is threatening her with. Because that's clearly what I see: Cooper is threatening Rose. Then she shoves him hard and he stumbles backwards, cursing her. He starts back toward her, his face contorted in anger before he stops short, with a surprised expression on his face. He looks behind and seems confused for a moment, and throws up his hands and storms off.

It takes me a few minutes to flag one of the Auxilliary officers to watch over the Womyn booth and by the time I return to the MCU there's a crowd gathering in front. People are running and pushing, and an ambulance with its lights flashing is trying to drive up through the throngs of pedestrians. I push through the group and see Decker, crouched next to the body of a man. My view is partially blocked by the paramedic team as they rush in. Decker stands up and gets out of the way and I see the man is Cooper. He's lying on his side, clutching his chest. His face is red and contorted in pain.

"What happened?" I'm out of breath.

Decker shrugs. "He staggered up here, looking like he was in a lot of pain. He was clutching at his chest and looked flushed. I saw him go into his pocket, like maybe he was looking for his phone or something, and then he… just… fell over. He was convulsing when I ran up to him. I shouted for them to call 911," he points to one of the Auxilliary Officers. "And I started to do CPR, but…"

We both watch as the paramedics work on Cooper, trying to stabilize him or maybe even bring him back. They use the defibrillator and for a moment I think they have a heartbeat, but I know from the looks they exchange that Cooper is already dead. They bring over a stretcher and load him onto it and into the ambulance. Within seconds he's being driven away, siren and lights flashing. That's likely for show, to make it look like he'll be okay. But there's no rush to get him anywhere.

I stand with Decker and watch as the crowds slowly disperse. The excitement is over for now, or at least it has moved on and they stroll off in search of more at the Fair. The buskers start playing again, and I can hear the hawkers and carnival barkers, calling for people to guess their weight or try their luck and win a prize. But Cooper's luck has run out.

"Heart attack?" I speculate.

Decker shrugs. "No idea," he says. "He sure looked like a candidate for one. Overweight. A big drinker."

"With anger management issues," I add. "Maybe his blood

pressure wasn't so great." As far as I can see, Cooper had been a time bomb for years, just waiting to explode. It's a miracle he hadn't had a heart attack years ago, if in fact that's what killed him. There are lots of people who'd have liked to see him dead, me among them.

THIRTY TWO

DETECTIVES AGU AND Vogel sit across from me in the office. I've briefed them on everything I've learned so far on the Cobb investigation and have handed over all my notes and files.

"There is something else going on here," I add as I gather the papers together. "There's some connection between Cobb and Taiga and Leon Flores." I look at Agu to make sure he's listening. It's important to me that they understand my suspicions, but I can't read Agu's expression. "And Leon Flores and Anna Kozlowski's death. Maybe that's why she died."

"You're connecting Flores' murder to Anna Kozlowski?" Vogel says. He clearly thinks I'm exaggerating. I don't know him but I resent his smug attitude—and his chattiness. I also think I resent him because he's standing in my way. Vogel is the last Detective Constable hired on the Unit, so until he moves up to Sergeant, or more funding is found to hire another DC, I'm not getting a spot on the Homicide Unit.

"I know it sounds unlikely," I say. "But, yeah. I am."

I don't know if what I'm doing is helping my cause or hurting it. Sometimes Agu looks pleased by my ideas and my contributions. Other times I feel I'm annoying him, like I do Vogel and some of the other Detectives. As a young female DC, the odds of my getting the promotion aren't great anyway. Probably my trying too hard is making things worse, but I just can't help myself.

I leave them in the briefing room with my files and reports. Niagara Region is a small geographic area with—until recently, a small local police force that has suddenly had to grow very fast to keep up with the population boom. What was a group of small independent police districts is now all connected under the same umbrella, even though they have very different social and economic problems and histories. Niagara Falls has the casino, Fort Erie has the US border with the guns, drugs and gangs coming in. We even have the Six Nations Reserve sitting on the edge of the region, with its own issues that affect ours. There's a lot of movement and change going on in the region; I just hope there's going to be room for me.

I pop into the Green Bean to grab a coffee. In a few hours I'll be off shift and can change out of my uniform and resume my normal appearance, like Wonder Woman. Not that the uniform gives me any superpowers, but it does give a shape to my life. After work the plan is to get to the gym before an early night in front of the TV.

There's Doreen, seated at her usual table, so I go over for a quick chat while they make my drink.

"Hi there," I say.

Doreen smiles. "Sit down, take a load off," she says, her voice that now-familiar gravelly rasp.

"Sorry, can't today," I tell her. "I'm in a hurry."

"That's a shame. I was hoping to get the dirt on this," Doreen says, showing me a newspaper. There was a front page article about DC Cooper's death on the front page.

"Sorry you missed it?" I tease.

"I'd have enjoyed seeing that," Doreen says, and I don't think she's joking. "The paper makes him out to be a great guy."

"Well, the first two paragraphs do," I agree. "It gets a little more honest about him toward the end." I'd read the article earlier and it goes on to list many of Cooper's infractions, like the disciplinary hearings, the charges of insubordination, the docking of pay and his demotion to second-class Constable. He doesn't get off lightly and the real question anyone should have after reading it was *How did he manage to keep his job on the force?*

"Just goes to prove you can't believe everything you read," Doreen says. "Anyway, people tend to make heroes out of anyone after they're dead. It's not always true, is it?"

I shake my head. "No, it sure isn't." Still, Cooper was a dead cop, and there isn't much to be gained in talking him down. No matter what my personal feelings are about him I don't want to be the cop who talks down other police officers. That never ends well, as I've learned.

"Do you know what he died of yet?"

I laugh. "No! They haven't even done the autopsy."

"Autopsy?" Doreen looks worried. "Why bother? I heard he had a heart attack. Or maybe one of his criminal connections had him killed."

"I can't tell you," I say, trying to edge away. Even if I knew more about Cooper, I'm not about to share it with Doreen. "But I'll find out soon."

"Maybe someone in his personal life hated him enough to kill him. He was such an nasty piece of work… he's likely to have made enemies all over."

"How did you like the Fall Fair?" I ask, changing the subject. Doreen seems a little too interested in Cooper's death.

Doreen shakes her head. "I wasn't there."

"Really? I could have sworn I saw you…"

"I suppose one old lady looks like any other," she says. I feel that she's lying but can't understand why Doreen would deny being at the Fair.

"There are probably thousands of old ladies who look like me wandering the streets," Doreen says. Her voice has an edge.

I start to feel uncomfortable. Why is Doreen so irritable? I'm grateful when Phil calls me over. My coffee is ready and I can get away.

"Have you learned anything yet about who killed Anna?" Doreen demands before I could leave.

"It's only been…"

"Two days. Yeah, I know."

"Look," I begin. "I get it. She's one of your oldest friends. But the investigative process… it takes time. It's not like on TV. Hell, it takes days or even weeks sometimes for autopsy results to come through."

"I guess some old lady dying isn't a high priority for the Niagara police force."

I don't bother to deny it. It's clear to me that they've already decided Anna died accidentally. An old woman, visually impaired, somehow confused, had wandered into the fruit storage and died. But I believe there's something more to Anna's death than that, and Doreen believes it too.

"I can look into it," I say. "But you understand I'm not an investigator." *Yet*, I add, to myself.

"I thought you were a Detective?" Doreen eyes me suspiciously. Did I tell her that? I didn't remember doing so.

"I've passed my exam," I clarify. "But I haven't been assigned to any investigative team yet. Still waiting." She looks irritated and I'm about to leave when I have an idea.

"Maybe you can help me with something," I say. I know I shouldn't involve her, but there is a way she can help and she's obviously invested. "I was out at Taiga a few days ago…"

"The weed grower?"

I nod. "I was doing some background interviews there, for a case. And I saw some men. They were some kind of agricultural workers. Maybe temporary foreign workers."

Doreen shrugs. "Yeah, they hire hundreds of people around here."

"I saw those same guys at Anna's farm the day she died."

"Are you sure?" She shakes her head. "I know Anna's son hires workers every season. He brings them in from Mexico or Jamaica or wherever. But they only work for him."

"Well these were definitely the same guys," I insist. "Would you please bring me to Anna's farm, to talk with her son? Unofficially."

"Well honey, you'd have to bring me. You're the one who's driving."

THIRTY THREE

WE ARRIVE AT Kozlowski's farm and Doreen instructs me to drive up past the front, all the way to the back of the house. I park under a carport with a corrugated metal roof then help Doreen out of the passenger side, first pulling her walker out of the trunk and unfolding it. While she starts to push herself across the gravel driveway I stand and survey the farm.

"We used to run around this farm when we were kids, a hundred years ago or so," Doreen says. "Those are Mutsu." She points at the large greeny gold apples nearest me. "They aren't ripe until later this month. They're probably picking McIntosh and Empire now."

I can see down long rows of apple trees, stretching acres into the distance. Some are red and others are green, but I can't tell different types of apples apart unless they're in the grocery store with a label.

The back screen door slams as Peter Kozlowski comes out of the kitchen and sweeps Doreen up in a big hug. I leave them alone for a few minutes before Doreen beckons me over. Peter Kozlowski clearly recognizes me from the day his mother died.

"This is my friend Lucy," Doreen says.

"We've met," he says. He doesn't sound friendly.

"Can I talk to you, Mr. Kozlowski?"

He glares at me then spits on the ground. "I thought you weren't interested in what happened to my mother. It was just an accident, right?"

I feel ashamed, but not surprised. Clearly whoever was lead investigator into Anna's death hadn't been very empathetic. "I don't really know," I mumble. "It's not my case. I…"

"Then what are you doing here?" he interrupts me.

"There may be a connection to another case I'm investigating."

He looks skeptical. "What other case?"

I avoid the question. "Can you please tell me about the men who work for you? The migrant workers?"

"What about them?" He's wary. He doesn't want the police coming around and asking about his foreign workers.

I'm quick to reassure him. "I'm not from Immigration, Mr. Kozlowski. This is a murder investigation."

"And you think my guys have something to do with it?"

"They might have some information that will help."

"Well, they aren't going to talk to you," he says. "You're a cop."

"Okay. Let me talk to you then. Do the guys who work for you also work at Taiga?"

"No. That's not allowed." His look of alarm tells me he's lying. "They're in the country on closed work visas. They can only work here, for me."

I take a deep breath. "Okay, let me start again. I know the guys who work for you also work there. I've seen them myself." I hold up my hand to forestall his objections. "I'm sure you have some arrangement that you let them job share. I don't care about that."

His eyes flick nervously between Doreen and me.

"If you don't have enough work for them, they can go over there for some days," I continue. "Make some extra money?"

"At busy times," Doreen chimes in. "It all comes out in the wash, right? No harm done."

"There is no harm done," he snaps. "They're good workers. They send the money to their families back home. I help them out."

"Relax Mr. Kozlowski," I say. "I just need to know what's going on at Taiga. A man died there last week."

"Peter, please," Doreen says, laying her hand on his arm. "Help her out."

He thinks for a moment then nods. "I'll go get them," he says as he strides out into the orchard. Doreen makes her way up the back steps and takes a seat on the porch to wait. I follow but feel uncomfortable sitting down, so I stand beside her.

"Sit down for God's sake," she barks. "You look like you're here to arrest someone. I assume you don't want the poor bastards to run away when they lay eyes on you." I comply and try to make myself as unintimidating as possible, which is not easy to do when you're in a police uniform.

"So, who else died?" Doreen asks, once I've removed my hat and received her nod of approval. It takes me a second to understand. "You told him you were investigating a murder. Was that true?"

"It's true," I say. "A man was found dead on Taiga property last week."

Doreen raises her eyebrows. "Anyone I know?" she asks with a smile.

"You know everyone who's killed in town?"

"I know everyone," she chuckles. "Especially the ones who need killing." I doubt she's kidding.

A few minutes later three men follow Peter in from the orchard. They walk slowly, dragging their feet. Whatever he's told them, they aren't happy about coming to talk with me. When they got closer I can see it's the same three guys I'd seen at Taiga: Two were small Latinos and the third was the tall Jamaican, his dreadlocks stuffed up into a yellow, green and red striped Rastacap. They all look nervous and keep their eyes down as they climb the steps onto the back porch.

Kozlowski speaks to them in Spanish and they sit down, reluctantly.

"Can you please tell me what you do at Taiga?" I ask. They exchange a glance, obviously not eager to say anything. I look at Kozlowski for help. He speaks again in Spanish, encouraging them to talk.

"We trim the plants," the Jamaican finally answers, in English. "Mostly."

"That's it? Just trimming the plants?" The two other men say something to Kozlowski. They seem to understand English, but aren't willing to speak.

"When harvest comes, they'll do that too," Kozlowski translates. "And they are laying out irrigation lines, in the new rooms." The Jamaican rolls his eyes and glares at them. I realize they've said too much.

"New rooms?" My interest makes them clam up immediately and they look down at their hands.

I know how to wait. Minutes pass and I watch them patiently. Finally one of them speaks, in English.

"In the new grow rooms," he says.

I shrug. "So what's the big deal?" I ask. "They've got all sorts of grow rooms operating at Taiga."

"The unlicensed rooms," the Jamaican clarifies.

Now that is interesting. "Really? Unlicensed?"

Kozlowski leans back against the porch rail, his arms crossed. He looks off into the orchard, keeping an eye on the rest of the pickers.

"Taiga's only currently licensed for nine hundred thousand square feet of production," the Jamaican says. "They built three new rooms, but grow licenses aren't approved yet."

"How do you know this?" I ask. It didn't seem like it was the sort of information temporary foreign workers would have access to.

"One of the guys told me."

"One of the pickers? What guy?"

He smiles and shakes his head. "No man," he said. "This guy was a journalist. He was working on a story."

"Was his name Leon Flores?"

He nods. "Haven't seen him around lately though." He glances at Peter Kozlowski, his expression resentful. I wonder why.

"He's dead," I say. "Since last week."

Peter Kozlowski's head snaps around. "Dead?" He demands. "Are you sure?"

"I'm sure. He was found in the Canal," I say, surprised at Kozlowski's reaction. "You knew him?"

He rubs his eyes. "Dammit," he swears. "Yes. I knew him. He interviewed me last month, asking about temporary workers, how the program works. I helped him get work at Taiga, for his story. He went over with my guys, when they needed some extra workers for a few days."

It looks like Flores was working on a story that might expose Taiga's practices. I wonder if that was the reason for his death.

"So, these new rooms—the unlicensed ones," I ask. "Is Taiga growing cannabis in them?"

"Oh yeah." All three of the workers nod.

"And if the government finds out?"

"They could lose their license," Kozlowski says. "The product grown in those rooms would be trashed. They'd be fined."

"That's a big risk," I say. "Why would they take that chance?"

"Money, obviously," he laughs. "Since legalization there's been a huge demand, and no supply. But because of some stupid slow government bureaucracy they're supposed to wait another eight months or a year until someone stamps their permit?"

"I see your point, but it seems like a stupid chance to take."

"What's the big deal?" he says. "There's no actual harm done. They're using the exact same grow techniques, taking the same safety precautions, growing the same plants. Nothing's any different from the already licensed grow rooms. They're just missing the rubber stamp."

I know so much goes on under the police radar, and most of

it I don't care about. Government rules and bureaucratic crap. It makes no difference to me, or to anyone, unless someone gets hurt or killed. Then the game changes.

"So that's what's going on at Taiga," I say, thinking it over. "I imagine they'll be doing all they can to keep that quiet." I just wonder if they'd go as far as murdering Leon Flores and Maurice Cobb to do so.

"Are you going to report them? I need to know," Kozlowski demands as the men quickly turn and walk back to the orchard a lot faster than they came out.

"I think you need to keep your guys here, Mr. Kozlowski," I say, giving him a stern look so he does not miss my point. "It's better they don't go back to Taiga anytime soon."

THIRTY FOUR

DOREEN CAN TELL Lucy doesn't want to chat on the drive home, and that normally would suit her fine. But she wants to know more about the case Lucy's investigating, and figures she'll push until she gets shut down.

"So who was this dead guy you're investigating? This Cobb?"

"He was a research scientist," Lucy says after a moment.

"And he worked at Taiga?"

"And at Pelham Woods," she adds then looks like she regrets saying it.

"Doing what?"

"Security."

There has to be a story there. "A scientist doing security guard work?" Doreen says. "You're going to have to explain that one."

"He got fired from his previous job at Advik Therapeutics," Lucy says. "They said he was stealing formulas and selling them..."

Doreen gets it. "Probably nobody else would hire him. Couldn't get a reference and it was the only job he could get, with his record."

"But his ex-wife says he wasn't a thief. Says he reported some shady drug testing they were doing and he was fired and blacklisted because of it."

"Ex-wife?"

"She's living at Sophie's place now."

"The guy's a wife beater?" Doreen scoffs. "Then I have a hard time believing anything he says. I'd say he got what was coming to him."

Lucy shrugs. "Personally, I agree with you. However, that isn't the official position of the Niagara Regional police force."

"So you think maybe he saw something at Taiga too? Was going to blow the whistle on them, and that's what got him killed?"

"It's possible," Lucy says. "Maybe he had a come to Jesus moment after they charged him with assault on his wife. Maybe he was trying to make amends?"

They have to wait a few minutes as the Clarence Street Bridge over the canal is just coming down. A fifty-foot sailboat under motor goes past, its mast too tall to pass under the bridge. It's late for the boats to be out. Most of them are being lifted and stored in shrink-wrap already for the winter. Its name is the Nautilus, registered in Bermuda. Looks like it has a long sail ahead.

Doreen shakes her head. "Not in my experience. These assholes never change." She looks at Lucy out of the corner of her eye. How can she of all people believe that, even for a second? "Suddenly he grew a conscience? I call bullshit on that."

"And the other dead guy, the journalist you pulled out of the Canal," she continues after a minute. "He was working at Taiga too. Think there's a connection?"

Lucy smiles at her and doesn't answer. She is shutting her down. Fair enough. Doreen changes the subject.

"My goddaughter has a nice boat, something like that one," she says.

"Rose?" Lucy says. "I didn't know that. I imagine she probably doesn't get much time out on the water, working at the restaurant every day."

Doreen shrugs. "Days off. In the winter she takes it down to Barbados. Sophie's got a place there."

The sailboat clears the bridge and it begins to lower. Lucy starts the car and drives across, the tires making a sound as they roll across the metal bridge. Doreen stares out the window as they enter the East Village.

The refinery isn't very tall but it still manages to loom over the entire area. Everything falls in its shadow and it has shaped and defined the town for over a hundred years.

"What happened to your husband?" Lucy asks as they pull up in front of Doreen's house.

"He died. About fifty years ago." She gives Doreen a sympathetic pat on the arm.

"I'm sorry," she says.

"It was a long time ago," Doreen says. "The refinery killed him."

"He had a workplace accident?"

"No. Lung cancer." She sees Lucy look at her cigarette pack, sticking out of the side of her handbag. "He never smoked. It was exposure to the metals and toxins in the plant. Lots of people around here got sick."

Lucy gets the walker out of the trunk and unfolds it for Doreen then opens the door. "I read about it," she says. "There was a class action suit, right?"

"There was," Doreen says as she climbs out of the car. "The Ministry of the Environment ordered them to clean up a lot of the properties around here. Paid some compensation."

"Not enough I expect."

Doreen shakes her head as Lucy gets back into her car. As she drives off Doreen pushes her walker along the cracked concrete slabs along the side of the house into the backyard. It looks fine, just like any other backyard if anyone took a look. But the soil is sour all over the East Village. Toxic. The whole place is poisoned, just like the people in it. People like Doreen.

The refinery is just visible over the top of her neighbour's house. A huge old brick building that takes up most of a city block. It used to be the heartbeat of the entire town, years ago. Thousands of families depended on it and the loud shift change whistle could be heard blocks away. It hasn't blown in years.

When he first got sick nobody knew what it was. People were afraid to even say the word cancer back in the seventies. The refinery paid out some insurance and offered her a cash settlement. Doreen signed a release and took their money, shut her mouth and has kept it shut ever since. She had a son to raise, alone. The settlement paid off her mortgage and she went back to work at the hospital to support them both.

Many years later the citizens started the class action suit to sue the refinery for damages and compensation. The activists used to knock on her door, asking for her support, for Doreen to come out and speak at town meetings and sign their damn petitions, to force them to clean up the contaminated areas. But she never did.

Finally the refinery offered to remediate the soil at the house, but she refused. The last thing she needed by then was anyone excavating her backyard and replacing all the soil. She knew exactly what they'd find. They can do it after she's dead.

She should have fought, she thinks. Like she's fighting now. She just can't let things go on, getting worse all the time. People getting away with murder. It's time the truth came out. All of it, no matter who gets hurt. It's time.

THIRTY FIVE

I WAIT IN the reception area of the walk in clinic, with the patients who've come to see Dr. Maja Kaur. Her receptionist recognizes me from the many times I'd met Maja for lunch and she smiles but I don't go over for a chat. Maja and my relationship is now strictly professional and I have to get used to that, no matter how much it hurts.

The door to the examination room opens as Maja ushers a patient out. She stops short when she sees me then forces herself to smile. She gestures for me to follow her down the hall to her office.

"Detective Cooper's autopsy results are ready," she says after she closes the door.

I'm astonished. "Why so fast?" It normally takes at least a week depending on how many tests are required, and how busy the department is.

"He was a police officer," Maja replies. "He goes to the head of the line."

"Professional courtesy?"

"Yeeees... ." she laughs. "Even though he wasn't courteous, or much of a professional." I'd told her all about Cooper during the time we'd been a couple.

I smirk. "His reputation preceded him."

"And will live after him in memory." She shuffles a few papers then passes one to me.

"I'm going to take a wild guess and say it was a heart attack," I say, without looking at the document. I'm not interested in Cooper, or in what he died of. I want to get to whatever the she might tell me about Mrs. Kozlowski. Not that it's my case, exactly, but I do have a personal interest in what happened to her.

"Ten points for Gryffindor," Maja says. "At first that's exactly what I thought too…"

"At first… ?"

"And he did die because his heart stopped," she continues, ignoring the interruption. "I also found liver damage, which I think we can attribute to heavy drinking over many years. And there was damage to his nasal cartilage, septum and sinus cavity, likely from drug use." That all makes sense to me, given what I know of Cooper.

"It was definitely a heart attack," Maja says. "But what's interesting is what made it stop in the first place. I'd say it was Potassium Chloride. It causes severe arrhythmias and heart spasms, then the heart stops."

"He was *poisoned*?!"

"Indisputably," she says. "The post-mortem elevated potassium levels I found are typical since potassium is naturally released into blood stream after a severe heart attack. So at first I didn't notice it. "

"What made you take a second look?"

"I found a fresh injection mark on his abdomen," she says. "Probably insulin. He was borderline obese, and there are dozens of marks, which tells me he was a diabetic."

"Okay…" I'm not sure how that proves anything.

"Then I found a second fresh mark." She looks to me for a reaction and finds none. I'm baffled. "These insulin injections are taken once a day," she explains. "So he should only have one."

"Maybe he forgot," I suggest. "And gave himself a second one?"

"If that were the case," she says, "he would have shown some symptoms of an insulin overdose. And I understand that wasn't the case."

"What kind of symptoms?"

"Confusion, blurred vision, sweating, irritability, seizures…"

"He was always sweaty and irritable," I laugh. "It would be tough to even notice. Why do you think it was Potassium Chloride?"

"There are several things that could have been injected that would cause a heart attack. Like digoxin or digitalis. But there was no evidence of either of those in his system. Potassium chloride breaks down into potassium and sodium… which makes it virtually untraceable as well."

"Then how did you know… ?"

"Close inspection of the two fresh injection sites proves it."

"How quickly would he have died?"

"Within minutes of receiving the injection," she says.

I'm stunned. I'd been looking right at Cooper just a few minutes before he'd died, when he was arguing with Rose. Could she have had something to do with it? "So someone definitely injected him?"

"Twice," Maja laughs. "Somebody wasn't taking any chances. They gave him two shots."

"Or maybe there were two people."

She nods. "Yes, that's possible. It would have been extremely painful," she says. "An intense burning sensation I'd imagine, at least for a couple of minutes until his heart stopped."

"We're going to send him to Toronto," Maja continues. "For a full forensic autopsy."

"Really?" I'm surprised. "But you've already determined the cause of death."

"I'm just a simple country doctor, what do I know?" she says with a wry smile. "Cooper was a cop," she says. "Since his murder is unusual, we want to make sure we do a thorough investigative job, which means a forensic pathologist needs to investigate. All coroner-ordered autopsies now have to go to Toronto, now that they've shut down the unit in Hamilton."

I hear the irritation in her voice and understand. The closing of the unit now forced all autopsies to be done almost a hundred miles away at the new state of the art Forensic Services and Coroners Complex. The new facility had all the bells and whistles: the latest forensic technology, laboratories, ballistics, toxicology, a Level 3 Containment autopsy suite, in case of biohazards and even a forensic anthropologist on staff. And it was close to the airport, in case of any mass casualties like a plane crash. It was like something out of a television show. Unfortunately, it also means a lot of travel, longer processing times for post mortem results, and the loss of direct access to information that local police forces could use in solving crimes.

"So, basically, they are going to do the same tests you've just done," I say. "It'll just cost more, and get the same results."

"Exactly," she laughs. "In the interests of efficiency."

I smile at Maja, who's gathering her papers and hinting for me to leave. She looks happy. I wonder if it's because of the new person in her life and I feel bereft.

"How are you?" I ask. "Are you doing okay?" I hold my breath, not even sure what I want to hear, or what I can stand. *I'm fine? I miss you? I'm in love with someone new?*

She looks up in surprise and smiles. "I'm fine," she says.

"Good," I smile, half choking with relief. "I wonder if you have any information about another death," I begin, changing the subject.

Maja gives me a look. "Is it your case?" she asks. "Or is this off the record?"

"Well, technically..."I begin.

"I can't help you Lucy," she cuts me off. "You can't just expect me to share confidential information with you. It's not on."

"I was going to say, that technically it's not even a case," I say. "It's an old lady who was found dead, in her barn."

"Anna Kozlowski. I know," Maja says. "It's not a criminal matter. She died of asphyxia and it's an accidental death."

"Okay, thanks," I say. "And you're sure?"

Maja stares at me in disbelief. "Are you being serious right now? You're questioning my judgement?"

"Maja, I'm sorry," I say. "That's not what I meant. It's just that I know a friend of hers, an elderly lady who is really upset about what happened. I want to be able to reassure her, convince her it was an accident. She feels that no one is listening to her, because she's old."

Maja looks embarrassed about her outburst. "It was obvious at the scene what caused her death," she says after a moment. "There was no question, no suspicion of wrongdoing."

"But Anna Kozlowski had severe visual impairment," I say. "Her son says there's no way she'd ever have gone into the storage unit on her own. There was no reason for her to do so."

"When we got her back here I did a brief post-mortem examination," Maja says. "There were no contusions, no defensive injuries that I could see."

"So she didn't struggle with someone who might have been putting her in there."

Maja shakes her head. "There's no evidence of that."

"And no bruising?" She shrugs. So there were some bruises. "But, if she'd been grabbed, would there even be time for bruises to form, given how quickly she'd died from the nitrogen gas?"

"Elderly people bruise easily," Maja says. "She could have had them from bumping up against a door frame. Dating a bruise is costly and not something we're even set up to do at this hospital. For that I'd have to send her to Toronto, and for that to happen I'd have to be convinced we needed further investigation, which I'm not. The cause of her death is clear: asphyxia, caused by exposure to nitrogen gas in a low-oxygen environment. There's no evidence to support the theory she was murdered."

"Okay, thanks," I say. "I appreciate your help." She gives me a tight smile and turns away. I walk out the door, leaving everything unsaid. It's too late now anyway.

I get into the car and think over what I've just learned. So Cooper was injected at the Fair in the few minutes after I'd seen him. I may have even seen it happen, if I could believe Rose had done it.

Poor Rose. *Black Widow*, they called her. Now the rumours will start all over again, just like they'd done the last time. All the small minds in a small town, with nothing else to gossip about.

Could it have been Rose? Did she inject him in that moment when she shoved him away? But why would she want to kill Cooper? I try to think if I'd seen anything in her hand. Surely I would have noticed a syringe. And who'd given him the second injection? Was there someone behind him, in the crowd? I tried to remember the image of who'd been there, but I come up blank.

I flash on the memory of Rose, pushing into Cooper as he threatened her. Him falling back, wincing, coming for her again before walking away. The only other thing I can remember is seeing Maja at the booth, smiling and laughing with her new girlfriend. And how I'd been so upset I'd had to look away. And because of that I missed seeing whoever had injected Cooper.

THIRTY SIX

DOREEN MAKES SURE to sit on the sofa in the lounge that has a clear view past the nursing desk and into the dispensing room. She arrives right after breakfast, has taken her position and is waiting while Nadia is dressed by the care workers. She keeps one eye on the television that's blaring in the corner. The other eye she keeps on the nurse.

Katrina Mueller is on duty, as she is most days that Doreen visits. She seems to pick up a lot of extra shifts, which means she needs the money. Or it's to make sure no one else notices any discrepancies in the medication logs. Doreen has deduced that Katrina Mueller is stealing the patients' medication.

No wonder the patients are acting out more; they aren't getting the medication they need to treat their pain. The residents are mostly non-verbal and they can't even speak up for themselves, or tell where it hurt. All they can do is moan or yell or cry. She's seen it in Nadia, when her pain isn't being properly managed. She gets irritable, and screams or even hits, lashing out in pain.

Doreen knows it has to be the nurse. The medication is prescribed by the doctor and the pharmacist fills the prescriptions. It's only here, on the ward and in the dispensing room, where someone can make a switch. And from what Doreen has observed, it's simple to do. The nurse works alone. No one oversees her filling the medicine cart, or doing her audit, or is even with her during the time she spends in the dispensing room. She has lots of time to switch the medications. The patients never question what they are taking. They just open their mouths and swallow what they are given, whether it's in a tiny plastic cup or mixed into a spoon of applesauce.

Both Anna and Nadia said something was going on at Pelham Woods, but Doreen always discounted it. She'd disregarded what her friends said because one couldn't see and one couldn't remember. Now Anna is dead and Doreen is going to make it up to them.

Doreen remembers Anna had been sitting right here, turned to the left, facing the television. If she'd been looking out of the corner of her right eye, she'd have seen into the dispensing room. She'd have seen exactly what Doreen is looking at right now: Katrina Mueller switching the pills in a patient's blister pack and substituting them with different pills that look the same.

That's what Anna had seen that day. And she'd spoken up about it, but Doreen hadn't paid attention to her. But someone did. Someone heard her, and that someone made sure Anna wouldn't be able to tell anyone else.

Who'd been there that day? The video film crew. Lucy. Dr. Chowdhury. Cooper. Katrina Mueller. The rest of the patients and PSWs. That woman who came through delivering flowers. The therapy dog and its handler.

After Doreen saw nurse Mueller with Cooper, she knew something was off. It didn't take a genius to figure out whatever was going on between them wasn't legal. The way Doreen sees it, either the nurse is stealing drugs and Cooper was the buyer, or he was getting a kickback to keep quiet about the nurse's sideline. Now Cooper is dead; he's paid the price for his part in the scheme and Doreen is wondering how and when Katrina Mueller will pay.

Nadia wakes up and looks at Doreen. Her eyes are alert and she seems to recognize her.

"Hi Doreen," she says. "Is Anna here?" Doreen shakes her head.

"Not yet," she lies. "She's just on her way." Nadia nods and smiles happily.

"I've got a new dress for the dance," she says. "What are you wearing?"

Doreen smiles and pats her friend's knee. "Just you wait and see," she says. "It'll knock you out. It's blue, off the shoulder, with a full skirt. I made it myself."

Nadia laughs and starts to move her feet, dancing in her seat. Doreen looks back toward the nurse. She's pushing the medication cart along the hall. She glances over and smiles and Doreen thinks how lucky it is that Mueller can't read her mind.

THIRTY SEVEN

THIS TIME WHEN I arrive at Advik Therapeutics Joshi isn't in the lobby to greet me. And when his assistant brings me into his office he isn't the same smiling, friendly man who'd tried so hard to put me at my ease. He doesn't offer me coffee, to my disappointment. It had been delicious.

"How can I help you, Constable Gauthier?" he asks. He does not invite me to sit down.

"It's Detective Constable, actually," I say, taking a seat anyway. "I'm just here with some follow-up questions about Maurice Cobb. It won't take long."

Joshi raises his eyebrows and gives me a patient half-smile, to let me know how busy and important he is and how I'm intruding on his time.

"Anything I can do to help," he lies.

I flip open my notebook and pretend to read my notes. "Can you please tell me a bit more about the information you say he stole? My notes say that they were exploratory drugs and that he worked in product development. What sort of product?"

Joshi clearly does not want to answer. He moves some papers around on his desk then looks up at me. "Why is this important?" he asks. "The man is dead. It's got nothing to do with Advik Therapeutics. He left here last year."

I smile at him with exaggerated patience. I will wait him out. Most people can't tolerate silence and I know he'll talk. A long moment passes.

"He was doing research in pharmaceuticals to help manage symptoms of dementia." Joshi finally says. I smile and make a note. I already know this from my interview with Geraldine Bennett, but I want to hear him confirm it.

"And these drugs, the ones he was developing, and that you say he sold to one of your competitors. What happened to them? Was the project cancelled? Or are they still in development?"

He's clearly surprised by the question. "The clinical trials were stopped," he says. "Why would I continue to develop a product that I know has been compromised through his corporate espionage? That makes no sense." He leans back in his chair. "Detective Gauthier," he begins after a moment. "I have plans to take Advik Therapeutics public next year. We're planning an IPO, doing lots of promotion. I'm even shooting a series of videos. I absolutely cannot risk researching and developing a drug that we can't bring to market."

I reach into my pocket and extract the pills I found on Cobb's body. "Can you tell me what these are?" I slide the plastic baggie across his desk.

He looks at the bag, but does not pick it up. "No," he says. "Not beyond the obvious fact they are pills of some sort."

"They were found on Maurice Cobb's body," I say. I feel Joshi tense. "We've had them analyzed and have found they are," I read from my notes, "an organic chemical compound, typical of a butryphenone-type. Possibly related to a heterocyclic compound in a thiazine class. Maybe a dopamine receptor, something to treat movement disorders, or dementia."

Joshi shrugs. "They have nothing to do with Advik Therapeutics," he says, pushing the bag away.

"Based on the tests we've done and his research notes..." I say,

"We think this is the same medication he was developing for Advik. The medication that you say never went into production."

"Impossible," Joshi snaps. "You see there's no imprint on them. They are not ours." He looks out the window for a moment, considering. "If they are the same formulation," he begins, "then I suggest he kept some back. From when he worked here."

"Stole them you mean?"

"If you like."

"Mr. Joshi, you're suggesting he stole these pills from your lab a year ago, and for some reason hung onto them. And that he kept them in his pocket, where they were found after he died."

Joshi shrugs. "I have no idea. I barely knew the man."

It's interesting he's making such an effort to distance himself from Cobb. I make a motion as if I'm about to leave. The relief on Joshi's face is obvious. "Did you know he was working at Pelham Woods just before he died?" I say, settling back down and watching Joshi for a reaction. "That's one of your nursing homes, isn't it?"

He nods, trying to give nothing away. "I'm the owner, but my role is executive. I certainly don't manage any of the day-to-day operations."

This time I really do stand to leave. "And the illegal grow rooms at Taiga——what can you tell me about them?" He looks horrified. Sweat beads on his forehead and upper lip.

"That's absurd," he blusters. "Taiga would never risk that. Do you realize how dangerous that would be?"

"I do indeed, Mr. Joshi. That's why I bring it up." I wonder how quickly the work crew at Taiga will be able to tear out the illegal grow rooms, now that Joshi knows the police are aware of them. I've already called it in and they'll be at Taiga within the hour, if not sooner. But for now, I can try to use it as leverage.

"Why would Taiga risk losing their license for some illegal rooms?" he asks.

"You tell me. I don't know, Mr. Joshi," I say. "I understand there are licenses pending on those rooms… but that they have not yet been issued. And you're growing in them, am I right?"

Joshi looks away. "I'm just a shareholder."

"You're the CEO, Mr. Joshi. Taiga is owned by Advik Therapeutics. You've just said you're going public this year, or trying to. A scandal around illegal grows and non-compliance with government regulations won't help your share price, will it?"

He glares at me then glances at his phone. I can read his mind. I know he's willing me to leave so he can get on the phone and order them to tear out the rooms, or remove any plants that are in there, or whatever he needs to do to cover up. Pity he's going to be too late.

"Mr. Joshi, either you didn't know about the illegal grow rooms, which indicates a staggering level of executive incompetence on your part," I say. "Or you gambled you'd manage to get away with it, grow and sell the product, carry on until the license was approved."

"One of your competitors was hit with a noncompliance report last year," I continue, rubbing it in. "You do know what happened to them, don't you? Over ten thousand kilograms of their product had to be incinerated. That's a huge financial loss. And they lost their licensed producer status." I *tsk* a few times, shaking my head. "For doing the exact same thing as you're doing now."

I look at him sternly, making my point. "Growing cannabis in unlicensed rooms, even if your license is pending, is illegal."

"I am aware of the law, Detective Gauthier."

"Well that's good to know Mr. Joshi," I say over my shoulder as I leave his office. I pull out my phone and glance back as the door closed. He has picked up the phone and is punching in some numbers. I wonder which would be first: Taiga to start the cover up, or his lawyer to cover his ass.

I now have two motives for someone to kill Maurice Cobb: covering up illegal grow rooms at Taiga, and whatever was going on with the pharmaceutical scam at Pelham Woods. And that someone in both cases was Amit Joshi.

I turn just as I'm stepping out the door. "One last thing, Mr. Joshi," I say. He looks up, a guilty expression on his face. "What can you tell me about Leon Flores?"

"I've never heard of him," he says. But the panic in his eyes tells another story.

THIRTY EIGHT

DOREEN SEES KATRINA Mueller heading down the hall, pushing her medication cart. She waits as the care worker takes Nadia down the hall to the toilet then follows them and does what she'd been planning to do. It only takes a moment before she's pushing her walker back down to the lounge and taking her seat on the sofa.

As much as she loves her old friend, dealing with her incontinence and changing her diaper is a job she's not going to take on. She knows that after the bathroom visit they'll have to go to Nadia's room to change her pants. That usually takes at least twenty minutes, and that's if Nadia cooperates with the clothing change. Which, as often as not, she refuses to do. She'll fuss about the clothing options and make it difficult for them to dress her. Sometimes she'll hit out in frustration or burst into tears. It's like dressing an uncooperative toddler. So usually the care workers just leave a change of clothes out for her and let her dress herself while they go help another patient. They'll return in ten or fifteen minutes once she's ready to return to the lounge.

Faintly at first, then growing louder and louder, Doreen hears a piercing scream. Someone is wailing, her voice rising and falling as she comes running toward the patient lounge. It's the care worker and she's hysterical, screaming about someone being dead.

Doreen shakes her head in irritation. Why all the fuss? Surely people die all the time at Pelham Woods. It's full of old people who are already mostly dead anyway. Still the woman continues to scream and two care workers run down the hall to help, followed by three patients who are drawn by the noise and excitement. Doreen remains where she is on the couch. She doesn't need to see it.

Within a few minutes a security guard, some administrators wearing lanyards, and Dr. Chowdhury also arrive, followed by two uniformed police officers.

One of them is Lucy. Doreen raises her hand in greeting, but Lucy doesn't respond. She's talking into her phone, then she speaks to the other officer and the two of them go down the hall.

After a few minutes Doreen stands and walks to Nadia's room, looking for her friend. The police and administrative staff are too involved in the drama to notice her pass by, pushing her walker down the carpeted hallway. She turns at the public bathroom and goes into the third room on the left, where Nadia is sitting on her bed, wearing a fresh adult diaper but no pants. She's waiting patiently for someone to come back and finish changing her. Her white ankle socks are soaked in blood.

The tile floor of her room is awash in red and more is streaming from under the door of her closet. Doreen hesitates at the threshold of the room. She doesn't want to get blood on the wheels of her walker.

"Nadia," she calls to her friend. "What's happened?"

Nadia smiles. She has a large knife on her lap and it's covered in blood.

Doreen cranes her neck and can just see into the closet where the body of nurse Katrina Mueller lies, her throat slashed.

"Excuse me," she hears a voice behind her. It's Lucy. "You'll have to move away from here." Doreen feels a hand on her shoulder as she pulls her back out into the hall.

"Hello Lucy," Doreen says.

Lucy jumps in surprise. "Doreen? What are you doing here?"

Then she catches herself, and acts like a police officer. "You'll have to leave. Immediately. Please go back to the lounge."

Doreen turns and wheels the walker up the hallway. She sees she's leaving some bloody tracks on the carpet. Oh well, it can't be helped. She pauses and turns to look over her shoulder. Lucy stands in the doorway, staring at Nadia, and at the knife. Her face is pale and she looks frozen, paralyzed by what she sees. Her eyes are wide and somehow unseeing, yet still she stares. Doreen can see her sway slightly, as if she's about to pass out. The other officer touches her on the shoulder.

"Are you okay?" he asks. Lucy snaps out of it and brushes him off.

"I'm fine," she says. But Doreen knows she isn't fine. Seeing the bloody knife has been a terrible shock to her. As it would be, she understands only too well.

Doreen goes back to the lounge and sits down facing the television. There's no more need for her to see into the dispensary room.

THIRTY NINE

IN THE TIME it takes me to secure the scene and take some preliminary photos, Nadia has fallen asleep on her bed. She lies on her side in the fetal position, completely unaware as her blood soaked socks are removed and the knife pulled from her lap and bagged.

"She doesn't have any blood on her," Decker remarks as we observe the Crime Scene Unit at work. "Just her socks."

"How is that even possible?" I say. "There'd be arterial spray from a throat slash like that."

"She must have come up behind her," he says. "Maybe that would account for it."

"Maybe." I'm skeptical. "But you'd need to know something about anatomy, like a nurse or a doctor. I'm not sure Ms. Efimov knows anything at this point."

Several patients try to come into the room while we work, drawn by the activity. It's unlikely any of them even know what has happened; they just see people moving around, hear raised voices and are interested in the hive of workers doing what they usually do at crime scenes. After a while they lose interest and wander back to their rooms or are led away to the patient lounge and parked back in front of the television.

The Crime Scene Unit arrives and begins their investigation. They remove nurse Mueller's body and I get out of the way, leaving

Decker to ensure the scene remains secure. I go to the nursing desk and find Dr. Chowdhury is still waiting there, as I'd instructed him. He looks impatient, frustrated and terrified. Standing behind him is Amit Joshi, sweating as if he's just run a mile.

"Dr. Chowdhury," I begin. "I'd like a list of the medications Nadia Efimov is on." He nods. "And those of Donald and Alan—I'm afraid I don't know their last names. I'd also like samples of their medications, to take away for testing."

Chowdhury looks horrified. "I can't possibly allow that," he blusters, glancing at Joshi for support. "Patient confidentiality precludes that kind of disclosure."

"Doctor, there's been a murder—of your nurse, Katrina Mueller," I snap. I've got no patience for his bullshit. "It seems that it was committed by Nadia Efimov. In the past week I've visited this facility on two separate occasions and on both of them I personally witnessed violent outbursts by two of your residents." Chowdhury's eyes are shifting back and forth between Amit Joshi and me as he tries to process what I'm saying and think of what he should do.

"I… I need to think about it…" Joshi mumbles after a moment. "Speak to our lawyer…"

"What exactly is there to *think about*?"

"I have to consider Pelham Wood's reputation," he says. "This could look very bad…"

"*Look* bad?" I laugh. "Trust me. It *is* bad. It's very bad." I get out my phone. Whatever he's hiding I'm not going to stand for it. If I have to call in the Homicide Unit myself, I will. Of course, I'd much rather proceed with the investigation on my own, but I'm not above bluffing. "Doctor, you will give me samples of the medication I requested immediately, or I will arrest you for obstruction. How *bad* do you think that will look?"

After my initial shock at seeing Katrina Mueller's body I'm able to focus on my job. Seeing her lying there in the pool of blood was like being trapped in a nightmare and I froze as I felt the panic threatening to overwhelm me. *Don't look down. Just breathe. Don't look at the blood.*

When no one was looking I took a rescue Lorazepam to stave off an attack and got to work. After a couple of hours going back and forth between Nadia Efimov's room, the dispensing room, Dr. Chowdhury's office and the main administration office of Pelham Woods, I've done all I can at the scene. The Crime Scene unit is still collecting evidence and the care workers have bathed Nadia and moved her into another room until hers can be cleaned and restored to a state she can live in again.

Nadia has been sedated and is asleep in her new bed, pending a psychiatric and medical interview. There's no point in arresting her. It's evident she's not in her right mind; if she were she wouldn't even be a resident at Pelham Woods. There will definitely be an investigation by the Ministry of Health into conditions at the facility, especially into how a patient with dementia had been able to access a knife and kill a nurse, but that's beyond my scope.

I'm heading toward the elevators when I notice Doreen, still sitting in the patient lounge.

"Doreen." I crouch next to her chair. "You need to go home. There's nothing you can do here." The old woman must be exhausted. She's been here for hours.

"I didn't really know what else to do," Doreen says, her voice small and quiet. "And I want to make sure Nadia's okay." She looks frail and confused. Has she even had anything to eat or drink?

"Let me drive you home." I hold out my hand to help Doreen up. "We'll grab something to eat on the way. Do you like fast food?"

"I could murder a fish sandwich," Doreen says, her eyes lighting up. Her hand flies up to cover her mouth. "I'm sorry."

"Don't worry about it. And French fries?" Doreen nods eagerly as we walk together to the elevator.

We drive through McDonalds on the way, and eat it in Doreen's living room, sitting together on the sofa. Getting Doreen out of the car and up her front steps was a struggle. I had to juggle the walker and the bag of take out food, with my one arm supporting Doreen, who seemed very unsteady on her feet. But once she's rested and has a bite to eat she seems to rally and get some colour back in her papery white cheeks.

"It's funny," Doreen says, chewing the last of her fish sandwich. I can't believe how long it has taken her to eat it. Everything she does is in slow motion. Maybe that's just what getting old is like. "You're a ginger, like me. Or like I used to be before my hair went grey." I nod. I hate my colouring. The red hair and pale skin with freckles. Every summer I'll get a bad sunburn, never a tan like the rest of my friends.

"Your last name—Gauthier... doesn't fit your colouring does it? You look like you should be a Scot."

I shake my head. "My parents are French Canadian, from New Brunswick."

Doreen looks at me for a moment then she takes a photo from the end table and passes it over to me. It's a school photo of a red-haired young boy, taken in front of the greyish blue background. He's smiling for the camera, showing his missing front teeth. He doesn't look like a boy who's going to end up with a long criminal record.

"This is my son," she says. It's one of the only photos I have of him." The photo looks like the ones I used to have, of myself as a schoolgirl. But that was a long time ago and they're all lost now. I don't even know what has happened to them.

"We didn't have cell phone cameras in our day," Doreen continues. "It was a big deal to take a snapshot—you had to buy the film, and pay to have it developed. That's if you could afford to have a camera, which I definitely could not. So I'd pay for the school photos once a year, or most years, when we had the money for it."

Doreen stands and goes toward the kitchen. "I'm going to make us some tea," she says. "Why don't you look through that old photo album to pass the time?"

I shrug and flip open the photo album that lays on Doreen's coffee table. I don't remember seeing it the last time I was there—what, three days ago? Doreen must have been looking through it, revisiting happier times. Or has she left it out specifically for me to see? I give my head a shake. Doreen had no way of knowing I'd ever come back to visit her, so why would she leave an album out deliberately?

Still, my ever-present anxiety prickles along the back of my neck as I slide the album closer. It has a coiled binding and is covered in vibrant yellow and pink fabric in a pattern right out of the seventies. It had probably been expensive when it was new. An investment in the future, to record and protect all the good times and precious memories they hoped life would bring them.

I listen to Doreen rustling around the kitchen as I turn the pages of the album. There are pitifully few photos inside, so maybe not so many good times to preserve. They are discoloured snapshots taken in the sixties, when colour film first became affordable. Most of the photos are of a trio of young women, at dances or the beach or high school graduation. The few photos have all been carefully preserved with photo corners to hold them in place, and most have little notations printed below. *Anna's new car* or *Beach Party Victoria Day 1967*.

There's a graduation photo of Doreen in a starched nurse's uniform, complete with white shoes, white stockings and a tall white cap. Nurses these days all wear green hospital scrubs and running shoes, but back then times were clearly different.

There are a few pictures of a young Doreen with a man, taken at what looks like a city hall wedding with only two witnesses in attendance: Anna and Nadia. I guess Doreen's parents hadn't attended the wedding. Doreen wears a simple white dress and a small hat with a veil, very sixties, very Jacqueline Onassis. She is smiling and happy.

The groom looks stunned, as if he doesn't know what's happening to him and is too afraid to ask.

"How long were you married?" I call out to her.

"Less than five years." The scream of the kettle cuts her off and I wait until she gets it off the boil. "We met at a dance. My parents never approved of him. Didn't think he was good enough for me, because he worked at the refinery, like his father did."

"I grew up on the other side of town. My father was a doctor. They thought I could do better." The clatter of mugs and cutlery punctuates her sentences. "But, that's not how it worked out. I met him. He was a good dancer. Had a nice car. They didn't come to my wedding. I was pregnant, of course."

Sounds like a very familiar story. How many marriages and families began that same way, and not just in the East Village.

"I had big plans to get out of the East Village," she says. "We all did. I never made it. Obviously."

I turn another page and find a photo of a woman with a little girl on her lap. The child is around three or four years old, and has bright red hair and chubby legs covered in freckles. The woman is my mother.

I look up and see Doreen standing in the doorway, holding two mugs of tea.

"Why do you have this picture?" I demand. I point at the photo and I can see my hand is shaking. My heart is pounding and I have to fight to keep my breath steady.

"It's okay, Lucy," Doreen says. "I can explain."

"That's my mother," I shout. "That's me! Why do you have a picture of us?" How does Doreen have this picture? A photo of my real mother. I don't even have one myself. Everything from that time of my life is lost, had been left behind in the terrible aftermath of blood and death and destruction that changed my life.

Doreen calmly places the mugs on the table and sits across from me.

"When I met you that day at the Green Bean," Doreen begins, keeping her voice low and calm. "I recognized you right away. It was your eyes."

"*Recognized* me? You *knew* me, knew my mother?"

Doreen nods. "I've lived here a very long time," she says as she reaches over and turns the page of the photo album. There's a photo of Doreen, with a young boy on her lap. A boy with red hair, like mine.

I feel the tingle of an adrenaline rush down my torso. My breath is rapid and shallow and I'm afraid I'll pass out. I reach into my pocket for my vial of Tylenol. That's where I keep my rescue medication hidden. I take one and put it under my tongue.

Doreen watches me, her expression full of pity.

"Is that Lorazepam?" she asks. "What's the dose?"

"Two milligrams." Her eyebrows rise in surprise. It's a lot, but I need it.

"Just keep breathing," she says. "Deep breaths. Slowly." She watches me quietly for a few minutes. "I was a nurse," she says. "It's fine. You'll be fine."

"I don't understand," I say, after my head clears a bit. "What do you mean, you *recognized me*. What about *my eyes*?"

"They are just like his," she finally says. I stare at the photos, willing myself to calm down as Doreen takes the two pictures and places them side by side on the table. "You look just like my son did, when he was a boy."

I'm unable to speak. I just stare at the photo of the red haired boy, next to that of me with my mother.

"I knew he was seeing a young woman in the neighbourhood," Doreen continues. "I hoped it was nothing serious. I didn't want him to ruin anyone's life, with the way he was carrying on. To tell you the truth I was relieved when he moved away from town and started living out at a farmhouse with some of this buddies. I'd hear stories about them tearing up the town, getting into trouble." She shakes her head at the memory. "My son turned out bad."

"When I saw your mum was pregnant and I put two and two together. He never stepped up and helped her out," she says. "Not him."

"I watched you growing up, saw you playing over there at the park with your friends. Of course I kept my distance," she says sadly. "I didn't want to upset anyone."

"I used to slip some cash in an envelope when I had it, and put it through her mailbox. Your mother was living with you in her parents' house, with her brother."

I nod. "Yeah, my uncle. He died…"

"I know. Drug overdose," Doreen says when I look up in surprise. "Everyone in the East Village knew everyone's business then. Some of us still do," she chuckles. "Your mother met your stepfather, when you were around six or seven, maybe. He moved in and I guess he paid the bills. People around here seemed to like him fine."

Doreen looks at me, her gaze steady.

"Yeah, everybody loved him," I whisper. I've never felt so tired. The rescue medication must be working. "He was a great guy."

"Except he wasn't," Doreen says. "I know what went on in that house."

I flash back to the beatings, the blood on the stairs, the broken dishes and the pot roasts flung against the wall, my mother crying.

"And that's why you had to do it. You had to kill him."

He's drunk again. He gives her mother a vicious beating and she's lying on the floor, unconscious. He opens his zipper. He's going to take a piss on her, again. Lucy is on the stairs. He looks up at her, his eyes are bloodshot. He starts to pull out his belt. Is he going to strap her? She doesn't know. She's frozen on the stairs. The phone rings and he staggers to the living room to answer it. Lucy runs to her mother, cradles her head, kneeling in all the blood. So much blood. Her mother doesn't move.

It'll be okay, Lucy says. I'll fix it. It's going to be okay. She goes to the kitchen and gets a knife.

She steps over her mother's body and she goes into the living room. He's lying on the couch, with a beer in one hand and a cigarette in the other. His eyes are closed. She goes over and sticks the carving knife into the center of his chest, right into where she thinks his heart would be. She leans on it with all her weight as shoves it deep into his body. He opens his eyes in drunken surprise, stares at her and he keeps staring, even after she knows he's gone. She goes back to her mother, who hasn't moved because she is dead.

It's going to be okay, she whispers to her. I fixed it.

"After it happened, you were taken into care," Doreen says.

I barely even remember the police coming. There was a blur of people in the house. I rode in an ambulance and stayed in the hospital. Some woman from Child Protective Services took me to a group home and I became a Ward of the Crown.

"I heard you'd been adopted, and your name was changed. I understand why. They wanted to give you a fresh start." Doreen drinks her tea. "I never said anything about who your father was. I knew it was the best thing for you. Getting you out of the East Village." Her eyes search mine, pleading for understanding.

"Never thought you'd become a police officer though," she laughs. "Could have knocked me over with a feather when I first saw you in uniform. My son must be rolling in his grave."

FORTY

LATE THAT NIGHT I lie in bed, wide awake. I left Doreen's as soon as I was able to walk without feeling like I was going to pass out. The old woman had looked disappointed as I'd rushed off, but honestly, what did she expect? A loving reunion? For me to burst into tears and fling myself into her arms, the grandmother I never knew? It was all I could do to leave without punching a hole in the wall in rage and frustration.

By the time I was home I couldn't even remember leaving Doreen's house. My intense anxiety often interrupts my working memory. I lose short-term information, but I'm left with a feeling of absence, of loss, and of impending doom. I know something bad has happened, but I don't even want to think about what it might be. It always comes back later, washing over me in a cold flood of reality.

I poured myself a glass of wine then downed it in a few big gulps. Yes, it's contra-indicated to mix alcohol and Lorazepam, not to mention the SSRI I'm on, but at that point I didn't care. I sank into the couch, prepared to drink the rest of the bottle, and that's exactly what I'd done.

I awoke a few hours later, the pattern of the cushion imprinted into my cheek. I dragged myself into the kitchen, stood at the sink and drank two glasses of water, staring at my reflection in the window. My eyes were hollow and my hair was a mess. I looked like a ghost, haunting my own life.

The worst thing that could happen, the thing I'd always feared, was that someone would find out the truth about my past. Now, like some cosmic joke, I find out that not only did someone already know, and had known all along, but the past was even worse than I'd thought. My real father turned out to be a low-life biker criminal. I also found out I have a blood relative—a grandmother. I couldn't decide how I felt about that. This odd, intense old woman, with her sharp eyes and raspy voice, wasn't anyone's idea of a grandmother.

I'd gone up the stairs and lay on my bed, knowing I wouldn't sleep. The bedside clock said three fifteen. It was only a couple hours until my alarm would ring and I'd have to grab my gym clothes and go for my workout before my shift began at seven. I lay in the darkness, looking out the window at the sliver of the new moon.

At the time it happened, I was too young to understand the legal process as it played out. I remembered spending time in a hospital, which I now understood had been an involuntary psychiatric hold. They'd kept me in the pediatric ward and lots of doctors talked to me, for days and weeks on end. I learned much later that some of the doctors and the Crown Attorney had wanted to see me committed to a secure treatment program, because I'd willfully committed an act that caused a person's death. They were sticking to the letter of the law.

I was lucky I was only eleven years old when it happened. That's how I always thought of it, as something that *happened*. Never as something I did. If I'd been eight months older, I'd have been charged under Youth Criminal Justice Act and there could have been a trial, possibly even one in adult court. I could have even been sent to an adult federal prison, if I'd been found guilty. But since I was only eleven, they'd have sent me home to my mother, if I still had one.

But the law saw the mother was dead, at the hands of the

stepfather. The stepfather was dead, at the hands of the child. Since there was no other family, I became a Ward of the Crown, and after a stay in a closed custody facility I was placed into a group home, with a conditional discharge and probation.

There's no legal requirement for me to disclose the information, so I never have, not to anyone, particularly when I'd applied to the police force. I'd lied and they've never found out. But it haunts me every day, the fear that someone could find out about my past, and it will cost me the job. Not to mention my failure to disclose my anxiety and depression, and the medications I'm on. My juvenile record is now permanently sealed by the RCMP. Technically speaking, I don't even have a criminal record; whatever happened to me was over seventeen years ago and it was all under a different name. Nobody even remembers it now. Except Doreen.

Doreen. How long has she known who I am? How long has she been watching me, trying to find the right way to approach, and the least painful way to introduce herself? I don't think she wanted to hurt me, to shock me. She probably just needed to meet me, her granddaughter—if I'm to believe her story. And I do, every word of it. All the pieces fit and she knows things nobody else does. And the picture she showed me says it all.

Maybe I'm a bad seed. Knowing what I now do, about my biological father, is it any surprise I'd gotten into trouble? I'd seen McAlpine's record in the MCU the day of the Fair. If his blood is running through my veins it's no wonder I'd killed, and spent every day since lying about it, to the police force and to myself.

I feel my heart racing as the panic threatens to drown me and I wonder if I dare to take another Lorazepam.

FORTY ONE

I LOOK LIKE death warmed over in morning when I report for duty, and I feel worse. I didn't manage to drag myself to the gym. When my alarm went off I'd just dropped off into a heavy, dreamless sleep, the kind you fall into like a deep well, drowning in darkness. I couldn't even move out of bed, much less face the thought of leg day with cardio.

My anxiety is a beast constantly clawing, trying to tear its way out of the cage in my mind. Whenever I have a panic attack I'm exhausted for hours. And if I need to take rescue medication, like my Lorazepam, it's even worse. Sure, it calms me down in a few minutes, but it leaves me so tired I can't even think. I can barely function the next day. But anything is better than the blind animal panic that threatens to take over whenever I have an attack. Between my usual SSRI, the wine and the rescue Lorazepam I'd taken yesterday my central nervous system took a beating. Add to that the extra Ativan I maybe shouldn't have self-prescribed, it's no wonder I'm having a hard time functioning.

Agu sticks his head into the hallway when he sees me through the glass. "Good morning Detective Constable Gauthier," he says. "Can you please join us? I'd like you to tell us about what happened yesterday."

I'm confused. Yesterday? The incident at Pelham Woods is

hardly a homicide, except in the strictly technical sense. But I follow Agu into the briefing room and take a seat with DC Vogel and a Detective Sergeant named Evans.

"Thank you for joining us, Detective Constable Gauthier," Agu says, his voice deep and resonant. He still sounds just like Darth Vader. I smile and look around the room. Most of the team members are looking at their phones or notebooks, not at me. "Gauthier's the one who figured out it wasn't a suicide, and who led the search team to find the murder weapon," Agu adds. For a moment it actually feels like he is praising me, but I put it down to my exhaustion. "So, what can you tell us about yesterday? When you made some inquiries into Maurice Cobb's employment at Taiga," Agu prompts.

So much has happened since my visit to Taiga I've lost track and have to pause to collect my thoughts. "I went to Taiga to inquire about Cobb's employment, as you said. When I was there, I noticed some suspicious activity, involving some of their workers. I also discovered a connection from Taiga to Leon Flores, the journalist who was found in the canal." Everyone in the room is now watching me with interest.

"I made further inquiries and learned that Taiga had several illegal grow rooms, which I reported to Special Investigative Services. I believe they made their own investigation."

Vogel bursts out laughing. "Yeah, they raided the place."

"Who gave you that information, Gauthier?" I hesitate, unsure how to respond. I don't want to involve the workers, or get Peter Kozlowski involved, but I'm not sure I have a choice.

"I became suspicious while I was speaking with the son of Anna Kozlowski."

"The accidental death out on Concession 6?" DS Evans interrupts. "The old lady at the apple farm?"

"Yes. But I'm not sure it was an accident…" They all turn to look at me and I stop talking. I'm on thin ice here. I'm just a lowly DC, who's inserted herself into an investigation without being asked. That's the kind of thing that can get me into deep trouble with Bruni.

"Go on," Agu orders.

"I met Mrs. Kozlowski a while ago," I begin, trying to find a way to tell the story directly so it makes sense. "She's a friend of a woman I know." *My grandmother, as it turns out.* "Kozlowski had macular degeneration and was practically blind, but her mind was sharp. I believe someone put her into the apple storage unit. That she was killed."

"Why would someone do that?"

"I believe she saw something when she was at Pelham Woods."

"You just told us she was blind Gauthier."

"Not completely blind," I clarify. "She could see out of the sides of her eyes." I demonstrate, by shifting in my seat. "Like, if she was facing in this direction, she couldn't see what was in front of her, but she could see peripherally." They nod in understanding.

"What's Pelham Woods?"

"It's a long term care facility, up on the escarpment. Something is going on there. And it has to do with Maurice Cobb." I fill them in on my suspicions, unformed as they are, and my findings about the drugs I'd had tested and confronted Amit Joshi with. When I finish talking Agu is silent. He's rubbing his face and I'm pretty sure he regrets inviting me into the briefing.

"There's a connection between Cobb and Pelham Woods," I continue. "Which is owned by Amit Joshi, who owns Advik Therapeutics and who also owns shares in Taiga. Cobb worked security at both Pelham Woods and Taiga, and he worked for Advik until last year." Agu is still silent, his dark eyes staring into the middle distance as he considers what I've said.

"So you think someone from Taiga or Pelham killed Cobb? And this Mrs. Kozlowski?" Agu finally says. "Why?"

"There's more," I say, holding up my hand. I hear Vogel groan.

"Yesterday a patient at Pelham Woods killed one of the nurses. And I have witnessed two other violent outbursts over the last week."

"Okay…" Agu l says, waiting for me to connect the dots.

"There's something going on with the meds, but I don't know what it is. I took samples yesterday, of all the medications of patients who I'd seen have violent behavior. Those results shouldn't take too long, I hope."

"I'll see if we can put a rush on them," Agu says, glancing at DS Evans, who makes a note on the whiteboard.

"Also," I go on. "The nurse who was killed yesterday, Katrina Mueller, fits the description of the woman who left Cobb's truck at Nickel Beach the night he died."

"The knife that killed Cobb was wiped clean. No prints on it," Agu says.

"I wonder if you showed her photo to Andre Dumont, Sir," I suggest. "Who I believe is still being held, if he'd be able to identify her." Again Agu nods to Evans, who makes a note.

"So, you're saying she killed him? Then ditched the knife and truck? Why?"

"I don't know," I shrug. "It just seems very convenient that she's now dead too. And one of my sources saw Cooper with Katrina Mueller. She said it looked … suspicious."

Vogel laughs out loud. "With *Cooper*? I'm not surprised it looked suspicious." A ripple of laughter runs through the room.

"So Cobb worked for Pelham Woods, like this nurse who was murdered," Agu recaps. "And you also think there's something going on with the medication patients are being given?"

"Actually Cobb wasn't an employee of Pelham Woods. He worked for a private security firm on contract. Limestone Security." The rest of the detectives exchange looks. "Limestone has contracts with Pelham Woods and Taiga, among other places."

"Shit," Agu says, dropping his head into his hands. "Cooper. Is he connected to all this too?"

"About Cooper..." I begin then stop, unsure if I should continue. I can assume they've had the preliminary autopsy results by now, if anyone's cared to look. I had an early look in thanks to my visit to Maja yesterday. But since Cooper was universally disliked it's entirely possible no one cares.

Agu's head snaps up and he glares at me. "What about Cooper?" he demands.

I feel the entire room staring at me and I flush as the anxiety starts to flood through me. "Well..." I clear my throat. "Since he was murdered, it's safe to assume..."

The room erupts in confusion.

"What did you just say?" Agu demands, holding up his hand for silence. "*Murdered*?! Gauthier," he glares at me. "I'll get to exactly how you learned this information later, but for now tell us what you know."

"I... we... well... the initial autopsy results came in for Detective Constable Cooper... before he was sent to the forensic pathologist for confirmation..." I stammer, afraid of what Agu will say to me *later*. "He definitely died from Potassium Chloride poisoning. Two separate injections were administered into his abdomen, a few minutes before his death."

"Ouch," someone says.

"So the question is, who killed him, and why."

"The line forms to the left," Vogel says. "Nobody liked the guy." Agu glares at him. "It's true," Vogel says defiantly, crossing his arms across his chest.

"He was still a police officer."

"Yeah, well, he shouldn't have been." The rest of the officers in the room avert their eyes. They all agree with Vogel, but what's the point in saying anything now?

FORTY TWO

AFTER I LEAVE the briefing room I get into the patrol car and drive over the canal bridge, heading east along Killaley. I'm assigned to traffic duty and I take up my usual spot in the speed trap around the bend. It won't require me to do much more than sit and wait for the beep of the radar to wake me up. And at least I'll be assured of issuing a few tickets, so nobody will know what I'm really up to with my time. I have plans to drop in at Kozlowski's farm again later to speak to the workers. But as I cross the bridge I found myself turning right and heading south into the East Village. I don't want to, in fact it's the last thing I feel like doing, but I know I have to see Doreen.

I didn't handle it well when I'd learned Doreen was my grandmother. It was a shock and I still haven't fully processed the information. But Doreen is a frail old woman; she doesn't deserve to be abandoned the way she was when I ran out on her. Especially after one of her oldest friends has just died and the other has killed someone.

I knock on the door and wait while Doreen fumbles with her walker on the other side. I hear locks opening and bolts being slid across. Poor Doreen. Living here in the East Village, in her crumbling house that she tries to fortify with some cheap deadbolts and chain locks from the Dollar Store.

"Oh, Lucy," Doreen says when she sees me on the porch. Her eyes well up with tears. "I was afraid I'd never see you again."

"I want to say sorry for running out on you yesterday," I say. "It was a shock… I didn't know how to handle it."

"Please, come in," Doreen holds the door open and ushers me inside. "Would you like some tea?"

"I'm on duty," I say, shaking my head. "I can only stay a minute." I follow Doreen into the kitchen and sit down at the wooden table. She puts the kettle on then sits down across from me. "How are you feeling today?" I ask. "After what happened yesterday with Nadia…"

Doreen shrugs. "I'm fine," she says. "And I'm sure Nadia has forgotten all about it. The only blessing that terrible disease can provide." I don't bother to say that it was likely the disease that made her kill Katrina Mueller in the first place. "I never liked that nurse anyway," she says.

"Why not?"

Doreen looks at me, with that familiar sharp gaze. "She was up to something. Switching medications. Maybe selling them."

"Whoa, Doreen," I say. "That's quite an accusation. What have you seen?"

"First of all, she was a bitch," says Doreen. "Nasty, uncaring, unfeeling. If you called her for pain medication she took her sweet fucking time giving it. Second, there was something shifty going on. I saw her coming out of that little medication room and I could tell she was hiding something in her pocket. I was a nurse for years. I know about medication." I remember the graduation photo I'd seen. I can't argue with Doreen on that.

The kettle boils and Doreen pours the hot water over a tea bag she's tossed into a stained mug. I really should get going back to work but find myself delaying. There are things I need to know and I've never had anyone to ask.

"Doreen," I find myself asking, "What happened to your son?" I can't bring myself to refer to him as my father.

"My son," Doreen echoes. Her back is to me, but I can tell she's trying to figure out how to respond. "Do you really want to know?" I nod, but I'm not really sure.

"His name was Scott," she says, as she shuffles back to the table and sits down. "He was a nice boy, so sweet and helpful after his father died. Then suddenly he wasn't." Doreen sighs and rubs her eyes. "Or maybe it just felt like it was sudden. I don't honestly know. I was working shifts at the hospital at the time, working as much as I could. We needed the money."

"He started getting into trouble when he got to middle school. Shoplifting, vandalism, breaking and entering. I used to find money and stuff he'd stolen, hidden in his room. He'd tell me he found them somewhere or he had a job and got paid in cash. He was a big strong boy so it seemed believable. Or maybe I just didn't want to know."

It's a very familiar scenario, one I've seen first hand from my years spent in the East Village on countless home visits. I feel a complete sense of unreality, a disconnect, like when I have one of my panic attacks. Nothing seems real. I don't know these people; my father and grandmother are strangers I just happen to be related to.

"It got worse," Doreen continues. "He left high school, and moved in with a bunch of his friends into a rented old farmhouse up on Ridge Road. I don't know how he managed. He told me he was working," she shrugs. "I didn't have a car, so I could never go up there to check on him. He only came home for a visit when he needed money or a meal."

"For years I'd hear about him and his friends, tearing up the town. He got himself a big motorcycle and his friends would ride around these streets, revving their engines. I'm pretty sure he was in a motorcycle gang. The Outlaws were big around here then." She sips her tea and looks around the kitchen, as if she's never seen it before. Her eyes are haunted.

"I heard he was working the door in one of the strip clubs in

Niagara Falls, so that told me he was working for criminals. Scott had turned mean, and he could take care of himself and anyone else that needed taking care of. People used to tell me the stories about him getting into fights in the tavern, or their farmhouse getting raided in a drug bust. After a while they stopped telling me about him. Probably thought it was better I didn't know. And they were right."

"What happened to him?"

Doreen shrugs. "The last time I saw him I'd come home from work and found him and his two buddies sitting in the living room, a case of beer and a bottle of whiskey on the table. They were watching the hockey game. I made them a nice dinner and they ate it in front of the television. That was over twenty-five years ago."

"And you think he's dead?"

"I know he is," Doreen says. "I'm relieved, if I'm honest. I spent years being afraid, every time I saw a police car or heard a siren. I was always waiting for the knock on the door."

So that was my father. Thank God he hadn't stuck around. My stepfather was bad enough.

FORTY THREE

I'M SITTING IN my patrol car at the side of the road, pulled back slightly into the shrubs, when an unmarked car pulls up beside me. It's Detective Sergeant Agu and DC Vogel. Agu rolls down his window and hands me a coffee.

"Thank you," I accept it with surprise.

"How's it going?" Agu smirks. "Any excitement?"

I shrug. "I don't know if you remember your days on traffic, Sir," I reply. "It's thrilling. Thanks for asking."

"I just wanted to share some information with you," he says. "About the Cobb case." I'm stunned. The fact that they are including me in the investigation is nothing short of a miracle.

"Nurse Katrina Mueller was selling drugs," Vogel says. "I've got a friend in the Drugs squad. They know her well. She's a real piece of work."

"Okay…" I encourage him to continue. So Doreen is right.

"She used to take the patients' prescribed pain meds—controlled substances of course—and substitute something over the counter. At her last job she was suspected of using and they demanded a urine test to prove she was clean. She gave a fake urine sample so was able to convince them it was some transcription error in the medication logs. They caught up with her in the end and she got fired."

I'm taken aback. "So how did she manage to get another nursing job dispensing medication? How does that work?"

Agu puts up his hands. "She was an addict, supposedly. That's considered an illness, not a crime. She got treatment, had some letters of reference, they gave her a job."

"I think maybe it's not easy to find qualified staff out here," Vogel says. "They took a chance."

"Who'd write her a letter of reference?" I ask, shaking my head.

Vogel and Agu exchange a look. "We had a look into her employment file at Pelham Woods. There's a letter in there signed by Cooper, saying she'd been rehabilitated."

"*Cooper*?!" I laugh. "I didn't know he was authorized to write letters on behalf of the police force." So Doreen was right. There was something going on between nurse Mueller and Cooper.

Vogel laughs. "He wasn't! The Chief is losing his shit over it."

"He stole the letterhead, printed it all up. It looks legit," Agu adds.

"So Cooper was definitely in on her scam," I say. "I assume he got a kickback, a percentage from her sales?" They nod in agreement. "What was she selling? Stuff she stole from Pelham?"

Vogel nods. "Probably," he says. "She dealt Fentanyl, Oxycodone, other opiates."

"It looks like she was doing her old scam of substituting a placebo in the patients' blister packs, and removing their pain medication and selling it."

I let that sink in. "She was letting those poor people suffer, knowing they are non-verbal and can't even complain. That's beyond low."

"We're looking into both of her and Cooper's financials," says Vogel. "Not sure what we'll find. It was likely all cash. They wouldn't be dumb enough to deposit money in the bank where it could be traced. We've also got warrants to search their homes."

"We know who killed Mueller," Agu says. "That's never been in question. But it's clearly not the same person who killed Cooper. Nadia Efimov can't even leave the facility, so I doubt there's a connection."

They're right of course. There's no way Nadia could have had anything to do with Cooper's murder at the Fall Fair. I'm not even sure how she'd managed to kill Mueller either, given the type of knife that was used. She'd have had no access to it.

"Could it have been Mueller who killed Cooper? As a nurse she'd have known how to inject him. Maybe their partnership wasn't going so well? She wanted to keep the money she made herself and not share with him."

Agu nods. "Definitely a possibility worth considering."

"And the samples I took from Pelham Woods yesterday?" I ask. "Have they been analyzed yet?"

"Yes," Agu says. "They're a match to the pills found on Maurice Cobb's body."

"So that confirms a link to Advik Therapeutics." I'm excited. "Somehow those pills, the ones that Cobb helped develop, are being dispensed to patients at Pelham Woods. Why?"

"Maybe somehow the nurse was working with Cobb," Vogel says. "He gave her a supply that he'd stolen and she was switching it. They split the money."

"I don't know," I'm hesitant to argue with Vogel. "It doesn't feel right. But I did just find out that Cobb had paid off his truck, in cash, just before he died."

"How much money are we talking about?"

"Forty grand or so."

Vogel whistles. "Doesn't seem like there'd be that kind of profit in whatever they were stealing from Pelham Woods."

"So where'd Cobb get that kind of money?" Agu asks.

I shake my head. "I have no idea, Sir. It makes no sense. Anyway, these pills are anti-psychotics. They don't have any street value."

"So why'd Cobb have them?"

"Maybe Mueller wasn't selling Cobb's pills." I feel the idea taking shape in my mind as I speak. "Maybe she was just switching them out, in the patient prescriptions."

"Why would she do that?"

"Because someone at Pelham Woods asked her to?" Agu and Vogel listen carefully as I brainstorm. "Let's say you had a ready supply of drugs that were originally designed to substitute for Risperidone or Haloperidol—the typically prescribed pills used to manage dementia…"

"I see where you are going," Vogel interrupts. "Using those other pills would save on your company's bottom line. But how much money would be saved, really? A few thousand? Ten thousand?"

"Possibly even more, which would be fiscally prudent, which is very important when you are trying to take your company public, like Advik Therapeutics is. Their CEO told me that when I interviewed him."

"I'm not buying that. A few thousand in savings isn't worth the risk," Agu says, shaking his head. "But it definitely looks like two separate, but related crimes were taking place, with nurse Mueller involved in both. She stole pain medication and sold it with Cooper, and she substituted the other stuff for Pelham, for whatever reason."

"There's another possibility," I say after a moment. "Cobb's ex-wife told me that Advik had stopped the clinical trials on the medication he'd developed, because the drug wasn't safe. That it had caused aggression and violent outbursts." Vogel and Agu's eyes light up as they see where I'm heading.

"Maybe Advik is still testing the drug now, and using the patients at Pelham Woods to do it."

"Maybe that's what Anna Kozlowski saw," I say. "Mueller switching those meds."

Agu and Vogel shrug, but they look like they are considering the possibility. Still neither of them wants to think of Anna's death as anything but an accident.

"Anna Kozlowski visited almost every day, and she was there for hours," I continue. "Who knows what she might have seen? And, I'd bet Mueller just assumed she was totally blind and might not have been as careful in front of her as she should have been while she was doing the substitutions."

"You're saying you think Mueller killed Anna Kozlowski, to cover up whatever she had going on with Cooper," Vogel says.

"It's possible," Agu says. "But they're both dead now, so it'll be tough to prove."

FORTY FOUR

ONCE AGU AND Vogel drive off, I call in a ***ten-seven*** and go out of service for my lunch break. I've written three speeding tickets, so my productivity is good enough that nobody will notice if I take a little longer than usual.

I drive out along Lakeshore Road, past Lowbanks and the Lakeview cottages where Leon Flores had rented his cottage. A few hundred yards along there's a road, prominently posted Private, with stone columns on either side. There's no gate, but there may as well be; it's clear that no one is welcome unless they belong. The prominent houses I'd seen from the beach at Flores' cottage are tucked in among the trees, and from this access road you can barely see them. They're all oriented toward the lake with expansive views over the water, and their rear entrances are modest and discreet. Apart from one that is, and that's where I'm headed.

Amit Joshi's house is a huge square box covered in faux stone that sits proudly in the middle of its lot, surrounded by gravel gardens and formal squares of immaculate lawn. All of the trees around it have been felled, so it's impossible to miss. It's the polar opposite of the luxurious casual style of the neighbouring beach houses, nestled behind mature trees and tall beach grasses. So this is the *Mistake on the Lake.* It's even uglier up close. Joshi's neighbours must hate him.

The patterned concrete driveway is packed with expensive cars and I park at the bottom, blocking them in. I'm not planning on staying long. A bouncy castle has been set up on the back lawn next to the pool, there's music playing and I hear the sound of kids laughing and screaming. There are chairs with hundreds of balloons tied to them, tables heaped with presents, loot bags and a large slab cake. It looks like one of Joshi's kids is having a party. Rather than knock on the front door I walk around the side of house to see what's going on.

Part of me wants to mess with Joshi. Having a uniformed police officer show up in the middle of your party can really put a damper on things and I like the idea of having the smug Joshi on the defensive. As I walk up to the house I hear a scream, followed by another. It's definitely not human so I don't panic, but it's loud and unpleasant. I look around for what might be making it and see there are several peacocks strutting across the lawn, as well as two peahens. One of the males raises his head and lets out another screech then gives himself a shake and slowly raises his massive tail and displays his glorious feathers to the modest peahens, who don't appear to have the slightest interest.

"Fucking peacocks," I mutter. What else did I expect from Amit Joshi. I'm surprised it's possible to dislike him more than I already do.

As soon as I turn the corner I see there's a clown performing magic for about twenty little kids, who are sitting on the lawn in front of him. They are rolling around, laughing hysterically at his jokes, while the parents sit behind on chairs, drinking wine with pained smiles. Nobody over the age of ten likes a clown. Joshi is sitting with his mother and another couple. Today he's wearing what I assume is his casual wear: a traditional Indian men's kurta pyjama with a Nehru collar, in a bright blue patterned silk fabric.

The clown sees me, loses his concentration and drops one of the rings he's juggling, but then he rallies and I doubt the kids even notice. Joshi's face darkens when he sees me and he moves quickly to intercept me before I can spoil the party.

"What can I do for you today, Detective Gauthier?" He says once he's ushered me into the kitchen and closed the sliding door behind us. His voice is cold, but he's being careful to at least appear to cooperate. "I've already told you everything I can about Maurice Cobb, and as you can see it's a special occasion."

I smile and look around for a moment, knowing it will frustrate him. "I'm here on another matter."

"What is it?"

"It's about Leon Flores," I say, pulling out my notebook. There's no mistaking the flash of alarm in his eyes. He blinks and looks up at the ceiling, acting like he's considering the question.

"No. Never heard of him," he says after a moment, but it's an act. I can see Flores' name has struck home. "Why? Who is he?"

"That's what you said the last time I mentioned him. In your office," I say. "He's an investigative journalist. He was living in a cottage just down the beach from you." I point in the direction of Flores' place and see that Joshi looks very nervous. He is silent, which tells me he's afraid to give anything away. The normal response would be to ask why I'm interested, or why I'm asking him. I wait a moment longer to let him sweat.

"He was writing a piece on migrant workers in the region," I say. I watch his eyes shifting around the room. "And he worked for a time at Taiga."

"I wouldn't know about that," he said. "You'll have to speak to the Human Resources people…"

"He's dead, Mr. Joshi," I interrupt him. "He was found beaten and drowned in the Canal." Joshi goes pale and he abruptly walks over to the table filled with glasses, pitchers of juice and bottles of wine.

"May I offer you anything," he says. He's pouring himself a glass of lemonade and I can see his hands are shaking. I wait until he's composed himself and wonder what he's afraid of.

"It's interesting," I begin. "He had a clear view of your home from his place on the beach. And we found a pair of binoculars. We believe he was killed as a result of what he was investigating." Joshi sits down heavily, slumping into the chair.

"I don't know anything about it," he says. "I never met him." I nod, noting that he's changed his story slightly.

"You never met him or you never heard of him?" I prod, but he just shrugs and stares out the window.

"If there were any concerns about someone investigating Taiga," he begins. He's speaking hypothetically, I notice. "They would have been turned over to my security team for follow up. It's not something I'd manage. They'd have taken care of it."

"And that would be Limestone Security, if I remember correctly."

He nods. I wonder if Cooper's company had *taken care of* Flores, once they'd somehow learned he was a threat to Taiga. If they'd been tipped off that he was an investigative journalist working on a story that could expose them they might have been highly motivated to shut Flores up. Is that what happened to Cobb too? Did Limestone Security ensure he didn't tell anyone about the drug switching at Pelham Woods? Maybe they didn't feel that firing him was good enough and wanted a more permanent way to ensure his silence. Having Cobb conveniently kill himself took care of that problem.

"Well, thank you for clarifying that," I begin and can't miss the obvious relief that washes over Joshi as he thinks I'm leaving. But I'm not. I make a show of flipping the page of my notebook as I look for something.

"On another note," I begin and Joshi turns to me. I can see he looks worried. "Tests have determined conclusively that the pills found on Maurice Cobb's body are identical to those we retrieved from the medication cabinet at Pelham Woods."

He looks pale, but he tries to bluff. "And exactly what are you implying?" he asks.

"That the staff at Pelham Woods were dispensing medication made by Advik Therapeutics, which had failed its clinical trials and was not approved for use in treatment."

"You clearly have no understanding of how his works," he says, doubling down on his bluff. "These patients are our test subjects. We are conducting clinical trials now, at Pelham Woods."

"I'm quite sure you are testing medications on the patients," I say and he smiles in relief, thinking it's worked. "But not legally. I very much doubt you have signed consent from them or their families, but we can easily check that." Joshi goes pale. "And that's what Maurice Cobb discovered when he worked at Pelham Woods. Which is why you had him fired, to make sure he couldn't reveal what you are up to. Maybe you got your security company to deal with him as well." Joshi doesn't respond.

I keep my eye on him as I push harder. "What did it matter if the patients start going crazy? Who cares? They're demented anyway, right?"

"I didn't even know Maurice Cobb was working there," Joshi protests. "I'm an Executive, I don't get involved..."

"...in the day to day operations," I interrupt him, finishing his sentence. "Just like at Taiga, right? Another example of your fine executive oversight. Where the illegal grow rooms have now been raided I understand."

He sighs and straightens his posture. He's clearly been coached by his legal and public relations teams and knows what he shouldn't say and how he should spin the situation. "*Illegal*," he says. "That's really a question of semantics, isn't it? The licenses were days away from being granted. You make it sound like Taiga was running some black market grow-op. It's hardly the same thing."

I know he's right, but I don't care. Joshi is an entitled rich prick who thinks he should be allowed to get away with whatever he wants. I shrug. "Well Mr. Joshi," I say. "I don't get to make the rules. Neither do you."

He stares at me for a moment, calculating if he should take offense, but in the end he thinks better of it. "If there was any impropriety or, more likely an error of some kind made, this is the first I've heard of it," he says.

I shrug. "That's certainly possible," I say. "But we're re-checking all the medication, as well as the logs and prescriptions. We'll get to the bottom of it."

Joshi glances at his phone. Wondering about calling his lawyer, no doubt.

"Maurice Cobb got himself a job at Pelham Woods," I continue, pressing my advantage. "Because he suspected what you were doing and he found evidence that you were using the unapproved medication there. That's what the pills in his pocket were." Cobb had stolen the pills as evidence of what they were up to at Pelham Woods.

"You made a point of telling me that Cobb had been fired from Advik Therapeutics for *corporate espionage*, as you called it. But in fact he was a whistleblower, and you had him fired and blacklisted after he reported you. The product isn't safe and needs more research, but you were pushing it through because you wanted a big new product for when you take your company public. Maybe you even lied about the test data and the clinical trials you were conducting, who knows?" Joshi keeps his eye on the desk, refusing to meet my eye. "But it's certainly something we can check." I stare at him, waiting in silence until he finally raises his head and meets my eye. "And I wonder if that might have had something to do with how he died."

Joshi stares at me. He looks terrified. "I didn't kill him!" He sounds panicky and desperate. "And I have no idea how Cobb died." He covers his face with his hands, all his blustery confidence gone. "I never even knew he worked at Pelham until…"

"Until?"

"Until he started blackmailing me," Joshi says before he breaks down in tears.

I let him cry for a minute then slide a pile of paper napkins across the table to him. They have pink balloons and Happy Birthday printed on them. "When did this blackmail start Mr. Joshi?"

"Just after he started working at Pelham Woods," Joshi sniffles.

"About five months ago." That might explain the cash that Cobb suddenly had to pay off his truck.

"And how do you know it was Maurice Cobb?" Joshi shrugs, which I interpret that he doesn't know for sure. "Did he speak to you, or meet with you, to demand money?"

Joshi shakes his head. "I got notes, slipped under my car windscreen at first," he says. "Then some emails."

"And what did they say?" I ask. "Did you keep any of them?"

He shakes his head. "They said they knew what was going on, and they demanded money."

"How much?"

"They asked for thirty thousand dollars," he whispers. "The first time."

I'm impressed. "How many times?"

"Four, so far," he says.

"Mr. Joshi," I say. "You keep saying *they*, not Cobb. Who are *they*?"

"I thought it was just Cobb, at first," he says. "But after he... died, there was another note. So he must have been working with someone else. I thought maybe it was the nurse, Katrina Mueller." He starts to cry again.

"But now she's dead too," I say as Joshi nods, his head bobbing up and down. "And you've received another demand?"

"This morning," he whispers. "And the price went up. They want fifty thousand now."

"Any idea who it might be?" I ask.

"Who's left?" His shoulders shake with sobs and he buries his face in another napkin.

Poor Amit Joshi. Two people dead—Cobb and Mueller, and either of them could have been his blackmailer. Or maybe he thought they'd been, and only after he'd had them both killed did he realize his mistake. There's no way Joshi would have done it himself, he's not the type to get his hands bloody. He'd have someone look after it for him, someone like Cooper. There's no question he'd have done it, for a price. Is all of this connected to Amit Joshi and Advik Therapeutics? The deaths of Cobb, Mueller, Kozlowski and even Flores, are they all just part of a cover up by Limestone Security?

This time I really am leaving. I put my notebook away and slide more napkins over to Joshi. "Thank you for your time, Mr. Joshi. I'll let you get back to your party now." I glance back at him as I slide the glass doors closed behind me. He's already got his phone out. I wonder who's on speed dial—his lawyers to prepare a defense or his security team to *take care of things.*

FORTY FIVE

THERE'S NOTHING I can do about Joshi's being blackmailed, so I decide to tell Detective Agu about it and let them catch whoever it is. It's definitely out of my hands, even though it's likely linked to Maurice Cobb's death. I'll put money on it also being connected to the deaths of both Cooper and Mueller, but again—it's not my department. I'm just a lowly Detective Constable sitting in a patrol car. What I can still do, however, is make more inquiries into the death of Leon Flores. He didn't beat himself up and he didn't throw himself into the canal to drown.

After his death The Standard ran the series he'd written, and the last piece had been completed by the editorial team in his memory, using notes he'd filed online. His laptop still hasn't turned up and I doubt it ever will. The story he told of the life of the local migrant foreign workers was heartbreaking and makes me wonder whether Flores might have been beaten and killed by some racists who didn't like the fact that he was Latino. We don't get a lot of that sort of crime in the region, but times are changing and politics, especially south of the border, has been affecting everyone. People are polarized and there are a few who've become somehow empowered to share some of their ugly racist beliefs, without shame. Some might even have begun to act on them.

Or, maybe he'd learned something at Taiga that had gotten

him killed. Had he'd learned about the illegal grow? Is that enough reason to kill someone? Had Cooper's team taken care of shutting Flores up, permanently? I decide to look a little deeper into Limestone Security.

And, it's a stretch, but I wonder whether Flores' death is connected in some way with Anna Kozlowski's. There's no way she'd gone into the fruit storage on her own, so therefore someone put her in there, to make sure and shut her up. Her son knew Flores; he got him a job at Taiga. The only two possibilities that come to mind are: either she'd seen something at Pelham Woods, or she knew something about Taiga and whatever had led to the murder of Leon Flores. I decide I need to take another look around.

I drive out to Kozlowski's farm. When I arrive the place seems deserted. Probably the crew and workers are all out picking apples. There's no truck in the driveway, which tells me Peter Kozlowski is out. But why isn't anyone else around? It seems odd that at least a couple of farmhands aren't here or down in the orchard. When I strain my ears I don't hear a thing: no jitney engines, no radios blaring, no voices shouting. Weird, but at least I won't have to explain what I'm doing here.

I didn't get a chance to look over the crime scene when Anna's body was discovered, and it looks like there's no way I can do it now unless the controlled fruit storage is open and safely vented, but I have to satisfy my curiosity, to scratch that itch. I tell myself I'm not sneaking in, exactly, and anyway the barn door isn't locked so I slip inside.

The barn has to be about a hundred years old, from the look of the heavy hand hewn beams and posts that make up the structure. There are large gaps in some of the boards that form the walls, and beams of sunlight slice across the dim space, lighting the dust motes that dance in front of my eyes. It's so quiet I can hear my pulse pounding and my footsteps echo as I cross the wooden floor. Suddenly there's a series of loud clicks and some machinery starts to hum. I quickly fling myself behind some boxes and hide, my heart pounding in terror. After a moment I realize it's just the refrigeration unit's compressor kicking in.

I creep out from behind the boxes and survey the large fruit storage unit that spans the entire back half of the barn. The controlled atmosphere unit is the size of two semi trailers, and twice the height, so it just neatly tucks in under the roof joists. The end of the fruit storage has a set of double doors, just wide enough for a small truck to drive into, with a small plexiglass window next to them.

I peer inside but it's too dim to see anything, so I pull out my flashlight and shine it into the darkness. I can see large wooden crates full of apples, stacked on top of one another, reaching all the way to the top of the storage unit. The space is still only half full, since it's still early in the harvest. I hear the barn door slam shut. I freeze and instinctively go into a crouch, hoping I'm out of sight, praying whoever has come into the barn doesn't notice me, when I realize that anyone could have seen the patrol car parked outside, so my hiding is pointless. I stand up and try to pretend I have legitimate business in the barn, in case anyone asks. I'm definitely trespassing, and while I have a reasonable explanation for my being here, I'd really prefer to not having to use it. The compressors hum and I hear a loud fan kick in, but nothing else, so I relax and continue my search. It must have been the wind swinging the barn door closed.

I shine the flashlight across the hoses and tanks of nitrogen gas that help preserve the fruit. Not that I'm any kind of an expert, but everything looks normal to me. I turn my attention back to the storage unit and go over to the doors to try the handle. It's unlocked, which concerns me considering Anna Kozlowski has just died in there.

I head back over to the window again for a last look and I'm pressing my face up against the glass when I hear a noise directly behind me. As I spin to look someone hits me in the face and I go down. My head hits the wooden barn floor and I black out.

As I start to come to I feel myself being carried, being rolled along somehow, then I'm dumped onto a concrete floor and I hear a door slam. My eyes fly open and I know instantly where I am. Someone has put me inside the fruit storage unit.

I feel the panic surge through me as I realize I have to escape, or I'll end up like Anna Kozlowski. What had I read? There was less than 10% oxygen in here and the nitrogen gas would asphyxiate me in less than a minute. I hold my breath and rush to the door, pushing against it with all my strength. It's locked. My gun. I'll shoot the lock off and escape. But when I reach for my holster my weapon is gone.

I almost scream in frustration, but some reptilian part of my brain keeps my mouth tightly shut. I feel my lungs start to burn from holding my breath, but I don't dare breathe in the toxic gas. The seconds tick past as I rack my brain, desperately thinking of how I can escape. No one knows I'm in here, except the person who's trying to kill me. By the time anyone finds the patrol car I'll be dead.

I spin around and see the shadow of a hulking metal shape next to the wall. It's a forklift, probably what they use to stack the crates of apples. I run over to it and hop into the cab. The key's in the lock and I start the engine, throw it into reverse and gun it. The forklift rams against the double doors of the storage unit, knocking my breath out. The doors hold. I instinctively inhale and then try to stop myself. My lungs are bursting and I can't hold my breath any longer. I throw the engine into drive and pull forward as far as I can. I put it into reverse again and plough into the doors as fast as the engine will let me go. They break open and the forklift crashes through, just as I fall out of the cab onto the floor of the barn. I crawl as far away as I can from the storage unit and the wreckage of the forklift, gasping for air.

I manage to pull out my radio. ***999 Officer Needs Assistance 999 Kozlowski Farm Concession 6.*** Then I pass out.

FORTY SIX

WHEN I COME to I'm lying on a stretcher outside the barn with an oxygen mask on my face. The ambulance attendant smiles at me and pats my shoulder. It has started to rain and I'm thankful for the drops on my face. It means I'm alive.

"You'll be okay," she says. "You're safe."

I close my eyes and let myself drift off for a second. I try to remember what happened, starting with where I am. Why am I lying down? What is a paramedic doing there? Slowly it comes back to me: being hit, locked in the storage unit, the forklift. I open my eyes and look around.

There's an ambulance parked on the driveway, and two patrol cars who've come in response to my 999 call. Officers are going in and out of the barn, talking into their radios. They are in rain gear so it's difficult to tell them apart. Peter Kozlowski stands on the porch with two of his workers, sheltering under the roof. He's shaking his head and talking with Constable Decker and DS Quinn Agu. *Agu is here?* Damn it. I fall back and close my eyes. *Great. Just perfect.* This does not reflect well on me.

Things get worse when a few minutes later I notice him speaking with the paramedic. After she gives him the okay he comes over.

"Feel well enough to talk?" he asks.

"Yes, Sir."

"What the hell happened in there?" From the expression on his face I know the damage to the storage unit is serious.

"I came out to speak with Mr. Kozlowski," I lie. Or half-lie. I'm not entirely sure why I came out to the farm; it was a hunch. "I was looking for him in the barn when someone hit me. I didn't see who it was. I came to inside the storage unit… and I escaped. I don't really remember…"

"Decker says it looks like you were knocked out and they got you into the storage unit on a wheelbarrow. We found one inside. They locked you in and left. We're dusting for prints now. Maybe whoever did it was careless." He doesn't sound hopeful.

"Decker?" I'm confused. What does he have to do with it?

"He found you Gauthier," Agu says. "He was first on the scene." He gives me a stern look. "We found your weapon in the barn. I assume it was taken from you while you were unconscious?"

I nod. "I tried to use it to shoot out the lock, but it was gone. That's why I had to use the forklift."

"Clever thinking," he says. "If you hadn't, you'd be dead." He hands me back my weapon and I quickly holster it.

"Thank you, Sir." I'm grateful. He didn't have to do that. I could easily have been disciplined for losing my gun, if he'd chosen to report me.

Agu shrugs. "You weren't at fault," he says. "Nothing more to it." He looks back at the barn and surveys the scene before turning back to me. "You're going to have enough paperwork to deal with after this mess, without mentioning losing your weapon." That's true, I know. I dread the reports and interviews I'll be facing over the next while.

"What were you going to speak with Kozlowski about?" Agu asks. I'm careful. No one authorized me to investigate any further. Agu and Vogel had been kind enough to keep me up to date with the progress on the case, but my job is only to support the Detectives, not to take any initiative.

I don't see how I can lie and get away with it, so I admit the truth. "I was following up on something I learned earlier, about the Maurice Cobb case."

Agu looks angry. "That's not your role, Gauthier," he says. "You should have reported anything you learned to me or Vogel."

"Sorry, Sir." I'm chastened and angry with myself. If Agu sees me as a pain in the ass, instead of as a good investigator, it's unlikely I'll get the assignment I want in the Homicide Unit.

"What did you find out?" he asks, his tone softer. He probably feels sorry for me, lying on a stretcher like some pitiful amateur.

"I was speaking with Amit Joshi earlier," I begin then stop myself when I catch sight of Agu's expression. "Sorry, Sir," I mumble.

Agu shakes his head in disbelief. "Go on, Gauthier," he says. Another strike against me. He didn't authorize me to do that either.

"He told me he's being blackmailed," I say. "Over the pills found on Cobb's body. Advik Therapeutics is using those same drugs, without approval, at Pelham Woods. The patients there are being used as guinea pigs in the clinical trials."

Agu looks exasperated. "Does he know who's blackmailing him?"

I shake my head. "He says he thought it was Cobb. Then nurse Mueller."

"Who are now both dead." Agu looks at me, considering what I've just told him. "Do you think he had anything to do with that?"

"He's got a lot at stake, Sir."

"Who do you think wanted to kill you?" Agu asks. My blood runs cold. I hadn't thought of it. But it wasn't random. Someone followed me out to the farm, crept up behind me, knocked me out, and put me in the storage unit to die. Why? Was I getting too close to something? I hesitate, wondering if I should mention Limestone Security. So many police officers work for them, possibly even Agu and Vogel for all I know. I don't need another reason for them to think of me as not one of the team.

"I have no idea, Sir." This time I'm not lying. "You know as much as I do now."

"Good," he says. "Let's keep it that way. Make sure you don't go off on your own again. In the Homicide Unit we always work with a partner. Remember that."

I don't know what to say.

Agu is staring at the barn, lost in thought. "When did Joshi say this new blackmail demand arrived?"

"He said it was this morning."

"Leave this with me Gauthier," he says as he pulls out his phone. "We'll have to move fast." Then he's gone. They'll have to work with Joshi to set up a money drop, like the previous ones. But with any luck this time we'll be able to catch Joshi's blackmailer. And that will also give us Cobb's killer.

The paramedic returns once Agu has rejoined the investigating officers. "We're going to bring you into the hospital, just to check you out thoroughly. Is there anyone we can call for you? Family?" I feel the tears spring to my eyes. Who is there in my life? Who can I count on to be there for me? The only person is Maja. Or was Maja.

"Yes, please," I say. The paramedic punches in Maja's number and hands me the phone. It rings once then goes straight to voicemail. My heart breaks when I understand Maja has declined the call.

"Sorry," she says, averting her eyes. "Is there anyone else?"

FORTY SEVEN

I LIE ON a hospital bed in Emergency. Since I'm a police officer, I've been moved quickly through triage and into a room and the curtain is pulled across for privacy. I'm hooked up to a monitor that's measuring my blood pressure, heart rate and oxygen levels, and from what I can tell by watching the yellow and green lines that run across the screen, I'm absolutely fine.

I've already had a CT scan to make sure there's no head injury, and the Emergency doctor on duty doesn't think I have a concussion or any residual damage to my lungs and respiratory system from the nitrogen gas. I was lucky because the storage container had been partially vented by whoever had tried to kill me. They would have had to prop the door open in order to wheel me inside, so the nitrogen levels weren't as high as they should have been. That gave me a bit of extra time to escape. I'm now waiting until someone sees fit to discharge me.

I've tried sleeping, but that didn't work. I can barely sleep at home so why would I be able to do it here, with all the noise and activity. No cell phones work inside the area, thanks to the building structure and electromagnetic interference, so I can't look at social media. There aren't any magazines or books to read. I'm bored. I just want to go home, or get back to work, or do anything rather than be here.

As I lie there fidgeting, I hear voices rising outside. The sounds of people laughing and delighted squeals and outbursts as the nurses on duty rush to greet someone. A local celebrity must be making a visit through the hospital. Maybe it's a photo op with some politician, but there's no election happening currently. Or a sports star, they always get good publicity at hospitals.

It's so good to see you! It's been too long! You look great! Still going strong, eh?

And underneath it all is a familiar croaking raspy voice. The curtain is pulled aside and Doreen rolls her walker in.

Several nurses come in with her, helping her get settled, offering her a coffee, and giving her hugs. None of them even glance at me, much less offer me a coffee.

"Hi Lucy," Doreen growls. "Still alive?"

I nod. "Barely. You?"

"It appears I am," Doreen laughs. "But when I look in the mirror I'm not sure."

She reaches over and pats my arm then quickly withdraws her hand and smooths out the sheet covering me. Doreen isn't comfortable with sentiment or human contact either, that's clear. Maybe it's inherited. "Thank you for calling," she says.

When Maja didn't pick up, the only other person I could think of to call was Doreen. And that fact gave me a lot to reflect on as I lay in the hospital bed. Just over a week ago, I'd never met this odd, crazy cat lady person. An old woman who most people would think is homeless, definitely marginal. Who talks to herself and smells a bit funny. Who turned out to be my grandmother.

Now that Doreen is here I see a whole new side to her. All these people, they love her. It's clear from the expressions on the nurses' faces. Those who knew her couldn't give her a hug fast enough, and the young ones who'd started working long after Doreen had retired, stood back in admiration and curiosity. Had they heard stories?

Tales of Doreen's exploits? The woman is a legend, that much is obvious. This old weird smelling relic with crazy hair is a hero.

"Wow," I say. "You're like a rock star."

"They're just bored," she says, waving it off. "Anything to break up the monotony of looking after sick people." She gives me an appraising look. "Or those pretending to be sick so they can get some time off work."

I laugh. "That's me all right. Always skiving off."

"So what happened to you?" Doreen asks. Her sharp eyes scan the monitors and my appendages. "Did you get shot?"

"No. I was at Anna's farm, investigating. Someone knocked me out and shut me into the fruit storage." Doreen's eyes widen in shock.

"Christ on a bike," she says. "How'd you get out?" I tell her the story as briefly as I can, as Doreen shakes her head. "You could've died, just like Anna."

"I got lucky," I say.

"You sure did," a male voice says. Doreen and I look up and see it's Decker. He looks tired and irritated. "What the hell were you playing at, Gauthier?"

I hold up my hand to forestall any more questions. "I'm fine," I say. "It's all good." Decker and Doreen both snort.

The Emergency doctor squeezes into the narrow space at the end of my bed. "I'm discharging you," she says. "There's no reason to keep you any longer. You're stable and your vitals are good. But take it easy for the next few days, okay? If you find you are coughing excessively, have shortness of breath or feel dizzy, come back in."

"Perfect timing," says Decker. "I'll give you a lift home. Since your patrol car is now back at the station." He leaves to bring his car up to the entrance.

I get up as quickly as I'm able and within minutes Doreen and I are sitting in the back of Decker's patrol car, being driven to my place. My townhouse is literally two blocks away from the hospital and I could have walked, but I doubt Doreen could. And as it appears Doreen is now my caretaker so I can't very well leave her behind.

"It's been a while since I've been in the back of a police cruiser," Doreen rasps before bursting into laughter that sounds like a broken garbage disposal.

I catch Decker's smirk in the rearview mirror.

"What did you see Gauthier?" he asks.

"Nothing," I mumble. I'm embarrassed. "Not my finest moment."

"Seriously," he says. "You must have seen something. Heard something?" My eyes meet his and he looks away.

"I didn't see anyone." I'm irritated by his questions. What business is it of his? I don't need him making me feel like a rookie, like some screw up.

Thankfully Decker doesn't say anything else until he pulls up to my house.

"Here we are," he says. "Home Sweet Home." I don't remember telling him my address. I guess he'd looked it up at the station.

He helps us out of the car and into the front door then drives off, leaving me trailing behind Doreen and her walker.

"Why don't you lie down on the couch," Doreen says once we're inside. "And I'll make you some tea."

"I don't want any fucking tea," I groan. "There's wine in the fridge. I need a big glass." I look down at my dirty uniform and start toward the stairs. "I'm going to change. Be right back."

When I come back into the living room, I find Doreen has poured me a big glass of white wine, and laid out a few things to eat: some cheese and crackers, and a few olives and slices of salami.

I'm surprised. "You seem to know your way around," I say, taking a big gulp of wine. "It's like you've been here before."

Doreen quickly shakes her head. "Every kitchen is pretty much the same," she says. "Food's in the fridge, dishes in the cupboard."

"It's amazing I even have any groceries in my fridge," I say.

"I actually managed to get myself to the market on my day off this week."

"Well…" Doreen begins carefully. "I wouldn't say three bottles of wine, a few cheeses and cold cuts really counts as groceries."

I shrug. "It does around here."

"Are you okay to drink?" She asks, as I take another big swallow of wine.

"It's medicinal," I joke. Doreen doesn't laugh.

She looks around the living room, taking in the spartan furnishings, and the lack of personal items. There are no photos or artwork on the walls. Only the sofa and two matching chairs, as well as the coffee table, furnish the room. And the television mounted on the wall, of course. "When did you move in?" She asks.

"Almost four years ago." Doreen's eyes widen. "I don't spend a lot of time at home," I explain, which is a lie, but I have no other explanation for why I haven't really settled in and made the place my own.

Doreen nods. My phone flashes on and she sees the screen saver before I pick it up. It's a photo of me with Maja.

"Hi," I say. "Thanks for calling back." Doreen can only hear half of the conversation, but she probably feels the awkward tension between us.

"I didn't leave a message… It's okay… I know you're busy… I was just thinking of you… No, nothing's wrong… I understand… Bye." Doreen sneaks a glance at me and I hope she doesn't see the pain on my face.

"Friend of yours?"

"I thought so," I whisper. Doreen can tell my tongue is getting thick from the wine. "We were close."

"And you didn't want to tell her what happened to you today?"

"She was my first call," I admit. "But she's got someone else now."

Doreen nods in understanding. "What's her name?"

"Maja." My eyes flicker to Doreen, expecting judgement, but see nothing but pity.

"Love is love," she says, stroking my knee. "And it hurts."

I lean back into the cushions and close my eyes. God I'm so tired. And my head hurts.

"I don't want to be nosy," Doreen says. "But, the prescription you're on? Is it safe to drink alcohol with it?"

"Probably not." I shake my head and study Doreen through my half-closed eyes. She's watching me, her expression sad. "Nothing is ever safe," I say. "The pills help me keep the beast in its cage."

Doreen can see my eyes start to close and she reaches for the comforter that lay across the back of the couch. She's tucking it in around my legs when I wake back up. "I'm going to get you an Über," I say picking up my phone. "To get you home safely. Is that okay?"

Doreen nods as my fingers fly over the phone, placing the order for the car. She waits by the front door for it to arrive, watching me as I drift off to sleep.

FORTY EIGHT

DOREEN DOESN'T LIKE seeing Lucy pounding back the wine that way. It looks all too familiar. The girl is troubled, and it's no wonder why, when you look at everything she's been through. And where she's come from. And who her birth parents were. But the drinking, and whatever pills she's on, that has to stop. Not that Doreen ever had any luck making anyone stop doing what they wanted to do, even if it wasn't good for them. But it doesn't mean she isn't going to try.

The look Lucy had given her when Doreen asked about her drinking so much wine—it was pure Scott. The apple does not fall far from the tree.

She looks at Old Cat, fast asleep in the armchair by the electric fireplace. Scott used to sit in that same armchair, exactly where his father used to sit before he died. Drinking a beer and watching TV while I made him dinner. Drinking whisky and watching the game while I stayed in the kitchen. Drinking and smoking and swearing in her house until she finally had to take things into her own hands.

Doreen goes into the kitchen and fills the kettle and puts it on to boil. After a second she turns off the gas and decides she wants a stiff drink instead. She pours the whisky into a tall glass, tops it off with Coke and stands by the back door, looking at the blackbirds on the wire. They sit in a sad little row, hunched over in the rain.

Don't they know enough to shelter in a tree somewhere? Doreen guesses they just don't know what's good for them, like most people.

The garden is slowly going to sleep for the winter. Even the weeds have stopped growing and their leaves are turning yellow and brown. The roses along the fence are still throwing off a few late blooms, but the rambler rose bush on the garage is just a mass of thorny canes, twisting and snarled and impossible to prune. It looks like something out of a dark dream, a nightmare. That's where they're buried. In the winter, when the leaves are gone and the only things visible are the thorny canes crawling out of the earth like snakes; it's easy for her to imagine the dark hearts they grew from.

It was easy to kill them, she remembers, and fast. None of them ever suspected a thing, never even thought to look her way, as she made the food that put them to sleep. When the kitchen was full of their snores she'd smothered them with a pillow, one by one, until the house was silent.

The rest of it had taken a long time: the digging, dragging the three of them outside and across the grass and shoving them into the holes in the ground. Even though she was younger then, they were all heavy men. Doreen remembers how deep she'd dug, to make sure they'd stay buried. She'd topped the trench off with heaps of manure she'd got from one of the farmers in Wainfleet and planted the rambler roses. People thought she loved them since she grew so many. But Doreen hates roses. They're prickly and vicious, like her son. Maybe like her too.

She'd hidden their motorcycles in the garage for a long time. Didn't know what to do with them, not at first. She couldn't ride them and they were too big for her to handle anyway. But over time she'd managed it. She left one at the far end of the alley, with the keys in it. It was gone in a night. She sold Scott's, forging his signature on the ownership papers and signing it over to a guy she'd found in the autotrader magazine at the library. She'd told him her son had to go away for a long time. He assumed she'd meant jail, which made perfect sense if he knew her son.

After Scott disappeared, there were a few big guys knocking on the door, asking after him. He owed them money, and she'd told them over and over she didn't know where he was. One guy wouldn't take no for an answer and he kept coming back. When he'd threatened her she told him there was a bike in the garage and he could take it, sell it for what Scott owed them if he wanted. She didn't have any money; he could see that by looking around her place. So he did and that's the last Doreen saw of him or the bikes.

She hadn't killed anyone since. Not until the guy tried to rob her in the bus shelter. There'd been no need to and it had never come up. Which was surprising, when she thought about it, considering how things have always been in the East Village. The cops have never been any good at keeping order around here—not back when her son used to run wild, and things have only gotten worse since. That guy trying to rob her was a helpful reminder of how good it is to take things into your own hands. She'll never forget that again.

FORTY NINE

I SLINK INTO the briefing room, hoping nobody notices me and sit at the back, behind Vogel. He's tall enough, and more than wide enough, for me to hide behind. A large white board has been set up, with crime scene photos and the names of the victims printed on it. Detective Constable Cooper. Katrina Mueller. Anna Kozlowski. Leon Flores. All of them possibly related to the first murder—the death of Maurice Cobb.

"How are you feeling today, Gauthier?" Agu asks. He's seen me sneaking in. I bet he never misses a thing. "Better?"

"Good enough Sir," I say, but it's a lie. I feel like hell; hungover, exhausted and I've developed a cough, just like the Emergency doctor had predicted. But I'm not going back to the hospital; I'd decided that as soon as she made the suggestion.

"I'd just updated the team about what happened to you at Kozlowski's farm yesterday," Agu says. "We haven't found any prints in the barn or on the wheelbarrow, apart from yours and Constable Decker's."

"Decker's?" I'm confused.

"He found you, Gauthier. He was first on the scene," Vogel reminds me. "It makes perfect sense." I manage a weak smile. I'm getting paranoid.

"I've also given the team an update on your conversation with

Amit Joshi yesterday," Agu says. "The one you had before you went
out to the Kozlowski farm." I nod. "We're checking the bank records
of Mueller and Cooper, but so far nothing."

"I don't imagine there'll be a paper trail," I say. "Joshi would
have given them cash."

"And, unfortunately, we got nowhere with the Fraud team. They
worked with Joshi yesterday to set up a drop, but the blackmailer
never showed up."

"I guess the word got out," I say. "Or somehow Joshi gave it
away when the blackmailer called him?" The other possibility is that
someone on the inside tipped the blackmailer off, but I don't say
that aloud. Nobody likes a spoilsport.

Agu shrugs. "Either way, it was a dead end."

"Have you found any connection to the murder of Anna
Kozlowski?" I ask. "Any evidence at the farm?"

"We still don't know it was a murder," Vogel says.

"I do," I say, glaring at him. "I'm certain of it." The memory
of what happened to me at the farm was still raw. He turns away,
avoiding my eye. I'm not sure what kind of proof Vogel needs.
Another body?

"We've got no progress on the death of Constable Cooper," Agu
continues. "We do know he was killed by two injections of Potassium Chloride, and that it occurred at the Fall Fair, at some point
before he died in front of the MCU."

"Crime Stoppers has put out a call to the public asking for
information or anyone who might have seen Cooper at the Fair in
the time before his death. So far, nothing." I don't want to speak
up. I know that what I'd seen Rose do is very incriminating, but it
isn't conclusive. And I don't want to drag her through the court of
public opinion again. But I have a job to do.

"Sir," I interrupt Agu.

"Yes, Gauthier?"

"I may have witnessed something material at the Fall Fair," I say. "Just before DC Cooper died."

"Please, tell us."

"I was on foot patrol that day," I say. "And I happened to be standing near the Womyn Collective Farm booth. I'd just spoken with them, saying hello and having a chat, and was moving on when I saw Cooper approach the booth." Agu nods for me to continue. "Cooper and Rose Efimov appeared to have an argument. It was very brief. Then Cooper left."

"An argument? With Efimov?" Vogel repeats, sounding excited. "Did you hear what was said? Did it become physical?" Vogel had been one of the investigating officers at the Thorny Rose deaths. It isn't hard to see he still thinks Rose is guilty.

"No," I say. "I couldn't hear anything. I did see Cooper lean in across the counter, getting into Rose's face. He was very aggressive." The other officers nod. They knew Cooper and how aggressive he could be. "She shoved him back, to get him away."

"Did he fall or stumble?"

I shake my head. "Not at all. He just stepped back out of her face. He said something—I'd guess it was along the lines of *Fuck Off Bitch*. Then he left."

"Okay," Agu says. "Let's go talk to her. Gauthier, you're coming along."

Agu and Vogel meet me at the Thorny Rose. I don't like having to leave the patrol car in the restaurant parking lot. I know it doesn't leave a good impression with any of Rose's patrons if they see a police car there, but it can't be helped.

I'm there a few minutes before they arrive, so I walk around the restaurant gardens while I wait. Even now, in late September, everything is still beautiful and lush—immaculately cared for and groomed to perfection, exactly like I remember it.

When Maja and I had celebrated our anniversary here last year, we'd taken our bottle of wine out to the garden and sat among the roses, drinking and enjoying the hum of the bees and the sun on our faces. It was glorious, the best day of my life.

I hear the crunch of gravel in the driveway as a car pulls in and I walk back to meet Agu and Vogel. Together we walk into the restaurant and ask to speak to Rose Efimov. She emerges from the kitchen, and smiles when she recognizes me.

"Hi again," she says. "Good to see you Lucy." She glances at Agu and Vogel. "But I'm guessing this isn't going to be a visit I'll enjoy." Rose had been through the mill over the disappearance of her husband, and the subsequent scandal that followed it had rocked the entire area. She's right to be suspicious of the police.

"Let's go into the dining room," she suggests. "We can talk privately in there."

We decline her offer of coffee and sit down. Agu and Vogel get right into it, while I sit back. I don't really want to be here, but what I'd seen at the Fall Fair was incriminating, and I can't deny that Rose might have had motive to want Cooper dead, for revenge, if nothing else. Cooper's had been one of the loudest voices attacking her.

"We understand that you and DC Cooper had an argument at the Fall Fair," Agu says. "It became physical. He died just a few minutes later. Did you kill him Ms. Efimov?"

"No," Rose says. "That's ridiculous. Of course I didn't!" She turns to me. "You were there, tell them they're wrong."

"I'm sorry Rose," I say. "I wasn't close enough to hear anything. But I did see you and Cooper in a dispute. I saw you shove him."

Rose stares at me, her mouth agape. "I did shove him! He was a bastard and he came up to me, threatening me with the same bullshit you people were all over me for last year." She rakes her hands through her hair. "I pushed him away, told him to go fuck himself."

"And then what happened?"

"I watched him walk back to that big police van that was parked at the Fair."

"You were able to see him go to the Mobile Crime Unit?"

Rose nods. "Yes, I saw him go up the stairs and inside."

Agu and Vogel exchange a look. "You're sure?" Vogel asks. "The Fair was pretty well attended I understand. Lots of people. You didn't lose sight of him in the crowd?"

"No way," Rose insists. "I kept my eye on that creep all the way until he was out of sight, inside that big black van."

"What she says doesn't tally with what we know of how Cooper died," Vogel says once we're back at the station. "We know he died enroute to the MCU."

"How do we know this?" Agu asks.

"Constable Decker witnessed it," I say. "I was there too, but I arrived after the ambulance was already on the scene. He was lying outside the MCU, on the ground."

Vogel nods. "Decker says Cooper had arrived at the MCU, already sweating and staggering. That he'd fallen and died out front, before even setting foot inside. Something doesn't add up."

"Could Rose Efimov even have seen the MCU from the Womyn booth?" Agu asks.

"Good point, Sir," I say. "I'm not sure there was even a clear line of sight, let alone with a throng of people in the grounds, potentially obscuring her view. And the Fair is over so we can't confirm her statement."

"So the only witness we have contradicting Decker is Rose Efimov?" Vogel says. "She's not exactly reliable, is she?"

"What do you mean *she's not reliable*?" I object. "Why would you say that?"

Vogel looks embarrassed. "Well," he says. "You know what went on this past summer. Her husband going missing, those people dying... Constable Wright." He throws up his hands.

"And none of that had anything to do with her," I snap. "It was proven." Vogel shrugs. I get it. Don't bother him with the facts when he's already made up his mind. "Maybe Constable Decker got it wrong," I say, but Vogel ignores me and turns away to take a call on his cell phone.

"We've got the results back on the knife that killed Katrina Mueller," he says a moment later.

"It was tested for fingerprints?"

Vogel nods. "And Nadia Efimov's aren't on it."

FIFTY

MY JAW DROPS. "That's impossible. I saw her holding it on her lap. The nurse couldn't have been dead for more than a few minutes at that point." DC Evans is noting the information on the white board.

Vogel shrugs. "The knife was wiped clean. No prints on the handle."

"But there's no way Nadia Efimov could have done that," I say. "She doesn't have the cognitive ability to understand she should wipe the knife."

"Are you sure?" Agu asks, his eyebrow raised. "She had the *capacity* to somehow get hold of the knife in the first place, hide it in her room, and slash the nurse's throat. Why wouldn't she know to wipe it?"

"And then just sit on her bed, with it on her lap?" I remember seeing Nadia on the bed, in her diaper, her thin legs bare and her socks bloody. It was like one of my nightmares, but the pool of blood spreading slowly across the floor proved it to be real.

"Makes no sense to me either," Vogel says. "But she's got dementia, right? Who knows what happens to the brain."

I can't argue that. I'd seen my grandfather die over a period of years, saw how his mind became full of holes and unravelled like a moth-eaten sweater. "Those pills they were on," I say, thinking aloud.

"They're experimental, still in development. I was told the reason they were pulled from the study was because of the side effects."

"And what are they?"

"Aggression. Violent outbursts," I say. "I saw one patient pull a knife on another one last week. And one guy rammed his own head into a glass door."

Agu whistles. "Some side effects."

I nod. "The initial studies showed the drug seemed to reverse or slow brain degradation and test patients were able to reason and plan again."

"So the drug makes them both violent and capable of planning something, like a stabbing?" Agu says. "No wonder Advik stopped the trials."

Vogel looks skeptical. "But could it cause enough improvement to allow her to plan something like this? And enough reasoning ability to remember to wipe the knife?" he says. "But then to just sit down as if it never happened?" Everyone looks skeptical. It really doesn't seem possible that she'd done it.

"What if it wasn't Nadia Efimov at all?" I say, holding up my hand against their objections. "I know I'm the one who first thought she was guilty. I saw her with the bloody knife, practically standing over the body. It seemed obvious at the time. But what if it was someone else, someone who knew she'd be blamed for it?"

"Someone else who wanted the nurse dead," agrees Agu. "There's probably a long list of those people, given what we now know about Katrina Mueller."

"Who else was there at the time, Gauthier?" He nods to DC Evans to note anything new or relevant on the white board.

I think back to the day I was called into Pelham Woods, running through it in my mind, from our arrival at the facility. "We responded to the 911 call," I begin. "When I arrived at the scene, Constable Decker was already there. We came in through the lobby together and the team from Womyn was there, delivering flowers."

"Anyone of interest?"

"Cobb's ex-wife, Geraldine Bennett was there," I say, remembering her arranging the large bouquet in the front lobby. She was adding branches of crab apples and had her sharp pruning shears in her hand, cutting them to the right length. "And Sophie Tuinstra, the owner of Womyn." Evans dutifully makes note of both Bennett and Tuinstra.

"I'm sure we can discount them both," Agu says, nodding to Evans, who puts a line through both their names. "Go on."

"Decker and I came up in the elevator together. When the door opened there was Dr. Chowdhury and two care workers at the nursing station. I don't know their names but they are Polish, I think. One of them was hysterical." DS Evans struggles with the spelling of Chowdhury.

"The patient lounge was full of residents," I recall. "There were some visitors too… no idea who any of them are." I flash on seeing Doreen, waving at me from across the lounge. "Some of the residents kept coming into Nadia Efimov's room when we were trying to secure the scene."

"I guess they were looking for some excitement," Vogel jokes.

I smile in agreement. "Once the crime scene team arrived I spoke with Dr. Chowdhury at the nursing station. Amit Joshi was there, threatening to get their lawyers."

"So Joshi was there that day?" Agu says glancing at the white board to make sure Evans gets his name. "He'd have had motive to kill the nurse, if he thought she was blackmailing him."

"He did accuse her, when he first told me about the blackmail. And I could definitely see him conveniently trying to pin a killing he'd done on a patient with dementia," I agree. "But's it's a stretch thinking of Joshi managing to kill the nurse on the ward without being noticed. He'd have gotten blood all over his fancy suit."

"It's possible he wore a lab coat," Vogel suggests. "Mueller's death was premeditated, whoever did it. If Nadia Efimov can plan to steal a knife, Joshi could have worn something over his suit. It would have been simple to dispose of it in the laundry."

"Look into that," Agu instructs Evans before he turns back to me. "We'll need to interview Amit Joshi again," Agu agrees. "Vogel and I will speak with him this time." He raises his eyebrow at me. "I expect he's seen enough of you Gauthier," he says with a chuckle that goes around the briefing room. "We'll also talk to this doctor…"

"Chowdhury," I supply the name.

"Gauthier," Agu says. "Why don't you follow up with the flower ladies?" I groan inwardly. Typical. Give the female Detective the women to interview.

"Sir," I nod in acknowledgement. I really should be grateful he was bringing me into the investigation at all. I put up my hand.

"Anything else Gauthier?" Agu asks.

"Just that… the knife that killed Maurice Cobb was wiped too."

Vogel rolls his eyes. "Not everything is related to Cobb," he laughs.

"No…" I hesitate. "But someone killed both people, using the same method. And both victims were connected, through Pelham Woods and whatever was going on there with swapping out the medications. I'm just wondering if there are any other stabbings that might be connected."

"There was that dealer that was killed in the bus shelter last week," Evans pipes up. "That knife was found in a sewer near the scene. It was wiped clean."

Agu thinks for a moment. "What have we got on that case? Anything new? Anything that would tie in here?"

Vogel shrugs. "It's possible." He doesn't sound like he believes it. "The guy was a dealer, just street drugs. A user too. But… there may be a connection between him and Mueller. I'll look into it."

"Okay," says Agu. "We're looking into connections between Cobb, Mueller and this dealer—does he have a name?"

"Ernhardt," Sir," said Evans. "Justin Ernhardt. He's got a record going back to juvenile crime. Low-level stuff. He's never served any time, just probation and fines."

I put up my hand again. "Sir," I say when called upon. "We're presuming Cobb, Cooper and Mueller were all working together. Possibly even this Ernhardt, if he was dealing what they stole. But they're all dead. So who tried to kill me?"

"Someone else is involved," he agrees. "They may now be protecting themselves and killing off anyone else who they worked with, especially now that the operation has been exposed. Maybe they feel vulnerable, and are getting rid of their accomplices, cleaning up."

"So, that could be the same person who was blackmailing Joshi," I say, thinking aloud. "And who didn't fall for the Fraud squad's trap. Why do you suppose that was? Were they tipped off somehow?"

"That would mean either Joshi told them, or someone on our team did," Agu says.

"Joshi probably shared the information with his security company."

"Or maybe they just got cold feet." Agu holds up his hand. "Let's not jump to conclusions." He rubbed his eyes. "Since I've been in this role for the past five years, we've had an average of less than three homicides in the region in an entire year. But in the past week alone, we've had five: Cobb, Cooper, Mueller, Ernhardt and Flores.

"Six, Sir," I correct him. "You forgot Anna Kozlowski."

Agu is about to argue then changes his mind. "Agreed. Based on what happened to you Gauthier, we need to review our initial assumptions that it was an accident."

I clear my throat. "And, Sir," I begin then stop when Agu glares at me.

He sighs deeply. "Yes, Gauthier?"

"It's seven, actually. Last week there was another death, by overdose, at the Green Bean Cafe."

"And?"

"I'm not sure it was an accident…"

"Haven't we got enough real murders to deal with Gauthier?" Vogel interrupts, rolling his eyes. "Without you adding more?"

"The victim was Mark Sempe," I continue, with a glance at Vogel to make sure he doesn't interrupt again. "You've probably all heard of him—a local club promoter? And a pimp. I'm sure Vice know him well. He died of an overdose of heroin and Fentanyl. The Coroner flagged it as suspicious at the time because it was an oral dose. Someone could easily have slipped some in his coffee."

"Who was investigating?"

"Cooper," I say and the room falls quiet. "He took it over. Constable Decker and I responded to the call initially." Agu glances at Evans, who is dutifully writing everything down.

Agu exhales deeply, puffing out his cheeks. "So, we've got possible connections between Cooper, Mueller, Cobb and now both Ernhardt and this Sempe."

I nod. "And Anna Kozlowski. Sir. If we consider the possibility that she saw something at Pelham, or that someone thought she'd seen something."

"Good point," Agu agrees as he wraps up the briefing.

I hang back for a minute as everyone leaves the room, thinking about who had tipped off Joshi's blackmailer. It makes no sense that he'd have done it himself and I don't want to believe someone on our team had leaked the information. So who does that leave? Was the whole blackmail story fake? If it is, that means Amit Joshi is one hell of a good actor. And it puts us back to square one in terms of figuring out where the cash had come from to pay off Cobb's truck.

Could the leak be through Limestone Security? It's logical to think that Joshi would have told his security team about the blackmail. Maybe he'd even used them to deliver the cash. Just like he may have used them to *deal with* Leon Flores and Maurice Cobb.

I head out to the parking lot, along the concrete block hallway that leads out the back door, past the wall of honour. Rows of photos of academy graduations, retirements, and two memorials for officers who'd died—one in the line of duty, the other of illness. Then I have an idea.

Backing up to the start of the hall, I make a point of studying the years of new recruits and graduation photos. There it is, right in front of me: A photo of Cooper, standing next to Wright and Decker. They'd all joined District 6 the same year, twenty years ago. Wright is serving a life sentence, for corruption, trafficking and murder. Cooper is dead and the list of his offences is even longer. Also, his security company is somehow at the heart of all of these murders. That leaves Decker—the last man standing in that group of recruits. I've never heard Decker say a bad word about another cop. But he works for Limestone Security. He must know something, and yet he's never said a word. Decker is one of the old guys. He's loyal and probably believes in protecting the blue wall of silence. Or could there be some other reason he's staying quiet? He must have some information about Limestone Security that will help me make sense of what was going on at Pelham and Advik. I need to talk to Decker.

Once again I'm stuck at the Clarence Street Bridge, waiting for a freighter to pass along the canal. I'd driven out to the speed trap on Killaley, expecting to find Decker there, but had no luck. I'm reluctant to call dispatch and ask for the location of his unit, in case it sends up a red flag. For all I know he's having a nap somewhere, given the amount of overtime he's been working.

I sit behind the wheel of the patrol car and think about what I'd said in the briefing with Agu. I'm not the first person who'd thought Anna Kozlowski had been killed because she'd seen something. Doreen was. And it was Doreen who'd first said Katrina Mueller was up to something. She'd insisted there was something going on at Pelham Woods—and she was right.

She had also tried to warn me about Cooper, but I didn't listen.

I already knew how corrupt he was; I didn't think she had anything new to tell me. I'd dismissed her as just a lonely old woman with too much time on her hands.

Doreen had been right about a lot of things. My heart starts to beat faster as I realize she'd also been present when a lot of things happened.

She'd been there at the Green Bean, sitting at the table next to Sempe the day he died. She told me how she'd replaced Sempe's coffee after she'd spilled it. She could have slipped the drugs into his cup. But why would she have any motive to kill Sempe? And how would she even have heroin and Fentanyl? The idea is ridiculous and I try to put the idea out of my mind.

But it keeps pushing its way back in. I remember Doreen was also at Pelham Woods when Mueller was killed. She'd even showed up in Nadia's room while we were securing the scene, getting in my way, and she'd managed to get blood on her walker wheels in the process. I remember the trail left down the Pelham Woods carpeted hallway of her treads in blood. Had that been deliberate? So she'd have an explanation if we'd found Mueller's blood on her clothes?

Walker wheels. I flash back to my house that early morning just after I'd first met Doreen. I knew someone had been inside, and I'd seen those treads in the dew on my lawn. I'd thought then it was a stroller or a bike, possibly even Dennis Sharp's. But could it have been Doreen? The day she brought me home from the hospital she'd seemed so familiar with everything. She knew where things were, even though she'd brushed it off when I remarked on it.

And I could have sworn I'd seen Doreen at the Fall Fair, but she'd denied it. Could she have injected Cooper, at some point after he'd left the Womyn Booth? Doreen had worked as a nurse. She knows about injections. About poisons too, I'd bet.

But why would she do it? Why would Doreen want to kill Sempe? Or Mueller and Cooper? Then I understand. She believes they're behind Anna's death. Of course she'd kill them to avenge her friend's murder. She'd take it into her own hands and she'd do it in a heartbeat. Is she capable of taking action against whoever killed her friend?

What had she said to me? *I can take care of myself. They'll never see me coming.*

I pull out my cell phone and call Doreen's number. No answer. I try the coffee shop, but Phil tells me she hasn't been in today. There's only one other place she might be; I turn the car around and head out to Pelham Woods, my heart pounding.

If Doreen didn't do it, she might know who did. Both Mueller and Cooper are dead, but someone else is involved in the blackmail and in the drug scam. Maybe Doreen has figured out who that is. And maybe she's already taking action.

FIFTY ONE

I DRIVE ON autopilot, thinking hard. If Mueller and Cooper were selling narcotics that had been stolen from patients, who at Pelham Woods would have known about it? Only the two of them, and whoever was selling it for them on the street. Someone like Justin Ernhardt, stabbed to death in a bus shelter.

But if this is all about illegally testing the pharmaceuticals in development, Mueller would have known about it, and the other person in the loop would be whoever supplied her with the medication. Who would that be? Amit Joshi? Or is it someone else who works at Pelham? Who else had access to the drugs? Who else knew the patients' prescriptions? And who would have had to record the results of the tests? Could that have been left to Mueller?

I doubt Amit Joshi even has the technical ability to monitor clinical trials. I'd read he was some kind of a software engineer. That doesn't really fit. It would have to be someone with a research background, or training in medicine and pharmaceuticals. His wife Zahira has a PhD in Chemistry. Is she the one who's been involved with the trials? Or does the crime not go that far up in Advik Therapeutics? Maybe it's someone lower down corporate totem pole.

I leave the car in front of the entrance and walk quickly to the elevators. It's after five so the administrative staff have gone for the day, and all of the fake shops on Main Street are closed. It's eerie. The atrium is empty. Where is everyone?

When I arrive on the second floor it's like a ghost town. The patient lounge is empty and the nursing station deserted. I rush down the hall and look into the dining room then breathe a sigh of relief. All the patients and care workers are inside; it's dinner service. The tables are full and volunteers and aides are going around delivering meals and assisting patients who aren't able to feed themselves.

I run down the hall, peering into the patients' rooms. All are empty, their occupants now in the dining room, so I retreat to the nursing station. Where could Doreen be now? I glance toward the palliative wing and my heart starts to race. *Please no. Not in there.* I feel my anxiety mounting, my ears are ringing and trickles of sweat roll down my back as I walk toward the double doors. My breathing is shallow as I force myself to push open the doors.

Halfway down the hall there's a body lying in a pool of blood and I instinctively draw my weapon and run toward it. It's Dr. Chowdhury. He's been stabbed. When I crouch and find he's still breathing I get out my radio and call it in then proceed down the hall, gun drawn.

Most of the doors to the patient rooms are closed, as the residents inside wait to die. It's quiet and my feet make no noise on the carpeted hallway. Chowdhury must have been the link back to Advik Therapeutics. No doubt he was working directly with Amit Joshi, using Mueller to distribute the medication to the patients. Maybe he'd even turned a blind eye to her stealing the narcotics, as a quid pro quo.

Chowdhury was the last link to Joshi—the last bit that needed to be cleaned up. Was the plan to have his death attributed to another patient run amok? Then Joshi could quietly wrap up the experiment and pretend it had never happened. Maybe that had been the plan all along, once the drug tests were complete. But Cobb had discovered what they'd been doing. So he had to be silenced, as did all of the other participants, one by one. Joshi would have had Cooper and Limestone Security do the dirty work. But who was doing it now that Cooper is dead?

I hear a faint moan coming from a partially open door on the right hand side of the hall. Holding myself against the wall I push the door so it swings open and I can see inside. There's a man lying in a bed across the dimly lit room, his lips are moving but he makes no sound. He turns to look at me, his eyes burning into mine and it's all I can do not to scream. I back out into the hallway feeling drops of perspiration rolling down my back.

I push open the next door. The blinds are drawn and as my eyes adjust to the lack of light I see Decker, holding a knife on Doreen. She's clutching her walker and I can see her hands shaking with the effort of holding herself up. I'm not at all surprised. It's as if some part of me had known all along she'd be here at the end.

"Drop it Decker," I shout.

He shakes his head. "She killed the doctor," he says. "Call it in."

"No I didn't," Doreen whispers. "He's lying."

"Drop the knife," I repeat. Even if Doreen had killed Dr. Chowdhury, she needs to be taken into custody and charged, not dealt with by Decker in this way.

Decker complies and turns to me, showing me his open hands as the knife falls silently onto the carpet.

"Keep your hands where I can see them," I say and Decker laughs.

"You're kidding, right?"

"What's going on, Decker?" Something's off here. There's something I don't understand.

"The Doctor called me," he says. "I came in here looking for him and I saw him lying there…"

"Why'd he call you?" I interrupt. "Why you, specifically?" Decker hesitates and I know he's lying.

"C'mon Gauthier! I've been a cop in this town for a lot longer than you. He's known me for years."

"Through Limestone Security?"

"Sure. He wanted to tell me something… said he needed my help…" I can see Decker is making it up as he goes along. His eyes are flicking around the room, over to Doreen, then to me, assessing if I'm a threat. "Are you gonna call this in or what?" he demands.

I ignore the question and keep my gun trained on him. "Why are you here, Doreen?" I ask her.

"She's here to kill the doctor," Decker laughs. "Just like she killed the nurse."

"Why would she have done that?" I ask. "Doreen? Is that true?"

Decker starts to walk calmly toward me, placating me, his hand open. He's completely non-threatening but why do I feel he's going to attack me? I step back, hesitating when Doreen shoves her walker in front of him and he stumbles. In that instant she picks up the knife from the floor and holds it to Decker's throat.

"He did it," she says. "He's the one who stabbed the doctor. With this knife."

"Gauthier," Decker whispers. "Help me. She's insane."

"Doreen," I hold out my hand to her. "Please put the knife down."

She shakes her head. "If I do that I won't be able to kill him." Decker whimpers in fear.

"Why do you want to kill Constable Decker?"

Doreen presses the knife into Decker's neck, the tip right against his carotid artery. "He's working with that nurse and Cooper. They killed Anna."

"Decker?" I meet his eye.

"I don't know what she's talking about," he cries. "Gauthier, use your weapon!" I have a clear shot, but I'm not about to take it.

"He killed the doctor," Doreen says. "I saw him."

"Liar!" Decker hisses. "She did it. She's crazy."

"I was about to do it myself," Doreen admits. "But he beat me to it."

"Why would you want to kill Dr. Chowdhury?" I'm stalling, waiting for back up. I have no experience in hostage negotiations. I'm flying blind, just saying whatever comes into my mind.

"He helped them steal the pain medication," she says. "They were suffering."

"I know." I step forward, again extending my hand to Doreen. "They were also secretly testing new drugs on them, drugs to treat dementia."

"So you understand why I have to do this," she says, her eyes glittering in rage. "They all have to pay." Decker gasps in pain as Doreen presses the blade into his throat. A drop of blood trickles down his neck and I jump back expecting a gush of arterial spray. Doreen laughs and I exhale in relief. She could have killed Decker by now, but she hasn't. I understand she's giving me a chance to get to the bottom of this.

"What are you doing here Decker?" I ask, pointing my gun at him. Doreen smiles.

"I told you. I got a call." His eyes are wild with fear. "From the doctor." Decker knows we can check the phone records, so that's probably true.

"What about?"

"He was going to tell me about the narcotics thefts."

"Why would he call you? How do you even know each other?" Decker looks desperate, but can't come up with a plausible answer.

"Chowdhury was the last link that could lead to you," I say as it all becomes clear. "You'd already taken care of Cooper and Mueller and you wanted to make sure you'd covered your tracks." Everything makes sense now. Decker had been working with Cooper all along. Decker made no secret of his need for money, how he worked over-time and paid duty shifts he could get. Whatever it was he did for Limestone Security must have paid well.

"What are you talking about?" he whimpers. "I didn't do anything."

"I know you killed Cooper," I say. "You injected him with Potassium Chloride in the Mobile Control Unit. Then you followed him outside to watch him die."

"No, he never came inside, like I said."

I shake my head. "He was seen leaving the Womyn booth and going straight inside, where you were waiting for him." I believe Rose.

"You needed him gone. He was volatile, a troublemaker, always drawing attention to himself, and you didn't want the scrutiny. Cooper was a problem, had been for years. Maybe you wanted to push him out of the way so you could work directly with Mueller."

I'd dismissed Decker all these years as being just easy-going, with no ambition. How wrong I'd been. "You, Cooper, and Wright were all old friends. You three go way back—you all joined the force at the same time."

I shake my head at my own gullibility. "All those times I'd see you putting up with Cooper, I just put it down to you being such a good guy, so loyal. Must have been why you were so nice to me— you were really just trying to find out how much I knew." And now I have figured it out, most of it anyway. The question is, what am I supposed to do about it? Take the law into my own hands?

"You killed Anna Kozlowski too. I'm sure Mueller told you she'd seen something," I say and see Decker's eyes widen in surprise. "And I'm sure you're the one who tried to kill me too. Joshi told you to deal with me." Decker's rigid with fear and trying to shake his head in denial but the knife at this throat forces him to keep still. I study him for a moment, thinking it through.

"You were the first on the scene after I escaped the fruit storage at the apple farm. That's because you're the one who locked me in. That's why your prints were in the barn. You probably watched the whole time, waiting for me to die, until I escaped and called in for help."

I know that if I hadn't arrived in time, Doreen would be dead and Decker would hang the blame on her. Even if she'd somehow survived the law would believe Decker, because he's a cop. There's no evidence that will prove him guilty and they're already all happy to discount Rose's version of events the day Cooper died. Who'd believe Decker capable of anything like this? Good old Decker, always there, amiable and helpful. Always on the scene, the trustworthy cop. But some pieces don't fit.

"You didn't kill Mueller though," I slowly realize. "You weren't at Pelham Woods that day." I look at Doreen and it all starts to come together. "But you were. Why did you kill her Doreen?"

"I had to stop her." Doreen smiles. "I saw her switching the meds."

"You just made it look like Nadia had done it, because you knew she wouldn't be blamed. She wouldn't even remember anything about what happened."

"I brought my knife every day, until I saw my chance," Doreen says. "I've remembered you need to take life into your own hands Lucy," Doreen says. "Like you did with your stepfather."

She's right. Of course she's right. She knows my secrets and the lies I've told. She knows me better than I know myself. Doreen knows what I've done, and what I'm capable of, to put things right. Killing my stepfather wasn't a good thing, but it was the right thing, and it was the only thing I could do to achieve justice and to try and protect my mother. I had to take things into my own hands.

"Like you did with you son," I say, as the last pieces fall into place. "Where is he, Doreen? Where is your son?"

She smiles and relaxes her grip for a brief second. "In the backyard, under the roses."

"Doreen, put down the knife. It's over."

She shakes her head. "I'm not letting this creep get away with it," she snaps, jabbing the blade back into Decker's throat. I hear him gasp. "All these people suffering, in pain. And he's selling their drugs on the street. A cop, for god's sake. Who can you trust?"

"You can trust me, Doreen." She shakes her head.

"Gauthier, do something," Decker pleads. "You're going to believe some crazy old lady over me?" I can hear the sirens outside. It's only a matter of minutes before they rush in.

"You know who you are Lucy," Doreen says. "Do what you have to do." I hesitate. I do know who I am now, more than I've ever known. I can see all the parts of myself clearly, the good and especially the bad, and I know what I have to do. I pull the trigger and Decker falls, dead.

Blood spatters Doreen's face and she drops the knife in shock. I quickly step forward and pick it up then I wipe it clean and press it into Decker's hand.

"He was going to kill you Doreen," I say firmly, coaching her. "He thought you knew something. That Anna had told you what she'd seen." I grab her shoulder and give her a shake. "Do you understand me Doreen?"

Doreen nods as the doors swing open and officers enter, guns drawn. I place my weapon on the floor and raise my hands.

FIFTY TWO

DR. CHOWDHURY SURVIVED his wounds and once he was conscious he was happy to testify against Decker, which put me in the clear. There was no question that I'd been forced to shoot him while defending Doreen. Chowdhury also told the truth about the illegal clinical trials of Advik's experimental drugs at Pelham Woods, in exchange for a reduced sentence. The doctor had been in on it; he worked for Joshi, got paid for his silence, and for any data he shared regarding the trials.

Amit Joshi was removed from his role as CEO at Advik, on the insistence of the Board of Directors. They were attempting some damage control and a salvage operation, in the hope they could still take the company public. Joshi's wife Zahira stepped into his role as CEO with her brother as CFO. There was some possibility Joshi would serve jail time, but his lawyers would drag the case out for years and by the time it came to court no one would even remember what he'd done. If he even were sentenced at all it would be light. That's what money gets you.

Decker was blamed for the murders of Mueller and Cooper, and the attempted murder of Dr. Chowdhury. The other charges just fell into place after that, and even though I knew it was Doreen who'd killed Mueller, I didn't feel bad about letting Decker take the blame.

He may as well be hung for a sheep as for a lamb, and anyway he was already dead.

I thought either he or Cooper had probably killed Leon Flores as well, but we were never able to prove it and I had to let it go. There was no way Joshi would ever admit he'd asked Limestone Security to silence Flores, and I have to wonder if the overproduction at Taiga was really worth killing him for. Maybe they'd had been asked to watch Flores, or to warn him away. Maybe they'd just beaten him up and the drowning wasn't meant to happen. Maybe they'd taken things a bit too far. But Joshi is unlikely to tell the truth about what had happened and Decker isn't talking.

Doreen told me how she'd killed Ernhardt and Sempe, but I didn't turn her in. How could I? Why should I? The first death was an accident; she was a vulnerable old lady who'd fought back against a mugger. And Mark Sempe? What can I say, the world is better off without him in it. I look at it like Doreen was doing a public service.

I moved her into Pelham Woods as soon as a space became available. We found her a nice room in the retirement wing. She has a small studio apartment with a kitchenette and all she needs to do to visit Nadia is walk along Main Street and take the elevator upstairs. They even allow pets, so Old Cat came along.

I visit her regularly, and take her out for coffee, to the bank, and to get her groceries. Doreen is now keeping her eye on the residents at Pelham Woods, like she did in the East Village. Just like I keep an eye on the community in my job.

I helped her rent out the house; she can't sell it yet, in case the new owners start digging around in the garden. Between that money and her monthly pension she just can about afford to stay at Pelham Woods. She also gets some financial help from her godchildren: Peter Kozlowski and Rose. They both owe her a debt.

The house will be sold after Doreen's death. She's made a new Will, with me as her Executor, to help protect her secret. She wrote out a confession and sealed it, to be opened after her death, revealing the location of her son's body. My father's body. Once she's dead it won't matter anymore, if it ever did.

My learning the truth about my father, about her son, has released both of us from the past. We've both been caged by our secrets and now the door is open.

I called Maja. We're having dinner together soon, and I'm going to tell her the truth. My truth. All of it. If she's already gone, fine. I'll have to accept that. But I owe it to her, and to myself, to tell my story. Then maybe I'll be able to put it away forever.

FIFTY THREE

THE SIGN PAINTERS have just finished plastering the front window of the shop with an OPENING SOON sign. This is the location of Geraldine Bennett's new flower business, scheduled to open in a month. I sit in the car for a few minutes, watching as the sign guys pack up their ladders and load them onto the truck. I have to admit the exterior of the shop looks great.

The windows and door trim are painted a glossy black and through the panes of glass I can see the interior walls are being painted and some workmen are installing a counter.

The door swings open and Geraldine Bennett steps out, wearing a floral apron and a big smile. She is completely transformed. From a haggard, exhausted and frightened woman, she's become confident and happy, and justifiably proud of her new business venture. I feel a brief flash of guilt as I step out of the patrol car and cross the street.

"Hello, Ms. Bennett," I say. "The store looks great." Geraldine jumps in surprise and spins around. There's a flash of fear in her eyes.

"Thank you," she says, with an insincere smile. "Can I help you, Detective?"

"When's the Grand Opening?"

"Next month," she says. "Still need to get the fridges in. Hire some staff."

"You've done well for yourself," I say. "May I look inside?" I see the resistance in Bennett, but she manages to force a smile.

"Sure, come in," she says.

I walk around and say appropriately impressed things. "I'm curious," I say casually. "How did you manage to afford to open your own business?"

"I beg your pardon?" Bennett looks offended.

"Well, I don't mean to be rude, but you were living at Womyn for the past year. Abused spouse, no money, no job. And now…"

"I was staying at Womyn to escape my ex-husband's abuse," she snaps. "Money wasn't the issue."

I nod and hold Bennett's eye. "It will be easy for us to prove otherwise," I say. Bennett's eyes shift nervously.

"What do you mean?" she whispers.

"Did you know Amit Joshi was being blackmailed?" I say, changing the subject.

Bennett does her best to look surprised. "About what?"

"The fact that he has been carrying on clinical trials at Pelham Woods," I say. "Of the drug that your ex-husband had helped develop. We believe your husband was the blackmailer."

"That's ridiculous," she laughs. "Maurice was a bastard but completely incapable of blackmailing anyone. Anyway, he never had any money. Never helped the kids, never even paid his bills from what I've heard."

"Nevertheless," I continue. "Evidence points to him."

"What kind of *evidence*?"

"I'm not at liberty to share," I say with a smile.

"Is that why you think he was killed?" Bennett asks, a little too eagerly. "You think the person he was extorting money from got even, maybe fought back?"

"That would certainly be a convenient way to wrap it up," I say. "But, no. Maurice Cobb was blackmailing Amit Joshi for a time. But the blackmail continued even after his death."

"So you're saying he had a partner?"

"No. I think someone took over the blackmail business, after he was dead. Maybe that's even the reason he was killed."

"And who would that be?"

"You, Ms. Bennett," I say. "You killed your ex-husband." Geraldine's eyes narrow and she glances into the street behind me. There are no flashing lights, no sirens, no back up. She allows herself to relax.

"How did I do that?" She sounds flippant.

"You lured him out to the field somehow, maybe with a promise of reconciliation. For all I know, that was your special place at one time." Bennett flinches and know I've struck a nerve. "There was a lovely view."

"You had some drinks, just like when you were young. Smoked some weed. Had some more drinks. You slipped him a couple of your sleeping pills, crushed into his beer. You didn't drink much, if at all, to keep a clear head. And when he passed out you killed him. You slashed his arms, using your florist knife, and you left him to die. Alone, sitting on a lawn chair in the middle of a field."

The colour drains from Bennett's face.

"After he was dead, you took his truck and drove way, leaving it abandoned at Nickel Beach where you knew it would be stolen. And you tossed the knife into the marsh."

Bennett glares at me, her chin raised in defiance. "No, I did not."

"And the suicide note," I continues, ignoring her. "You must have brought it along that night. Which of course means you planned it." Bennett's jaw is set in anger and her eyes flash. She looks a lot stronger now than when I'd first met her, in the living room at the Womyn Shelter. I guess that's what happens when an abused woman takes her revenge. It must be empowering.

"It was a skillful forgery and who better than you to know his handwriting? It was also convenient that you were the one who confirmed that he'd written it."

"It makes perfect sense why you planned to kill him," I say. "You were afraid of him, especially once you realized he'd found out where you worked. You thought he'd come after you again. But you made a mistake. Maurice Cobb wasn't at Pelham Woods looking for you or trying to find out where you lived. He was after proof that Amit Joshi was testing the drugs illegally. So he could blackmail him. Which you found out all about, when you got him drunk."

"That was his biggest mistake, apart from the first one where he agreed to come out to the field with you that night. He told you about the blackmail scheme. He told you how he'd made money off Amit Joshi. He probably loved telling you all about it. Maybe he even thought you'd be proud of him. Making money off the guy who'd fired him and had him blacklisted."

I look around the store, pausing to admire the new fixtures and finishes.

"That's how you financed this new store of yours, isn't it? You took over the blackmail business, after he was dead."

Bennett turns her back on me, her arms crossed. "I was able to pay for this store thanks to a life insurance policy we took out, years ago. You'll never be able to prove otherwise."

"So you say," I shrug. "We'll see," I say with a smile before I walk out the door.

It's certainly possible Bennett had killed Cobb for that life insurance policy in the first place. That might have been the plan all along. The blackmail money would have just been a nice bonus.

I can only speculate that Bennett had been the blackmailer, since we'd never been able to catch whoever it was. There's no way I can prove she'd done any of it; I know that. What little evidence we even have is all circumstantial and easily explained away: The florist knife is common enough and there were no prints on it. The truck has disappeared. She had more than enough motive to see Cobb dead and she fit the description of the woman Andre Dumont had seen leaving the truck at Nickel Beach. But it isn't enough.

The investigation into Cobb's death will be closed, unless Agu can find a way to blame Decker for it. The department isn't going to waste any more resources going after Bennett, not just on my opinion. But I know the truth. Just like my grandmother, I never forget a thing. And I know how to wait.

ACKNOWLEDGEMENTS

woo hoo!

Thank you to my dear friend Martha Mason, who welcomed me into her beautiful family cottage on Lake Erie, which provided the inspiration for the Niagara Noir series. The characters and situations in this novel are my own invention and any mistakes in the book are my own.

I'm grateful to Dr. Sammy Barakat for his pharmaceutical and medical advice, and for his support over the years.

Thanks also to the Damonza team for fabulous cover design and formatting and to Lucy Dauman--whose early editorial comments and support made such a difference in the finished novel and helped me turn Blood Relative into a novel I'm very proud to share.

Most of all, I'm grateful to my mother for inspiring me with a love of reading and of books, and to my children for their love and support.

ABOUT THE AUTHOR

Liza Drozdov worked as a bookseller and book publicist, as a garden designer and a college professor, and as a producer of lifestyle television, before settling down to writing full-time. She lives in Oakville, Ontario.

www.lizadrozdov.com
www.twitter.com/lizadrozdov
instagram.com/lizadrozdov

Manufactured by Amazon.ca
Bolton, ON

19941108R00153